"I remember now," Deidre mumbled. "I remember—"

"Remembering won't help much if you pass out," Francis said. "Will you stop fighting me?"

But Deidre tried clumsily to free herself of his grip. "I remember I was trying to land a plane on your crummy airstrip."

"What d'you mean, crummy?"

"I damn well nearly killed myself!" she cried fiercely.

He shrugged. "You don't seem to have hurt your mouth very much."

"Do you have a smart answer for everything? I'm trying to tell you that I remember who you are," Deidre insisted.

"That's a relief."

"You're Francis MacIntire. Hey!"

"What is it this time, darling?" he growled.

"You owe me a hundred and seventy-five thousand dollars, Mr. MacIntire," she said sweetly, and thrust out her hand. "Pay up."

Dear Reader,

Spellbinders! That's what we're striving for. The editors at Silhouette are determined to capture your imagination and win your heart with every single book we publish. Each month, six Special Editions are chosen with *you* in mind.

Our authors are our inspiration. Writers such as Nora Roberts, Tracy Sinclair, Kathleen Eagle, Carole Halston and Linda Howard—to name but a few—are masters at creating endearing characters and heartrending love stories. Their characters are everyday people—just like you and me—whose lives have been touched by love, whose dreams and desires suddenly come true!

So find a cozy, quiet place to read, and create your own special moment with a Silhouette Special Edition.

Sincerely,

The Editors
SILHOUETTE BOOKS

LINDA SHAW
Santiago Heat

Silhouette Special Edition

Published by Silhouette Books New York

America's Publisher of Contemporary Romance

To Joe Player,
who helped Deidre land the plane
without killing herself.

SILHOUETTE BOOKS
300 East 42nd St., New York, N.Y. 10017

ISBN: 0-373-09403-5

First Silhouette Books printing September 1987

LINDA SHAW,

the mother of three, lives with her husband in Keene, Texas. A prolific author of both contemporary and historical fiction, when Linda isn't writing romantic novels, she's practicing or teaching the piano, violin or viola.

GUIANA
VENEZUELA
SURINAM
COLUMBIA
FRENCH GUIANA
ECUADOR
PERU
BRAZIL
BOLIVIA
CHILE
PARAGUAY
ARGENTINA
URUGUAY

Las Tablas
★
SANTIAGO
Rio Tepui ●

SOUTH AMERICA
Underlined places are fictitious.

Chapter One

On the second Thursday of April, Nicolas Noreiga arrived late to work.

It was a variation of the same old tune—a hangover. And a doozy. His churning stomach defied description. The top of his head felt like pigskin stretched over a Chocó war drum. And his eyes? *Dios,* they didn't belong in his head at all but in Manuel Alfonzo's pickling crock at the cantina.

Maria was to blame. Every time he got drunk Maria was to blame. The night before, she said he had a potato where his brain was supposed to be and that any woman with half a nose would know it was rotten. Never again. And this time he really meant it!

The truth was, he should have called in sick. To get to Panama's international airport, where he was a senior maintenance man, he had to ride the bus sixteen miles out of Panama City to Tecumen. What he didn't understand was why all the women and their wailing, wiggling children chose to ride his bus.

Maintenance wasn't really a bad job, though. Over four hundred passengers passed through the airport gates each year. To him that meant fourteen hundred dollars a year in honest labor. In bribes, kickbacks and skimming he pocketed another thousand.

Out of respect for his condition, he walked with great care through the airport gates and onto the tarmac near Gate Seven. He pushed back the bill of his cap and cupped his hands around his bloodshot eyes.

¡Jesu! A Douglas A-26 had begun its descent, and the throb of the big propellers was attracting attention all over his end of the concourse. Squinting, for anyone who knew about the Bay of Pigs knew of the famous "Invader," he watched it drop down to touch the runway in a flawless landing.

Some decorated World War II ace, no doubt. It was a publicity stunt, right? He shuffled to where another man waited to guide the warbird in.

"Where you been, *amigo*?" the worker asked in rippling Spanish as he lifted a two-way radio to his mouth and gave a series of directions.

Nicolas grinned to disguise the jackhammer working away in his head. "To the dentist."

The man snorted. *"Mentiroso."* Liar.

The bomber was taxiing along the runway now—a handsomely restored machine right down to the military paraphernalia of an eight-gunned nose and a top turret locked forward for strafing. In red, beneath the cockpit, was neatly painted *The Albatross*. A real museum piece, all right. The clamshell canopy revealed a single pilot.

From the opposite direction, a fuel truck rumbled in. Knowing his hangover wouldn't improve with coddling,

Nicolas painfully waved the vehicle on. Some of the other maintenance men also wandered over. One wondered aloud if an American film company was coming to Panama.

That was something to be considered. Everyone immediately set about figuring how much extra money might soon line their pockets.

Hardly had the plane come to rest than the canopy opened, and the pilot climbed out onto the wing. They all watched as the slim, helmeted figure wearing an olive drab jump suit topped with a zippered yellow flight jacket stooped to check the fuel tank.

Dios, I'm still drunk, Nicolas thought as he observed the gracefully tapered hips and the slender legs whipped into relief by the wind. Or else there was something terribly wrong with the World War II ace.

Then he noticed how narrowly the jacket spanned a trim waist, and the smallness of the gloved hands, the demure way the legs of the pants were strapped at the ankles above petite canvas sneakers.

The figure straightened, topping five feet by only four or five inches at most. From behind mirrored sunglasses it gazed about itself, noted the waiting men, dragged off its helmet and tucked it beneath its arm with a brisk, virile confidence.

A tumble of shoulder-length hair was caught by the wind and thrown out in a shimmering, fig-brown cloud.

Ah! Delighted laughter rippled all around as she caught the finger of a glove between her teeth and deftly pulled it off. Just as swiftly, she skinned off the second glove and slapped them both into the helmet.

Nicolas chuckled. He'd known it all along. Only Hollywood, California, would send a woman in a spiffy, spruced-up bomber to Panama City. They would all be rich. *¡Mucho abundancia!*

He moved slowly forward with the rest and checked out her stance. A good sign, her posture—gutsy, one of authority. He couldn't tell much about her breasts beneath the jump suit, but breasts weren't all that important if the rear was good, and hers was spectacular.

Her face, with its intelligent high brow and slightly upturned nose, was good, too—much nicer than Maria's. Her mouth could have been better, though; it was wide and full and sexy enough, but to be really outstanding it should have been all pouty and coy. Instead there was a twist of mistrust that wasn't particularly to his liking, as if her twenty-eight or so years had been lived the hard way, and she was putting everyone on notice that she had no intention of learning her lessons again.

She frowned at the fuel truck and disappeared into the cockpit. Seconds later a small ladder dropped through the doors beneath the nose. Climbing down it, she stepped limberly onto the tarmac.

One of the men placed his fingers between his teeth and whistled: the perennial international language. She whipped the glasses off her face, and the men abruptly found themselves confronted by a pair of no-nonsense, North American gray eyes.

Sacra madre, but she was a handful! Nicolas pressed a hand to his tumbling stomach. Since he spoke better English than any of the others, he considered it his patriotic duty to take charge of the situation and learn her business.

"Señorita," he said in a friendly way as he stepped forward and removed his cap, "I am Nicolas Noreiga. Welcome to Panama."

"Thank you," she said, and she glanced over her shoulder as the fuel truck backed laboriously into place. She started walking toward it.

"You are a movie producer from the States, yes?" Nicolas called to her cloud of hair. "You have made a most excellent choice, *señorita*. We are most genuinely happy you have come to our country."

The driver of the fuel truck stepped to the ground and began adjusting his hoses. Her interest was focused on him as she replied. "What? Oh, yes. I'm sorry. Thank you, *señor*."

Walking up, Nicolas extended his hand and his most sincere smile. "Please be assured that I, Nicolas Noreiga, am at your personal service."

"Well, I—" She darted another apprehensive glance at the truck, then turned, shook his hand with a smile and gave him her full attention. "Why, thank you. I appreciate that very much."

Nicolas double-checked her ring finger and wondered if she would be making a war movie. War movies required lots of extras. He wouldn't look bad in uniform—a little makeup, and he could let his hair grow longer. This could be his big chance.

"Night or day, *señorita*," he said carefully. "I am most serious. Feel free to call upon me." To make sure she didn't misunderstand, he closed his hand over hers and squeezed.

A frown nibbled at the tiny lines about her eyes and between her brows. Slipping free, she pushed back her hair and kept her head angled toward the tarmac. For a moment, Nicolas feared he'd screwed up.

But she smiled again. "You've been very helpful, Señor Noreiga." She took a long, deep breath and threw back her shoulders. "I will certainly remember, I give you my word."

Nicolas nodded happily and adjusted his cap to a more flattering angle. He settled his belt importantly about his waist as he congratulated himself. And to think he'd been upset by all that potato business. *Take that, Maria!*

* * *

Deidre Miles was in a hurry. She was almost always in a hurry—a learned condition, stemming from too much ambition, too little capital and not nearly enough hours in a day to cover either one. Panama City was her one stop between Dallas, Texas, and Santiago, South America.

She was also extremely nervous and had been from the beginning of the transaction six months ago between Francis MacIntire and herself. Walking on the edge of a razor blade could hardly be more risky than selling an A-26 through the mail. The last thing she'd needed was to confront an oversexed maintenance man who smelled suspiciously like the Miller Brewing Company.

Unzipping her flight jacket, she drew out a sheaf of papers and battled the wind for the top sheet. In the distance a jumbo jet was preparing for takeoff, and she looked up to see the technician guiding it out.

"The others will arrive soon?" the maintenance man was asking. "From California? Hollywood, California?"

"I'm afraid I'm not from Hollywood, Señor Noreiga," she said absently over the whine of the great engines.

The 747 set the air to shuddering, and for a few moments hearing anything was impossible. Turning, she lip-read the man's sagging disappointment. "Awww..."

She yelled, "My partner and I once provided a single prop that was blown up in a Tom Selleck movie. Does that count?"

"¿Qué?" He cupped his ear.

"Tom Selleck? Television? 'Magnum, P.I.'?"

When he showed his teeth in a blank smile, Deidre waved away her remark. The jet was airborne now, streaking toward the sky's flat bottom while the sun beat brightly upon its wings.

"It wasn't all that big a thing, anyway," she told him with a self-deprecating shrug. "Well, it's been very nice chatting with you, *señor*. Maybe you'll get your movie company next time."

Nicolas signaled his fellow workers that they might as well forgo dreams of endless wealth. But if she wasn't a movie producer, she was still rich, right? He might as well cut his losses if he could.

"This is truly an amazing craft, *señorita*," he said, trudging after her with an ingratiating laugh he used with all North Americans. "I must compliment you. It is most especially fantastic."

He'd touched upon the one thing that could break through Deidre's tough crust. To her, receiving a compliment on one of her planes was like being congratulated for having borne a beautiful child.

Tilting her head, she invited him to fall into step. "Why, thank you, *señor*. She is fantastic, isn't she?"

She could have added that he didn't know just how fantastic the *Albatross* really was. Usually she and Phillip Magaskin bought small, respectable planes like Spitfires or P-35s. Phillip, a fifty-five-year-old wizard mechanic she'd met when she worked at Bell Helicopter, did most of the manual labor. Though she wasn't too bad at mechanics herself, she generally did the selling and bookkeeping and worked the air shows.

Upon hearing that the A-26 was rusting away in a remote Mexican hangar, waiting to be hauled off for scrap, neither of them could resist. They plowed through the paperwork and brought the *Albatross* back to Dallas on four trucks.

Being featured in *Warbirds, International* was a sheer stroke of luck, of course. She and Phillip really had done a first-rate job of restoration, but it had been the magazine spread, complete with pictures and quotes, that snagged the contract with MacIntire. Naturally, their bank was delirious; the total of their outstanding debts was presently down to a mere hundred thousand dollars.

During the past six months she had received two letters from the wealthy Irishman from South America—professional correspondence, dictated and typed by a secretary. Her own replies were handwritten but on a letterhead that said Aero Classics, Restoration. The contract had been finalized through an agent MacIntire had sent to Dallas in his behalf.

Behind her now, Deidre sensed the fuel attendant placing the nozzle into the wing. In her pocket was only enough cash for this one stop, and she'd learned the hard way that fuel had a nasty way of sometimes not stretching as far as it should.

Noreiga called to her back as she walked away. "If you're not from Hollywood, you must be on your way to the air show in Brazil."

Shaking her head, Deidre kept her eyes riveted tenaciously to the truck's fuel gauge. "The *Albatross* is sold," she called over her shoulder. "Some Irishman in Santiago with more money than sense."

Noreiga hurried up and bestowed a persuasive smile as he jabbed his thumb toward the cockpit. "May I?"

The fuel technician was shuffling around on the wing in a way Deidre didn't like at all. She shrugged. "Sure. Check out anything you want to."

As he climbed into the cockpit, Deidre drew out a small pad from a pocket of her flight suit. She had already calculated how many gallons the plane would need to reach Santiago, and she stepped up to make a point of rechecking all her figures.

The technician looked at her with a tragic smirk.

She tried to smile like Mona Lisa. "Just making sure," she said.

"No hablo inglés, señorita."

Of course he understood English, the shyster! Men like him were such predictable creatures—always trying to rob her blind, thinking that she was a helpless woman who would never suspect. She had a separate vocabulary for men like that.

"I'll check it out when you're through," she said in her most meaningful tone.

"¿Qué?"

"You heard me."

While he finished, Deidre looked over the *Albatross*. Like most children, she had her faults, even if she had paid her dues in three wars. To begin with she was an unforgiving piece of machinery, and she was messy, always leaking oil, staining everyone's runways and riling the custodians.

For that reason, she carried wheel guards to place over the landing gear if she was going to remain parked for any length of time. Tucked away on board were also two emergency barrels of oil.

She inspected the landing gear, which was brand-new, as were the two engines at thirty thousand dollars apiece. The propellers were over seven thousand, themselves—each!—so she fully appreciated the bank's concern. *She* was concerned!

Another jet tore across the sky while she checked the hydraulic reservoirs and the oil tanks, which were predictably low. When the refueling was done and the oil had been replenished, the attendant wrote down his figures in a book, scribbled his name across the bottom of an invoice and sullenly thrust it at her.

Deidre smiled. He might have fudged on a gallon or two, but at least he hadn't soaked her for a hundred. She would go inside and pay the bill. Climbing into the cockpit, she wiped her hands on a terry towel and replaced her sunglasses.

"You will be departing now, *señorita*?" Noreiga questioned as she backed down the ladder and stepped lightly to the ground.

She waved her papers at him and said, "As soon as I take care of the bill, Señor Noreiga."

"*Bueno.*" His bow was eager to please. "In that case, I will most happily get you the permit myself."

A small confusion formed in the center of Deidre's chest. Reaching up, she pulled the dark glasses down the bridge of her nose. "What permit?"

His teeth glistened craftily. "You're departure permit, *señorita*. Of course."

"My what?"

"Allow me to explain." He laughed as if it brought him great pleasure to do her a favor. "In order for you to...what do you say? Skip? Yes, in order for you to skip the *inspección*, I must give you a special permit."

Was this some fancy come-on? Deidre wondered as she drew back in consternation. What was this hungover creature trying to pull? She punched out her words. "I've never had to have a special permit before."

"Oh, it could take hours." He shook his head in a deeply concerned way. "And if many others are waiting before you, it could perhaps be tomorrow before you leave. Panama City is a busy airport. *¿Comprende?* Without a special permit..." He turned down the edges of his mouth. "Much inconvenience."

To Deidre's horror, he actually fetched a clipboard from one of the other workmen and began walking around the fuselage of the *Albatross*, pausing here and there to write earnestly. He pointed with his pencil to the puddle of oil.

"A leak, *señorita*," he said and clucked woefully to himself. "This must all be checked out by me personally. I am responsibility... eh, *responsable*."

The wretch might be uncertain of the English word, Deidre thought as dread tightened more and more tightly between her temples, but he had a wolf's keen smell for old U.S. dollars. Damn!

She placed her body between him and the oil puddle and glared fiercely, her hands on her hips. "All A-26s leak oil like that," she adamantly declared. "It's their idiosyncrasy."

"*¿Qué?*" He squinted bloodshot eyes. "I wouldn't know about that."

Deidre's fury bubbled as he continued to poke about. What a stupid little dreamer she was, to think she could simply enter and leave a city with more than a hundred banks and secrecy laws more stringent than those of Switzerland. Millions of dollars in illicit drug money poured into Panama every year. Payoffs were a way of life here. One either came prepared, or one took one's business elsewhere.

Promising herself that she wouldn't lose control no matter what, she followed him. He walked to the tail and wrote down the registration number, then double-checked it. He drew his finger through the black soot of the exhaust stains on the nacelle, lifted it to his nose and sniffed.

"It's supposed to do that," she snapped belligerently.

He continued to write.

Incensed, Deidre pursed her mouth and tapped her lips with a finger. "Ah, *señor*... what was your name? Noreiga, yes. Tell me, Señor Noreiga, why do I have the sneaking suspicion that you know the perfect way to get around this *inspección*?"

Turning, and with a smile creasing his face, he struck his head with the heel of his hand, as if a brilliant idea had just occurred to him. "Now that you ask..." He dropped his voice to a conspiratorial mutter from the side of his mouth. "I wouldn't want it to get around, you understand. If certain people knew, I could... what you say?"

He sliced his throat with a finger. "I could get the axe."

"No kidding?" She pursed her mouth dryly.

"But for you, *señorita*?"

Deidre narrowed her eyes until they were bitter, steel-gray slits. "Bottom line, *señor*. How much?"

"Let me finish, please. For you, because you bravely fly this wonderful machine by yourself, I will make a grand favor."

"Golly gee, thanks," she sneered.

"Unless you wish to consider making *me* a grand favor." His hesitation was sticky with sexual innuendo, and to Deidre's astonishment he had the gall to lay his hand on her behind.

Deidre lowered her head as if she planned to gore him to death and said through gritted teeth, "If you don't move your hand in the next two seconds, you oversexed... man, the favor I'm going to do is scream at the top of my lungs, and I won't stop until they call the police. Which means, *señor*, that you will probably nurse that hangover in jail. I don't think they serve tequila in jail." She narrowed her eyes. "*¿Comprende?*"

He assumed a mistreated but practical resignation and removed his hand. "In that case..." Stepping so near her that Deidre could smell cheap whiskey on his breath, he glanced furtively over his shoulder. "I know for a fact that one of the big men at the top can be persuaded now and again." He held up his hand. "An honest man, you understand, but from time to time—"

"How much to buy this good, honest man who can be persuaded from time to time?" she interrupted.

"Four hundred. And take it from me, Nicolas Noreiga, it is a most generous bargain. *Mucho magnánimo.*"

Deidre's shock momentarily overpowered her outrage. She swallowed in disbelief and blinked. "Dollars?"

The corners of his mouth revealed vast disappointment at her naïveté. "Tsk, tsk. You did not think I meant pesos, *señorita*?"

Whirling around, Deidre gazed blindly at the sky. Ever since the day she'd buried her mother, she had begun amassing a long and elaborate history of shafts, most of them having come from men, beginning with her father, embellished considerably by John Desmond and topped off in grand fashion by a whole string of mechanics, clerks, bankers, landlords, salesmen and some idiot from North Dallas who insisted that she'd bought three thousand dollars' worth of aluminum siding.

Even with that imposing repertoire, she was still surprised whenever it came. She wasn't a fighter by nature. It always took its toll. It sometimes made her ill.

From over her shoulder, Noreiga was murmuring, "Some of the other unscrupulous gringos around here would charge you twice that."

Wetting her lips and swearing that he wouldn't see so much as a wisp of fear on her face, she dipped her words in acid as another jet hammered the sky. "One hundred and fifty dollars, you . . . you creep, and that's my bottom dollar!"

Nicolas Noreiga's laughter floated into the warm Panamanian morning. "Oh, *señorita*, what a sense of humor you have. Never have I seen an American lady with such a sense of humor. It is a grand joke, no?"

At her sides, Deidre curled her hands into furious fists. "You think this is a game? You think I have time to waste playing with you? Ohh ... why don't you just forget it! Go play with your pencil or something. I'll see this good, honest man at the top myself!"

She was a blaze of infuriated womanhood as she stomped doggedly toward the terminal.

"Three hundred!" he yelled to her back and hurried, panting, to catch up. "Three hundred, *señorita*. What a mean one you are. I will lose much money. I do not understand how you can do this."

A bitter smile was on Deidre's lips as she faced him. With no effort at all she could throw her hands into the air and give up on life, simply crawl into the safety of a closet.

But she had it coming on this one. Her conscience had warned her, hadn't it? A man with MacIntire's reputation? A man she hadn't trusted from the very beginning? Now she must pay for her sins.

"Two hundred dollars," she said with the most nasty, unnegotiable tone she possessed. "Take it or leave it."

He took it.

The country of Santiago was buried in the side of Brazil like an angry fist. All the way across the cordilleras—the mountain chains that wound between the *mesetas* and river valleys and long, fugitive gorges—Deidre cursed it. And herself. Then she cursed Nicolas Noreiga and her father and John Desmond and Francis MacIntire and everyone down to the salesman from North Dallas and his three thousand dollars of aluminum siding.

Well, what now? She was in a strange country and nearly broke. She had only enough fuel to find MacIntire's landing strip. Oh, her checkbook was in her attaché case, of course, but no one down here would take anything less than a certified check. *She* was the only fool who did that.

So, which was it to be? American Express or her old reliable bluff?

It wasn't as if she had no experience at bluffing. After Alice was buried and she had come to herself, alone with no money, no family and no friends who wanted a permanent houseguest, bluffing had become a way of life.

As had mistakes. At seventeen, one had such a blue-chip list to choose from. One of her most memorable had been marijuana. After she'd cleaned up that distinctly messy act, she made the most brilliant mistake of all: she married John Desmond.

How like her to search long and hard for the very thing that could hurt her the most, then go for it full throttle. She hadn't even been motivated by survival when she fell in love with John. She'd gone after him with the impatient innocence of a child, which she most certainly was not by then.

Strangely, though, she hadn't given up on marriage and children and the permanency that sometimes seemed like the Holy Grail. Sometimes she found herself actually searching a man's face and wondering if he could possibly be . . .

But nothing transitory, thank you very much. No casual, passing affairs while she waited for Mr. Right. It was all or nothing this time. Go for broke. Longevity, Deidre. You're in it for the duration.

Looking down, she realized with a start that she had crossed the Andes into Santiago's tablelands and bluffs. She quickly dispensed with her helmet and headset. Spreading out the maps Francis MacIntire had sent her, she found where he had marked the landing strip.

If she were skilled at handwriting analysis, she would be able to read the man's character from his script. How did a fat-cat opportunist write?

His agent, she had to admit, had been absolutely stunning. He had appeared at her apartment door in Dallas one day—a princely Hispanic, posed against the winter sunshine with a sexy aura guaranteed to turn a woman to gelatin. His suit hadn't cost a penny less than eight hundred dollars, and his diction was straight out of Harvard.

"Good afternoon, Miss Miles," he said eloquently. "I'm Joaquim. I represent Mr. Francis MacIntire. I believe you received a letter saying that I would call."

She had indeed received the letter, but she'd filed it away with all the other impossibilities of life.

"Come in," she invited, painfully aware of her threadbare jeans and prehistoric sweater.

Her apartment on lower Greenville Avenue was an attic over a health-food store. She had gutted the entire place, refinished the hardwood floor, painted the walls a pale peach and hung slender venetian blinds upon the gable windows. The furniture was what she could afford—a bed with an expensive mattress and box springs, a walnut table she had refinished herself, two cane-back chairs painted green and a truly extravagant throw rug.

Joaquim ducked his beautiful head when he walked through her door. He glanced around at the spaciousness. "I approve," he said.

Laughing, Deidre padded across the floor in her stocking feet. "If a person can survive the stairs, it's okay. The only thing I have to offer you is iced tea. Will that be all right?"

"I was hoping you would have some."

She could hardly tear her eyes off him as he sat down on one of her green chairs, extended his long, long legs, adjusted his marvelous creases and wrote her company a personal check for a hundred thousand dollars in Francis MacIntire's name.

When he finished he casually placed the deposit, face up, on the table beside him and extended his hand for the glass of tea she held. "That leaves a balance of a hundred and seventy-five thousand due upon delivery. Correct?"

Deidre gaped at the tiny piece of paper as if it were a mirage that would momentarily disappear. She had expected to work months selling the *Albatross*—advertising in all the magazines, mailing brochures, flying shows all over the country, then accepting a series of partial payments or trade-ins of other planes. Never cash on the barrel head.

It was, in fact, too good to be true. His glass of tea dripped condensation onto the table. She absently wiped it away and squinted at him.

"You're sure this is on the level?"

"You're not looking a gift horse in the mouth, are you, Miss Miles?"

"No, no. Of course not." She smiled lamely. "I just expected to be dealing with a bank or something, that's all."

"The check is good, I assure you."

"I'm sure it is. I just . . ."

"I represent a very wealthy man, Miss Miles. This is to be a gift, you see. An extremely important and sensitive gift."

Deidre didn't know of any human being worthy of such a gift. She angled him a disbelieving glance.

Smiling, he said, "You would have to understand some highly complex issues."

"I helped rebuild an A-26. I can understand complex issues."

Steepling his fingers, he tapped them against his magnificent nose. "You're aware, naturally, that Santiago has owned an Invader."

"So have Brazil, Chile, Colombia, Cuba, the Dominican Republic, Guatemala, Mexico, Nicaragua and Peru."

He laughed. "You've done your homework."

"I have my reasons." When he quizzed her with his brows Deidre shrugged.

"Then you have to know that my country is currently having a . . . shall we say, a bit of difficulty," he said.

Deidre waved a finger in retort. "I may be a working girl, but I keep abreast enough to know that you're talking about Francisco Araujo. From what I've heard, sir, your president should be put on someone's hit list."

All the teasing evaporated from his smile at her words, and his own came more slowly, as if each syllable were weighed precisely, like gold. "He has been, Miss Miles. A number of times."

She, too, sobered; there was something wrong here, but she couldn't put her finger on it. She grudgingly assumed a bit more of her tough-lady facade. "What does my selling Mr. MacIntire the *Albatross* have to do with President Araujo?"

"Mr. MacIntire is a good friend of the president."

"The gift is for him? The president?"

"Sort of."

Sort of? Sighing, Deidre turned away. Francisco Araujo's recent years in office were an international scandal. Even if half the gossip were true, he had to be a wildly extravagant and self-indulgent leader. Everyone wanted him out, but no one could get him out. If Francis MacIntire was this man's friend . . .

She wished he hadn't told her. She hesitated to call him by name. Was he Joaquim Something, or Something Joaquim?

"I'm sorry, Mr. Joaquim . . . sir," she said honestly. "As desperately as our company needs the money, I don't know if I could sleep nights knowing that I was part of anything that would benefit President Araujo."

"No mister."

"What?"

"Just plain Joaquim."

"Well, just plain Joaquim, I think I'm going to be forced to say no."

"I appreciate your integrity. As it happens, this machine that you and your partner have restored so beautifully is symbolic in a number of ways to my people. You see, my country is on the verge of a revolution."

"Your country is always on the verge of a revolution."

He chuckled mirthlessly. "Be that as it may, your own country has a high stake in keeping the peace. This machine of yours represents democracy's incredible ability to endure the worst of man's petty struggles."

That much was true. The *Albatross* had served democracy well during World War II, Korea and Vietnam.

"Besides being a symbol," he said more craftily, "it can also be turned into cold, hard cash. If that should ever be necessary."

She laughed suddenly and briefly. "That I understand, but from what I heard, your president has quite enough cash, and most of that is stolen from his own people."

As Joaquim fingered the check and cleared his throat, Deidre absently wiped condensation from the glass onto her jeans.

"Miss Miles, I would like to tell you more, but I'm going to have to ask you to trust me. The gift will not be misplaced, I assure you. And even if it were, can the man who manufactures cars in Detroit be held accountable if the automobile he made is used in a bank robbery?"

That was a convenient way of thinking, wasn't it? All's fair in love and capital gains? She should walk the man to the door right now.

Instead, she shrugged. "That's some summation you've got there, counselor."

His brows lifted skeptically. "How did you know?"

"You really are a lawyer?"

"Among other things. And you know that lawyers always tell the truth."

What a charmer he was! Deidre smiled. "Now I really don't trust you."

"Oh, yes you do."

Yes, she did, and she dropped her shoulders in bafflement. Where did a person draw the line? Was the man who made bullets guilty of murder when they killed?

She couldn't take her eyes off Francis MacIntire's check for a hundred thousand dollars. "When would you want it?" she asked briskly as her conscience hit her a bright blow in the back of her head.

"When can you deliver it?"

She frowned. "You wouldn't pick it up yourself?"

"I'm sorry. I don't fly planes, I only deliver hundred-thousand-dollar checks. What's the problem?"

Deidre nibbled her lower lip. "I'm not sure I have one."

"Well, there you are."

"It's just that..." She was totally honest now, no tough lady, no bristling businesswoman. "Well, the truth is, I might run into someone I don't particularly want to see."

"Really. May I ask whom?"

"Whom?" She threw back her head and laughed. "I'm sorry. No one I know says *whom*."

A twinkle appeared in his eyes. "*Whom* are you wanting to avoid, Miss Miles? Maybe I can make it easier."

Deidre pretended to clear her throat. "You might answer me one small question."

"If I can."

"The ambassador... the U.S. am—"

"Jonathan Miles? Ah, I see."

Lifting her head, Deidre pulled a face and shrugged. "My father, yes. I haven't heard from him in a number of years. I wasn't sure he was still there."

Retired Colonel Jonathan Miles had taken the post of U.S. ambassador to Santiago after divorcing her mother. Neither of them had dreamed he would stay there twenty years. Deidre wished Jonathan no ill will, but running into him was something she didn't particularly relish. Yet, the practical side of her brain considered the box of bills she and Phillip couldn't pay. And the work still to be done on the bomber.

"It's either make delivery, Miss Miles," Joaquim was urging, "or no contract."

Deidre swirled the ice in the glass. The truth of the matter was, she could probably drop down in Santiago, leave the *Albatross* and catch the first flight out, all without Jonathan ever finding out that she'd been in the country.

She pursed her mouth as she battled with her conscience. "Maybe I'd feel better if you told me something about this man you work for."

"Mr. MacIntire? He's a rancher."

"A big guy, huh?"

"He has over a million head of Zebu stock."

"That's big."

"Enough that his rice crops make a difference in the world's food supply."

Deidre nibbled at the inside of her lip. "A missionary, yet? Come on."

"Well, you asked. He's built a town. He provides jobs for a lot of people. In fact, his enterprises are so large that they've necessitated bringing in his family—three of his brothers and his parents."

She tapped the end of her nose. "My kind of guy. I guess he can afford to buy expensive toys if he wants to."

He didn't appreciate her comments. He drew in a long, thoughtful breath. "Actually, I'm surprised you haven't heard of him."

"I don't keep up with the ten most wanted men."

Rising, he leaned forward and nudged the check toward her. "Look, Miss Miles, if you decide you can't deliver the plane, you can always tear the check up."

He started gracefully toward her door. Staring at his beautiful back, Deidre envisioned financial ruin if she didn't say something quickly. What was the use of a conscience if it starved to death? Damn!

"Six months," she blurted, and hurried after him.

Turning, keeping his hand on the doorknob, he had the grace not to throw her cynicism up to her. "Will that be enough?"

"Phillip and I work fast." Dear Lord, don't let her regret this.

"Very good, then. We have an agreement." He extended a strong bronzed hand, and, after nervously wiping the sweat from the glass onto the front of her top, Deidre shook it. Then, because he was an absolutely charming man and she'd come on a little strong, she invited him to dinner.

"I would love to, Miss Miles," he declined so graciously that she flushed, "but I have a return flight booked. Perhaps we could have dinner in Santiago?"

"Perhaps."

"Till then?"

"Give my thanks to Mr. MacIntire."

"Of course."

As the door clicked shut, and Deidre listened to the sound of his feet lightly taking the stairs, she leaned back against the wall and didn't know if she'd done the right thing or not.

But it was sold! After three years of work that she and Phillip had juggled between quicker money jobs, the big one was sold. Maybe now things would be better. Maybe now she wouldn't have to scratch and claw just to make a dime.

"Joaquim," she murmured and nodded her approval. But how about Francis MacIntire? Buying an A-26, then giving it to a despot? She pictured an obnoxious, overweight man in a three-piece suit and a Stetson and Tony Lama rattlesnake-skin boots. And a diamond pinkie ring on his fat little finger—she mustn't forget that.

She wouldn't trust the man if he'd sent platinum as a deposit. But she did trust Joaquim.

She glanced down at her fingers, which were half-frozen from the melted ice. She'd forgotten to give Joaquim his glass of tea! Laughing, she twirled around her airy room in a silly little dance, waltzed over to the telephone and called Phillip.

"Phillip, old man," she'd said in Joaquim's precise Harvard accent. "Don't hyperventilate. I've got the most smashing news."

Chapter Two

It was the spilled milk theory all over again, Deidre bleakly told herself at three thousand feet. She had to put Nicolas Noreiga and his extortion behind her. Crying over the wretch was a waste of good saline.

"Longevity, Deidre baby," she stubbornly said aloud, a child whistling in the dark. "Forget the lowlife. Or come back to haunt him."

Except that she couldn't, and she wouldn't, and life wasn't fair, and she was shin deep in milk again.

Below her, a lush carpet of jungle spread between fingers of bare wilderness where peasants had hacked away the rain forest. Except for a half dozen or so cities, Santiago consisted mainly of unmarked villages whose landing strips were so remote they were probably used for smuggling. The boat landings were even more suspicious looking.

By the time she was flying over the places MacIntire had marked on the maps, however, the landscape began subtly to change. Here, hundreds of sparkling lakes were interspersed with lavish contrasts—richly cultivated pasture against areas of wildest jungle. Great herds of cattle dotted the grassland, so many they were impossible to estimate. Following the contours of the wilderness, rice fields were laid out in enormous paisley patterns that stretched for miles.

She spotted the deep, slow-moving river, Rio Tepuí, where a rainbow-laced cloud of mist rose to meet her. The town, which carried the same name, gave the appearance of considerable sophistication, with its hydroelectric plant hunched on the river and the deep-water port accommodating big boats from the Amazon that could transport the town's produce to market.

The ranch of the Irishman was a town in itself. Ten miles beyond Rio Tepuí, it sprawled over the top of a hill. Being the friend of a president had its certain little niceties, eh, Mac?

A muster of *tuyuyú*, five-foot Jabiru storks, rose from one of the lakes and formed a cloud beneath her. Deidre kept an anxious eye on them as she scoured the terrain, searching for the airstrip. The birds could be as dangerous as a wind shear.

There! Two miles away, the strip angled off the edge of the jungle where bulldozers had recently been at work. A large hangar lay to the east, approached by a road that twisted drunkenly through the trees.

From a distance, the hangar appeared guarded. A small plane was parked at one end of the runway, apparently having just landed, and vehicles looking like Monopoly pieces were pulling off the road and parking haphazardly alongside it.

Banking wide, Deidre dropped to eight hundred feet and lowered the landing gear and her flaps a quarter. The *Al-*

batross was mushy now and as slow to respond as a surly drunk. Rarely did she land one of these big planes without experiencing a fresh respect for the pilots who'd flown the first ones over the South Pacific.

From the corner of her eye, as she dropped her flaps another quarter, she spied a cloud of dust spinning out from behind two trucks. They had whipped into the fenced area of the hangar and were racing alongside the runway.

She was being met by the *Albatross*'s new owner? Well, well. People seemed to be collecting from all over—from out of the nearby fields and peasant huts, from the clumps of jungle fringe. They were all moving toward the airstrip.

Look sharp, sweetie. There's going to be a ceremony.

In seconds, she was down to a hundred feet. Then sixty. Fifty. At thirty, she detected another flurry, from the sentries this time. Men were spilling out of the trucks. The truck in the lead, an old World War II relic, actually had a gun mounted on the top. Some jerk was clowning around with it, swinging it about and aiming at the small plane.

Good grief! What was happening here? The men spilling from the vehicles were in uniform. Why uniformed men? They were swinging guns up to their shoulders. Some were dropping to one knee and aiming.

Deidre's heart jerked in confused alarm. Men were racing toward the end of the runway now, and she wanted to shout at them to get back, but, to her shock, she caught sight of the plane she thought had just landed—a 210 Centurion. It hadn't landed at all but was preparing for a reckless, insane takeoff.

"No!" she screamed as it hurtled down the runway straight toward her.

It couldn't happen. It would be a head-on collision to end all collisions. The men on the ground were firing relentlessly now, and from the crowd arms were waving with a frenzy.

In a split-second decision, acting more on instinct than logic, Deidre cut the power and gritted her teeth. She would hit too hard, but dear God, better to lose nose gear than her own nose.

As she thought it, she did it. Adrenaline burst into her veins as she dipped down to touch the runway. The Centurion zoomed over her head and streaked into the sky.

Instinctively she ducked, but now an equally catastrophic dilemma confronted her—the old World War II truck that had been parked at the end of the strip, mocking her like some smiling barricade of TNT It was whipping around on the runway and heading toward her. The gunner was still seated ludicrously on his perch, except that now he was swinging his gun toward her.

Deidre's breath was trapped in her lungs. Without even thinking, she jammed the throttles wide open and dropped the flaps full down. Like a comet flung out of orbit, the *Albatross* ballooned up over the truck, then thudded heavily back to earth.

Inside the cockpit Deidre was thrown first one way, then another, while beneath her the nose gear gave way with a sickening crunch. Two feet of the precious, seven-thousand-dollar propellers bent like licorice sticks as the belly of the fuselage skidded along the runway. There was an excruciating shriek of metal, which seemed to go on forever, then the plane came to rest with a final scream and turned crossways, her nose down and bleeding, as wounded and vulnerable as a beached whale.

For some moments, Deidre didn't move. From beginning to end it had lasted the space of a few heartbeats. As the metal finally stopped weeping, she thought she saw more vehicles screeching up to surround the *Albatross*.

Land Rovers? she wondered in a daze. Pickups? Jeeps? More people running toward her?

Hardly able to believe that she was even alive, she lifted a hand to a place on her head, and her fingers came away bloody. Through a blur she saw sunlight fractured through the windshield...blinding light...fresh air...hands...voices.

The next thing she knew, they were pulling her out of the cockpit—strange, uniformed men touching her in impersonal ways. She felt an eerie awareness of something important that she must address herself to but could not remember.

Someone chattered in incomprehensible Spanish. She flailed at someone's khaki-clad chest.

"Leave me alone!" she groaned. "I'm all right."

"She's regaining consciousness," a man's voice said, not in the national Spanish but in precise, clipped English.

She was placed upon her feet by strong brown hands. "I never lost it," she heard her own voice snarling back. She struck at a faceless person. "Leave me alone."

"She's bleeding."

Of course I'm bleeding, imbecile! But, oddly enough, there was little pain, only a weird illusion of floating.

"Get first aid," the English voice briskly commanded. "Private Campos, the jeep. ¡Rápido!"

Through a fog, Deidre saw that the hangar was sheet metal, a remarkably sturdy building with electric lines swooping from a pole near the road. Another small plane and a helicopter were parked inside. Then she saw that the men in uniform, who were scattered unevenly over the turf, hadn't lowered their weapons; they were observing her with hard, shuttered faces.

Not understanding, she gazed blankly at the civilians who looked on—thirty, perhaps, all of them men. Some had formed a column along the shady side of the hangar, and some waited along the parked vehicles: black men, brown men, white men—a veritable sea of slouches and booted feet.

Towering above them all was the tall, beautiful Hispanic who had appeared at her apartment door. Now he wasn't wearing a Fifth Avenue suit but denim pants covered with dust. Over them were chaps cut into strips. His shirt sleeves were rolled to his elbows, and his skin was burnished and gleamed like purest bronze in the sun.

"Joaquim!" she said in a fervent breath of relief.

The shake of his head was almost imperceptible.

Stunned, Deidre pulled up short. The Amazon heat took on a new, more perilous dimension. It seeped into her blood through the pores of her skin and sent hysteria bubbling up in her throat. What was going on here? Why had Joaquim pulled back? Did that mean the deal with MacIntire was off?

Unable to breathe, she fumbled with the zipper of her flight jacket. She had to get out of some of her clothes before she fainted.

"*Señorita,*" the English voice said icily as she was groping for the metal tab, "please stand exactly where you are. Do not move. My men have orders to shoot. I don't think either one of us would find that very pleasant, do you?"

It was a scene from the movie that lost money for the producer but won eight Oscars for the Academy. Not the one where the rags-to-riches heroine became an international humanitarian whose biography was written by David Halberstam, but the one where the silly American pilot was taken prisoner in a strange land and never heard of again.

"*Lento, lento.*" The voice grated along the edge of Deidre's nerves. "Nice and slow now. I like to see hands. Keep them high, *señorita.* I said up!"

"All right!" Deidre's words were packed hard in her chest, squeezed into a ball that she could scarcely get her voice around. "I'm turning, see? I'm turning." Then, in a whimper that appalled her, she moaned, "Oh, please..."

"Ah." His chuckle sounded satisfied. "Very good. You seem to have a brain in that pretty head of yours, *señorita*. It would be a real shame to put a hole in it."

Did it ever fail? Deidre wondered hysterically. Whenever some sadist was about to let her have it, he always prefaced it with a remark about how intelligent she was. Or how pretty.

Surely a woman of your intelligence, Miss Miles, can see that if the university made an exception in your case, we would have to make exceptions for everyone.

Look at this from an intelligent point of view, Mrs. Desmond, er... Miss Miles. The police have neither the manpower nor the time to look for your husband. Ah, exhusband... whatever he is.

A good-looking woman like you, Miss Miles? Why, I bet you could find a dozen roommates who would be glad to share the new rent. If you get my drift.

With her arms sagging, Deidre saw the uniformed men closing in to form a barricade around her. Guns were in their hands—not pistols, but vile black things that had to be held with both hands.

She visualized herself lying facedown on the ground. *Poor Deidre, she was such an intelligent girl, so pretty—what a shame. And just when she was getting the hang of it.*

Her courage snapped like a brittle twig. "I'm just a pilot," she pleaded. "I haven't done anything. This is a terrible mistake. Please, listen to me." She slowly swiveled toward her tormentor.

"Listen?" His mockery sent a chill chasing up her spine. "Do you know, most of our trouble here in Santiago is because of pilots? Why, you would not believe the things that are flown into our country, *señorita*. Just once I'd like to hear one of you people say to me, '*Sí*, I am carrying cocaine. I am carrying weapons.' Now, why don't you save us both a lot of time?''

"You think I'm smuggling *drugs*?" In clammy disbelief, Deidre completed her pirouette.

The owner of the clipped English voice was the kind of man no one could possibly like, a small figure of half a dozen badly mixed cultures that made his complexion nearly mauve. His tight, blood-chilling smile was that of a fanatic. Beneath the visor of his military cap his needle-sharp eyes missed nothing.

But his hands were effeminate, almost pretty. Deidre wondered how many bribes had crossed *his* palms. Somehow she didn't think he could be bought off as easily as Nicolas Noreiga. His quirt, which he rested meticulously on the toe of his spit-shined boot, was an affectation he didn't even need. Attila the Hun could hardly have been more terrifying.

"Allow me to introduce myself," he said with the oiliness of self-importance. "I am Captain Candido Malta, commander of the President's Special Task Forces. It is my unpleasant duty to inform you, *señorita*, that unless you can give me a satisfactory reason for landing a military plane in Rio Tepuí, I shall be forced to place you under arrest."

Deidre looked up at the hot, unforgiving sky and felt the hair rise on the back of her neck. "I am Deidre Miles."

"Indeed?"

"I'm from the United States. I came here on business," she added bitterly.

"I see." The captain tucked his quirt into an armpit with a look that said nothing she could say or do would surprise him.

The guards inched nearer to form a more threatening cordon. Deidre dizzily wondered if she could gather enough courage to make an escape—something spectacular that would live on after she was gone. She could hurl herself through the men and dash for the plane amid the chatter of submachine-gun fire. She would zigzag, like Alan Arkin did in *The In-laws,* and wouldn't even sustain a graze. Everyone knew what crummy shots villains were.

"And if you want to arrest someone, Captain Malta," she declared with rising desperation, "I suggest you try catching the idiot who nearly made me crash."

"Oh, I fully intend to do that."

"And let me also remind you that I'm a citizen of the United States."

His voice was thick with self-esteem. "I'm afraid we're not quite as impressed with that fact as you are."

Deidre saw her picture on the cover of *Time,* with the caption: "Death of American Civilian Triggers War." It occurred to her that running into her father after fifteen years wasn't so unattractive an idea as it had once been.

"I demand to be taken to the American embassy, Captain," she ordered with a haughtiness that would have won one of the Oscars. "Immediately. Do you hear? I'm a citizen of the United States."

"Oh, do please stop saying that."

"But you have no right to hold me at gunpoint like this!" she shrieked.

"Perhaps." His eyes grew intimidatingly smaller. "Would you now be so kind as to produce your identification?"

Deidre blinked. Was this a good sign? "My papers are in the cockpit." Like the most pathetic kind of ingenue— Would you tango on a tightrope, please? Yes, I'd be delighted—she started to get them.

At a single snap of Malta's quirt against a palm, one of the guards stepped into her path.

"Oh!" She gasped and stumbled back, her eyes wide.

"You, Private!" the officer called imperiously over his shoulder to another man as Deidre's heart thrashed in her chest. "Fetch her papers from the aircraft. *Ponte en marcha.*" Get going.

"Oh, hell, I'll get the bloody papers."

The voice that shattered the tension was like a clap of thunder bursting from a cloudless sky. Even as Deidre jerked around to see who owned it, a murmur rose from those who watched.

One of the Anglos was elbowing his way through the crowd. With a long-legged, vagabond grace, he stepped from among them and strolled across the turf. From her dizzy haze, Deidre wondered how he had the courage to intervene in her behalf against Attila. But then she saw that he seemed quite capable of taking care of himself. There was something about the aura he exuded. He didn't attract attention; it was his already, and he appeared comfortable at the center of it. Could he possibly be the Irishman she'd come to meet?

No. This man wasn't rich or even well-to-do. He certainly wasn't wealthy enough to afford something like the *Albatross*, Deidre decided as she noted his threadbare bush jacket, its pockets and flaps wilted dismally with age, and his slim bush pants pushed limply into scuffed riding boots.

There was no way of telling how old he was. Forty? Forty-five? Sun and wind had weathered him, and the lines webbing his icy blue eyes were time-tracked and permanent. The black of his sideburns was streaked with gray. The creases on his cheeks and forehead, blending in fascinating harmony with his rugged nose and jaw, created an indelible impression of that thing called experience, much of which had obviously not been to his liking.

What did it matter who he was or how old? He was coming to help. He was rolling up one of his sleeves as he walked, bunching it absently about the biceps of a suntanned arm. He touched the brim of his hat to her in polite acknowledgment.

Deidre thought with some disappointment that the hat matched the rest of him only too well—a battered felt affair, flat-crowned and wide-brimmed, much like that of the common gaucho.

She flashed him a wan, hopeful smile.

He did not return it.

Well! How rude!

She angrily snatched her attention back to Candido Malta, but, to her astonishment, the disdainful military face was not nearly so arrogant now. His bones were suddenly prominent beneath taut skin, as if they were ready to pierce through the sleek facade. The sides of his mouth pinched downward. His eyes were so slitted that she could not see them.

The Anglo inclined his head. "With your permission, that is, Captain." As he drawled the lazy challenge several men with baggy pants and flowing shirts moved in to form a rank behind him.

The tension crystallized like vapor around the site of an explosion. Even the mosquitoes seemed to stop their bloodthirsty humming as if to see what would happen.

The captain laid a hand casually upon his holster. Deidre didn't dare draw a breath.

"Very well," he said with a face-saving gesture of boredom. He fluttered his fingers. "Be quick about it."

The wide, curved mouth of the Anglo twisted in a smirk. With a touch of his hat, he moved negligently away, looking again at Deidre as he passed, but differently this time: swiftly, elementally, marking everything at a glance, but not just the usual things men looked at—not her mouth and her breasts, her belly and all the feminine apparatus below that. She suspected he truly *saw* her, as few men, or anyone else, had ever taken the trouble to do.

A small, dormant creature stirred somewhere inside her, but Deidre thrust it back into its dark corner and took an impulsive step after the white man, calling, "Sir, my ID is . . ."

Where? Clamping her mouth shut and feeling like a fool when he turned, she pasted a dumb smile on her face. She didn't have the faintest idea where her identification was. On a clipboard? Beneath the seat?

A lift of his shoulder said he could find the papers on his own.

Disappointment washed over Deidre in a wave, not because she couldn't remember, but because the encounter should have meant more. And wasn't that just great? Her fate, maybe even her life, hung in the balance between a power-crazed army officer and a cocky cynic who looked as if he could easily be an ivory smuggler on the Amazon River, and she was worried about meaningful encounters!

He disappeared into the cockpit. The peasants positioned themselves at the bottom rung of the ladder. Turning to face Candido Malta without the slightest trace of fear or apprehension, they spread their feet with a curiously military bearing.

From behind a burgeoning pain in her temples, Deidre realized that something was terribly inconsistent in the scene. An important equation wasn't balancing. Who in the name of common sense was in control here, anyway?

The sun was ruthless now. The jungle heat was much different from the Texas burn she was used to; it wrapped tentacles around her and pulled at her limbs, making them so heavy that she could scarcely stay on her feet. As she once again reached for the zipper of her jump suit and gave it a raspy jerk, a soft metallic click sounded behind her left ear.

In slow motion, she lifted her head and looked over her shoulder into the muzzle of an automatic rifle. Oh, Lord! She sucked in her breath with a harsh sound.

"I wouldn't touch the jacket, *señorita*," Malta said with lethal condescension. "In fact, if I were you, I would stand perfectly still and not touch anything until I tell you to."

Deidre's face felt as if it would crack. "But I was just—"

" I now what you were doing." He motioned for another guard to step forward.

Over her shoulder, Deidre threw a desperate glance to the *Albatross*, but now the Anglo was nowhere to be seen. His men watched with dull, impassive faces.

"I don't have a gun in my pocket, for pity's sake!" she protested.

With a flick of his quirt, Malta ordered the second man to position himself in front of her. Corporal's bars were stitched to the sleeve of a shirt that was splotchy with sweat. He gripped her by the shoulders.

His grin was a sour, scavenger's leer. Deidre could almost see the roots of his teeth. Her eyes flew wide, and an even worse fear filled her. When he began slapping his hands over her body, she struck out at him with wild, righteous fists.

"Just a dad-gummed minute!" she cried. "Get your filthy hands off me!"

The man's response was to consult his captain.

"Continue, Corporal," Candido coolly ordered.

The corporal caught her wrist in a grasp that brought tears swimming to Deidre's eyes. She wasn't tough now; she was terrified. Longevity, Deidre, she told herself as he clapped his rude hands to the sides of her thighs. First order of the day: Stay alive. Clear your mind of him. Pretend he doesn't exist. He isn't touching you. You aren't this body. You're inside, and no one can hurt you there.

As he moved over her waist, then her breasts, lingering over their curves much more than necessary, Deidre kept her eyes fixed, trancelike, upon his face and stared straight through it.

He finished quickly after that, skimming over her back and the slope of her hips. Deidre flinched when he made a final sweep up the inside of her legs, but he seemed to have lost interest.

Presently he stripped off her jacket and searched the pockets. He opened all the zippers on the sides and on the sleeves. By the time the Anglo returned from the plane, Deidre was so deep into her self-induced hypnosis, only the whispery stir of Malta's guards alerted her to his presence.

She looked distractedly over her shoulder, and her eyes, like steel to magnet, found him.

He was hardly recognizable as he stepped through the barrier of men and hesitated, the sheaf of her papers in his hand. Where before he had been graceful, he was now furiously intent. An ugly snarl pulled his lips back from his teeth as he took stock of her dazed misery, her hands extended pitifully into the air, her still-spread feet, her jacket in the guilty corporal's hands.

No one breathed as he strode angrily across the grass. No sounds came from the hangar or from the area of parked vehicles. The jungle air hovered, still and close and aching with danger.

Slowly, almost imperceptibly, Candido's men pulled back, leaving her alone in the center with the corporal. They arranged themselves in a loose formation behind their captain, and Candido Malta, not removing his gaze for a moment from the dangerous Anglo, muttered an order from the corner of his mouth.

They could have been two small armies facing each other, and Deidre decided it wasn't the first time; old hatreds, like old buildings, had a certain character to them. Oh, she'd known better, hadn't she? She'd had all kinds of reservations about coming here, but no, she had to be greedy. She had to sell the big one.

The Anglo stopped deliberately before the corporal, but the man was staring into the never-never land where all good soldiers stare.

He plucked the jacket from the corporal's hands and draped it across the shelf of Deidre's half-extended arm. "You can put your hands down now, Miss Miles," he said gently.

Blinking at him, Deidre absently slapped at a mosquito on her neck. How did he know who she was? Of course, her papers.

But before she could say or do anything, the Anglo said to the corporal with heart-stopping softness, "Tell me, Juan Geisel, did you put your hands on this woman?"

Juan Geisel continued to stare. For a reason Deidre didn't totally understand, she took a trembling step toward the back of the man who was befriending her. Her intention was to touch the roll of his sleeve, but his authority affected her, too, for she stood with her hand outstretched, unable to.

"Sir," she whispered to the back of his head, "please let it go. I'm all right. It doesn't matter."

"Stay back," he ordered as if he'd been taking care of her for years.

"But it's a stupid misunderstanding. The captain thought I was carrying a weapon or something. Please, it's not worth it."

When he finally did turn to face her, outlined against the iron-fisted sky with his feet dangerously parted and every muscle in his body alert with strain, Deidre's brain sifted through all it had known before. She found nothing to justify the look he gave her—as if many things had passed between them, of which this was only the least; a whole lifetime of closeness, countless and infinite intimacies that forged a chain of history, a background of passions that melted time and made anything possible.

"Deidre," he said quietly, branding her with the burn of his look, "don't tell me what you're worth. Please, stay where you are, and be quiet."

Never before had Deidre obeyed a man as she did him. She was so helpless before the impact of his strength, she guessed she would have proffered her very soul if he'd asked for it.

Turning to the corporal, he said with the same pleasant manner as before, "I'll ask you one more time, Juan, did you touch this woman?"

Sweat trickled down Juan's cheeks, and he blinked rapidly, flicked his tongue across his lips. "I had orders to search her," he declared flatly to the sky. "I obey orders."

"Well, obey mine then." The demand was infinitely more frightening because of its quietness. "Apologize to Miss Miles."

Even the onlookers were shocked at such a command. Deidre thought she sensed them closing in, pressing nearer.

Juan wasn't leering now, and he cocked his head with uncertainty. "*¿Qué?* What did you say?"

"I don't give orders twice," the Anglo replied with perilous tranquility. "You know that, Juan."

Alarmed, Juan glanced at his commanding officer for orders, but Candido Malta was swimming in his own impotent rage. To Deidre, he seemed to have grown smaller.

With his head ducked, he seemed stamped with exhaustion and dark with bitterness.

Juan assessed the threat of the Anglo's determined jaw and gauged the distance of hostile peasants. "But, *señor*—"

"Do it!" The order cracked like a whip. "You stand on my land, Juan Geisel. You insult my guest."

My land? My guest? Deidre was drowning in confusion.

Knowing now that he wouldn't be receiving help from his fellow soldiers, Juan suddenly reversed tactics and laughingly placated with his hands; it was all a ridiculously funny mistake that could be corrected if both parties would only take the time to sit down and talk.

"Señor MacIntire..." He was wheedling in a joking singsong.

Too much was happening for Deidre's battered, overheated senses. Juan was suddenly stepping back so that a distance was between himself and the Anglo. With a slap of his hand to the holster riding his hip, he was flicking the snaps and fumbling to free the gun. With a reaction more swift and immeasurably more decisive, the Anglo swung back his arm and brought his hand hard across the corporal's face in a splintering, open-handed slap.

No man would tolerate such an insult, of course. A man could accept a fist in the teeth, yes, or a knee to the kidney, a mangled arm and torn-off fingernails, but never a palm upon a jaw.

Juan's head snapped backward as if jerked with a wire. His hand that held the gun dropped to his side, and when he realized what had happened and the disgrace that went with it, he screamed as if he had been shot. "You son of a pig!"

The Anglo didn't move. He did not reply. When he struck Juan across the face the second time, it was with the back of the same hand.

Never in her life had Deidre witnessed such a shocking scene, and she guessed that none of the rest of them had either. Voices rose, then silenced as quickly. Candido's guards rushed forward in unison, their guns drawn and at the ready.

Deidre expected Francis MacIntire to at least step back, to at least . . . *MacIntire!*

At last her addled brain caught up. This man was Francis MacIntire! But he wasn't fat and obnoxious. He wasn't wearing the Stetson, the Tony Lama boots, the pinky ring. . . .

Tears of passionate rage stood in Juan's eyes now. Slowly he lifted the gun and, holding it steady with both hands, aimed it dead-center at Francis MacIntire's chest.

"If you use that thing, Juan," MacIntire said through a flash of bared teeth, "you'd better kill me within the first second."

The Irishman's hat had fallen to the ground, and Deidre was as aware of his wild black curls as of her papers scattered on the crushed grass that was sending its acrid pungency into her nostrils. Candido Malta looked as if he could commit murder with his bare hands, but, with a jerk of his head, he commanded his men to lower their weapons.

A dozen guns swung downward. Blundering, booted feet stepped back.

Deidre wished she could run, screaming, from the scene, but the fascination of violence wove a web around her melting senses. No man, real or fantasized, had ever defended her before, and coupled with the Irishman's virile possessiveness—or perhaps because of it—she experienced a whole series of bizarre, superimposed images, all of them intensely sexual: herself belonging to such a man, being swept up in his powerful arms and being carried away by him, being adored and made his captive queen, never needing or wanting anything ever again, surrendering to his urgency in the heat of the night, thrilling to his outlaw hunger, her own hunger.

"No more, *señor. Me pesa, señorita.*" Juan obediently surrendered and hung his head. "I'm sorry."

Deidre had no reply for such a confession.

Sidling sideways like a crab, Juan stumbled away to nurse his mortification. Deidre was still in the backlash of her outrageous fantasies, and she didn't know what to do. Thank the man? Smile and pretend nothing had happened? Follow Juan Geisel's good example and simply disappear?

Francis MacIntire stooped for his hat while his men gathered up her fluttering papers. When he straightened, the skin was drawn tautly over the granite of his cheekbones, and Deidre thought she read pain.

She was unable to take her eyes off him. He walked with slow deliberation to his men and collected her papers, then heeled sharply and returned to the indignant captain.

"I think you'd better take a look at these, Candido," he said with wry insolence as he thrust them into the starched front of the uniform, "before you make a bigger fool of yourself."

Chapter Three

As Francis looked into the deep, liquid pools of Deidre Miles's gray eyes, it occurred to him to wonder just how much longer people would tolerate his outlandish macho performances.

Years before, when he'd first come to Santiago with Mary Beth and Sean, he'd been young enough and arrogant enough to be impressed with stunts such as the one he'd just pulled. But he was hardly that man any longer, was he?— that brash, self-centered young hellion who'd been born fighting.

Not that he'd ever cared all that much about what people thought; if he'd been guilty of that, he wouldn't have come to Santiago in the first place. Life had never been easy for the MacIntires. A minority, though a closely knit family clan, they'd told themselves it didn't matter that they were never accepted by the elite Boston WASPs who lived blocks away but who might as well have been on another planet.

For three generations MacIntires educated themselves in Boston's public schools and served their country in the armed forces. They built houses and bakeries and canning factories and trucking companies. Some became policemen on the block. But the MacIntire men still tended to marry good Irish girls and raise more Irish Catholics.

Promising to follow suit, at nineteen, without a penny to his name, Francis had one day found himself drafted into the army. The Korean war was winding down. "Happy Days" and "The Fonz" were for real back then. What a thrill it was to put on the uniform and set the cap at a rakish angle and listen to all the girls say how much like Burt Lancaster he looked.

He shipped out believing in three things: himself, the good old American way and the back seat of a '49 Ford. When he'd found himself flying over the Korean mountains, however, he was a plain GI Joe in a bomber exactly like the A-26 Deidre Miles had just landed on his airstrip. It was a routine mission. Who could have predicted that the pilot and the copilot would both be killed in a sudden burst of antiaircraft fire?

A funny thing, when crashing is imminent one isn't too inclined to worry about things like experience and expertise. The nearest he'd come to flying was back home when Harvey Blair let him take the controls of his Cessna for ten minutes.

But if he was going down, he damn sure wouldn't be sitting and wringing his hands while his life passed before his eyes. Without a moment's hesitation, he dragged John Anderson's body out of the seat and took over.

He almost pulled it off. "A miraculous crash landing," they'd congratulated when he woke up with a rebuilt hip.

At last, the MacIntire clan had its American hero, and Boston opened its loving arms. Now bankers wanted to loan him money. One of the small aircraft businesses gave him a Piper Cub to endorse their line. Fashionable hostesses put him at the top of their guest lists. Some even asked him to stay the night.

With his fine sense of fair play insulted, Francis returned home on a crutch and thumbed his nose at the society that had refused to accept his family before. Oh, he accepted the loans and the Piper Cub, but he didn't endorse the line, and if he stayed the night with any of the hostesses it wasn't for pleasure, it was for revenge.

In the end, however, he'd married one of those genteel Boston socialites. He brought her to this backward country in South America. Mary Beth hadn't wanted to come, but she did because she loved him. He built himself an empire, then he buried Mary Beth.

That was when he climbed off his arrogant horse. He began to learn a few things. He grew twenty years older.

Buying the A-26 was one of the most risky things he'd done in a long time. It served a dual purpose, actually. Francisco Araujo, his friend, his patron, his nemesis, was a good man going bad. Not only could he not bear to watch it any longer, but the rest of the country couldn't either. And that was the crux of it all; in one month—Araujo did not know this—he planned to present the plane to the president as a farewell gift.

A balm for his conscience? A cop-out?

Precisely. He owed a lot to Santiago and its people. And he owed Araujo, whether he liked to admit it or not. But once the tables were clean, he, Francis Collins MacIntire, learner of lessons, deserter of ships, thrower-in of towels, was withdrawing his support from the president, and whatever happened, happened.

He wasn't blind to the possible repercussions. For months officials in the State Department had been after him to throw his support behind Carlos Navarro in the next election. The U.S. leaned to paranoia when the left went communist, the right went fanatical and the president was left helplessly in the middle. But he didn't like Navarro.

The U.S. wouldn't be happy about his decision to pull out, but then, neither would his family, and for different reasons. His own son, a doctor, brilliantly educated, the only child he had and ever would have, believed that he'd become corrupted by Araujo. Sean had left home. Now he was up in the hills, giving free medical care to the rebels who sought to overthrow Araujo.

The truth was, he was nearly fifty years old. He was lonely. He was tired. At times he wondered if he hadn't lost his nerve. He hadn't sat at the controls of a plane in ten years. Sometimes in the night he awoke in a cold sweat and lived the nightmare of the crash all over again. Vultures were wheeling high over his life, and he stood holding a spear to keep them at bay.

He'd arrived late at the airstrip today. Sean had been seen in Las Tablas getting medical supplies. He was hoping to find him. Just in time, he'd climbed out of the Land Rover to see Deidre Miles landing an A-26 and nearly getting herself killed by his own son in the process.

But her handling of the big plane had been a virtuoso performance. Par excellence, and he should know. What he really took his hat off to her for, though, was the way she'd stood up to Candido—some spunky little mongoose, feistily baring its teeth at a king cobra. After that, he would have burned in hell before he'd leave her in the hands of a mongrel like Juan Geisel.

Behind him now, he could feel Joaquim's thoughts burning into his back: *Poor Francis, he's entering some embarrassing phase now. We'll all have to watch him make a fool of himself. Next he'll be going out to buy blue jeans and a cowboy hat and a white Porsche.*

"That was stupid thing to do, my fine North American friend," Candido Malta was saying as he accepted the papers from Francis without so much as a glance at them.

"Only one among many, eh, Candido?" Francis smiled nastily at the captain but focused upon Deidre Miles; she had no color, like a faded photograph in a thin silver frame one finds in the attic. He had to get her out of here, quickly.

"My land, Candido," he heard himself say, "my stupidity. Also my plane. Now, if you'll excuse me . . ."

"Your land?" came the guarded challenge.

"Bought and paid for. Miss Miles? Deidre?"

The captain came as close to a smile as Francis had ever seen. "I hate to disillusion you, Mr. MacIntire, but this land is not yours. That's the trouble with you foreigners, you know. You come down here and say, 'I own this jungle.' You don't own the jungle. You don't own the trees. You don't own the water. No one owns it."

Not for an instant did Francis underestimate the enemy he had in Candido Malta. The man was completely without morals and devoid of any grace whatsoever. He was cruel; he was clever. To back him against the wall another inch would only ensure that he would jump out like a fighting rat.

"Really, Candido?" He made himself laugh and at the same time tried to reassure Deidre with a smile. "Maybe that's the reason men keep stealing it."

"Go home where you belong, Irishman." There was no smile on the captain's face now. He looked capable of terrible things. "An airplane took off from this strip a few minutes ago," he said darkly. "I don't suppose you know anything about that."

"Of course I do."

"We think it was Sean MacIntire."

"Is that a fact?"

As Deidre stood watching the struggle between the two men, she thought there was something to be said for a less civilized age when men could shoot each other and be done with it. Sweat was springing from the roots of her hair now and dripping from her chin and drizzling between her shoulder blades. If she stood out here much longer they would have to carry her away in a body bag.

"I do own this air strip," Francis MacIntire was telling the captain with bored negligence, "but I can't always control who comes onto it. Quite often it's without my authorization. Sometimes not even to my liking." He turned up his hand in insolence as blatant as a yawn.

The trap door of Malta's mouth snapped shut. He lowered his eyes to the papers in his hands, and when he spoke, Deidre mistakenly assumed that he spoke to her.

"Do not push your luck," he said. "Time is running out. Go home before something tragic happens."

Just as Deidre opened her mouth to protest such threats, the captain lifted his head. The penetration of his gaze into Francis MacIntire was murderous.

"If you don't care about yourself, think of your family. Your son is living on borrowed time."

Son? Now Deidre began to perceive something of the history between the two men. She expected a brash display from the Irishman, but at the mention of his son, he became oddly vulnerable.

"Ambition brings a man to his knees, Candido," he warned softly. "Take care that the same time doesn't run out for you, too."

The captain's laughter wasn't a pleasant sound. "But I'm more clever than you, Irishman. Araujo, you see, trusts me."

"Then he is a fool."

Candido Malta brought down his quirt with a whistle that made Deidre flinch. Her motion attracted the attention of both men. The officer withdrew a pair of reading glasses from his pocket and held them to his eyes as they moved over the papers he held.

"Miles?" he questioned, and he looked at her.

But Deidre was preoccupied with the way MacIntire was studying her. It was as if the two awarenesses, MacIntire's and her own, once joined, could not be broken.

What do you see, Irishman? she wanted to say. *Are you looking on the inside of me? Do you see that I'm a fraud? That I'm not tough at all but am a confused mass of hinges opening on all kinds of strange fears? Do you see that I am at this moment wanting to go to you, to have the security of your arm around me?*

Breathlessly, she answered Candido, "Yes."

Candido Malta gestured to one of his men, who withdrew a pad from the breast pocket of his tunic and began to write. He said, "The American ambassador to Santiago is named Miles."

The implication of his remark jerked Deidre back to reality. "Really?" she said with a fragile pretense of disinterest. "What a coincidence."

Had the Irishman smiled? She was sure he had.

"'Aero Classics'?" The officer also smiled, but not pleasantly. "Come now, Señorita Miles. Why don't you tell us who you really work for?"

"I don't know what you mean. What're you saying?"

"It's no secret that your government is desperate to see that our country does not league itself with the communists."

"Look here, I don't know anything about that."

He slapped the side of his leg with the quirt—once, twice. He drew a noisy breath through his nose. "You leave me no choice then, *señorita*. I must request that you come with me to Las Tablas for questioning."

Deidre felt as if the mosquitoes buzzing around her face had drunk half her blood. She brushed at them and looked in wonder at Francis MacIntire. "Can he do that?"

"Bringing a military plane into a foreign country without proper authorization is no cause?" the captain demanded.

"What?" She tried to focus more clearly.

"This plane—" he waved vaguely over his shoulder at the aircraft "—is a bomber, *señorita*."

"Of course it is, but—"

"One of the most reliable."

"Yes, but—"

"And it appears to be completely functional."

"That—"

He gestured theatrically. "Our democracy is a small one. This plane is exactly what it needs."

"Now, just a minute!"

"Did the CIA send you to Santiago?"

Until hearing *CIA*, Deidre supposed that down deep she believed she would come out of it all unscathed. That was the trouble with her—she never learned. She knew better than to trust people, but she invariably did, and then she was neck deep in trouble.

As naturally as the sunflower turns its face to the source of its strength, she turned to Francis MacIntire. *Help me*, she signaled him in dazed misery.

Do you trust me?

Must I?

Yes.

I trust you, then.

He pushed back the brim of his hat with a jaunty thumb and shifted his weight. "I really hate to bring this up, Candido," he said and embraced her with a look, "right when we're all having so much fun and all, but you know and I know that you don't have any authorization to hold Miss Miles. You came here on a wild-goose chase. Admit it. Well, the goose has flown the coop, so to speak, and unless you wish to press formal charges against my business associate, I'm going to inform my very good friend, the president, and my other good friend, the secretary of interior, that you and your goons went on an insane shooting spree and nearly killed all of us. If that doesn't work, maybe I will just go home. But let me tell you something, *Capitán*, if I do go home, I'll pack up my factories and my hydroelectric plants and my engineers and—" He sighed heavily and shook his head. "And then I will leave you to yourselves. Now, if you'll excuse us, please."

All of his threats couldn't have been idle, Deidre thought in foggy astonishment. At least some of them were practical enough that the officer clearly burned with hatred.

"You're interfering with national security here, *Mister* MacIntire!" he hissed.

Without warning, MacIntire tipped back his head in laughter so spontaneous that Deidre started. A rousing, habit-forming sound, it rolled out of him like music and rippled through the crowd.

Presently it dwindled, however, and the crowd exchanged shrugs and wondering grimaces. The soldiers flicked looks back and forth. After a moment, Francis MacIntire wiped a hand across his mouth and sighed as if he couldn't quite rid himself of the moment's hilarity.

Enthralled, finding a smile on her own face, Deidre was surprised when he motioned for her to come stand beside him. With her ears ringing, she moved near enough that he could reach out and cup her elbow. He was quite tall.

"With all due respect, Candido," he said, "I think Miss Miles has been in the sun long enough. And you have been on my land long enough."

Candido Malta's quirt sliced the hot air with a whistle. "Don't threaten me."

The Irishman had been drawing her gently away with his hand upon her wrist. Turning, he said softly, "I never make threats. If you want to accuse anyone of aiding the rebels, Candido, make it count. Accuse me."

The silence was like the inside of a skull. The veins through Malta's neck stood out like cords, and his voice softened to the sweetness of poison. "One of these days, you will push too far."

"I must remember to be especially careful then, eh?"

"And when that happens, I'll put you in front of a firing squad."

"Tsk, tsk. Today is the day of the soft sell, Candido. Haven't you heard?"

Whether out of weariness or defeat, Deidre did not know, Candido brought his heels hard together and visibly swallowed his rage.

"I will release the woman in your recognizance," he declared loudly for all to hear. "She may not leave the area without consulting me, and she may not leave the country until clearance is obtained from President Araujo himself."

The captain's madness touched Deidre like a cold breath. "But I was returning home tomorrow," she protested.

"I'm sorry, *señorita*." His sullen bow shifted the cause of her dilemma from himself to Francis MacIntire. "I have no choice. I will notify you when you are free to leave. Now, by the authority granted to me by the sovereign state of Santiago, I am impounding this aircraft.''

Impounding the plane? Deidre instinctively laid her hand on the rough fold of Francis MacIntire's sleeve. If she couldn't deliver the *Albatross*, she couldn't get back her investment. And if she didn't get back her money, how was she going to get back home?

"He can't do that, can he?" she asked.

Before he could reply, Candido, with a command that required little dialogue, made a series of motions to his men with the end of his quirt and neatly dispatched them in all directions. With their guns the squad motioned for the onlookers to make way. The peasants quickly obeyed. The guards swarmed over the turf and ordered MacIntire's sentries to let them through.

Deidre felt her fingers groping for the Irishman. His hand closed upon hers—powerful and unhurried, capable. "Keep cool," he murmured. "It'll come to nothing."

To her further bafflement, Joaquim appeared suddenly from nowhere, and this time he smiled sheepishly at her. "Hello, Miss Miles. I'm sorry that I—"

"I'm posting sentries here at the hangar," Malta was declaring.

The roar in Deidre's ears grew louder. Insects seemed to swarm everywhere, and the sun was burning deeply into her brain, blistering her eyelids and the top of her lip. Her feet suddenly seemed to be going in two different directions at once, and the ground shifted—a blur of the most lovely shade of green.

She clawed unwittingly at the collar of her jump suit. The next thing she knew was the pressure of a hard chest straining against her cheek and her head lolling back upon a shoulder that felt completely trustworthy. She was pleasantly aware of the smell of tobacco blending with the pungency of dust and sweat.

Had she fainted? If she hadn't, she had come dangerously near it. But everything seemed quite pleasant from the safety of the Irishman's arms. The feel of him walking with her was pleasant. His chuckle as he looked down at her was pleasant.

"You do have style, Deidre Miles," he murmured as the crowd parted before them like the walls of the Red Sea. "I'll have to give you that. A little like Don Quixote, perhaps, but stylish."

How pleasant, Deidre thought and closed her eyes. How very pleasant.

Chapter Four

Under any circumstances, Deidre would have been appalled to wake up and find her head, facedown, in a man's lap. But to regain consciousness and realize that she didn't know the man, didn't know the lap and had no idea how she'd come into contact with either one, disoriented her even more.

She lifted her head and promptly struck it against the steering wheel.

"Easy, girl."

A deep male voice drifted through a swirl that kept trying to suck her down into its warm, seductive depths. "You're all right now, Deidre," it rumbled reassuringly. "You're with me. Nothing can happen to you now."

Deidre wasn't at all certain about that. At this moment, she wasn't sure she was even conscious. Perhaps it was all a dream. Perhaps she was slithering down an Alice-in-

Wonderland shaft, where she would be as weightless as air and would meet a weird rabbit.

Fingers speared abruptly into her hair—masterful fingers that were used to doing whatever they pleased. They shaped about her head like a steel trap. It was no dream!

Her eyes flew wildly open, and she saw that a masculine garment was bunched roughly beneath her cheek. Its texture was erotic in a crazy sort of way, as was its heady smell and the tingling vibrations passing through his iron-hard thigh and into her head.

Where was she? Why was she here? What had happened? Had she been drugged? No, but she felt absolutely terrible! Why couldn't she remember?

She tried to pinpoint the last thing she'd done. A white cloud of storks formed upon the screen of her memory. Yes, and fields of rice. Ah, it was coming back now. Santiago...lakes...jungle...a gun, and a man.

This man?

The hand upon her head was suddenly not to be borne any longer. Fighting herself free, Deidre scrambled from his lap and scratched, kicked, clawed and fell, pell-mell, onto her own side of the vehicle.

"Not the wheel!" he yelled.

She had sent the thing spinning with her foot. He grabbed it, swerving the Land Rover hard as it skidded sideways. Behind them, two more vehicles also went skidding toward the ditch. A horn blared raucously.

The tires took a final bite of gravel, and the shuddering stopped as swiftly as it began. The man, signaling the drivers behind him, threw her a smirking reproach.

"I don't suppose anyone's ever mentioned the fact that you're a little cross when you first wake up?" he said.

"I don't wake up with people," she snapped indignantly.

His brows lifted with mock surprise. "Indeed."

With a shrug and a grind of gears, he straightened the wheel, and the tires spun in the loose gravel, sending them forward.

With a sigh of relief she didn't quite trust, Deidre flicked her eyes back and forth. Men followed closely behind them in two jeeps. In the back of the Rover, along with a roll of barbed wire, some fence stretchers and a wooden carpenter's box of tools, her flight bag was scuttling around. Along with her attaché case and jacket. On the floor at her feet lay a pair of cowhide gloves and a high-powered rifle in a handsome leather case.

She sucked in her breath. Easy, Deidre, her instincts warned like a friend who gives useless advice. Don't go flying off the handle now. All this could have a perfectly logical explanation.

Arranging her expression in what she hoped was tranquility, she lifted her chin and gazed beyond the road. On one side, cattle grazed serenely, knee deep in rich verdure that crossed and recrossed a stream needling through willow trees. Thatched roofs huddled together in a cluster of brown, as if they must take comfort from one another.

On the other side rose the steep woods of the jungle, a wild tangle that glistened with trees almost unrecognizable in their majesty. At their edge, like some bridal wreath cast aside by an eager lover, a lacy waterfall spilled off a nearby precipice into the river.

Peasants stopped working to look up from the fields as the Rover passed, waving and yelling, *"¡Señor, señor!"*

Yes, *señor*, Deidre thought glumly. *Señor*, whoever he was, was a man to be reckoned with, and she was in no shape to do battle with a monolith. She was eerily outside herself, two women, one a ghostly double somewhere very high looking down at a man and a woman riding to no-where.

Fanning at the heat, she gently cleared her throat and cautiously slid her gaze around.

He was driving with one hand. The other was braced along the opening of the window. His hawkish profile was vaguely familiar below the flapping brim of his hat, and more than a little overwhelming. He could be a mercenary. His hands were quick and efficient upon the wheel. His wrists, surprisingly beautiful, were tapered into powerful, torqued forearms that looked capable of unspeakable things. How much should she fear what he could do to her?

"Are you all right?" he called over the rush of the wind as he divided his attention between the road and her.

"What?"

"Are you okay?"

He had to be joking. Deidre calculated her chances of reaching her case without arousing his suspicions. But there was nothing there to help her, God knew, and as she racked her brain for some way to protect herself, the Land Rover abruptly hit a hole in the road.

He drew a whistling breath through his teeth as she flew high from her seat and came down with a crunching *thunk*.

"Sorry about that," he said, snatching a glance.

The distress in Deidre's head instantly traded places with that in her stomach. "Stop this thing," she mumbled to her fickle knees, which wouldn't stay pressed together.

"Here?"

Holding onto her legs with all her strength, she looked up and shrieked, "I'm going to be sick!"

With a slam to the brakes he brought everything to a skidding stop. He thrust his arm across her breasts to pre-vent her from being hurled against the dash.

"Hang on, lass."

Once again the vehicles behind them screeched, and the wheels of the Rover had scarcely stopped turning when Deidre kicked her way through the opening and swung her legs to the ground. The dust from the road caught up with her like the backwash of a tidal wave.

Beating it back with both arms, she staggered toward the rear bumper. She couldn't remember what she'd last eaten or where, but she knew with a miserable certainty that she would soon find out.

Please, she prayed as she clung to the metal and squeezed her eyes tightly shut, if there's mercy anywhere, don't let anyone look at me.

No sooner had she braced herself than two hands gripped her firmly by the shoulders. With an ease Deidre found mortifying, he turned her into the hollow of his body and braced his legs against her own collapsing ones. Drawing her hair aside, he cupped her forehead in a callused, comforting palm and took the whole of her weight upon himself.

"It's okay," he said.

"I don't—"

"It's okay, Deidre."

Deidre's pride quickly met the same unhappy fate as her lunch. She didn't question how he knew her name. He probably knew everything, including what she'd had for lunch.

When it was over she groped for her sleeve to blot her mouth. He thrust a handkerchief into her hand.

"Thank you," she whispered weakly.

"My pleasure," he murmured, chuckling.

Recovering enough to take an ungraceful step away from him, Deidre lifted the back of her hand and blotted the sweat streaming down her face. She plucked at the damp tendrils of hair that clung to her jaw and pushed them back.

"I think I should tell you," she announced with one of her best and most convincing bluffs, "that I don't take kindly to being teased."

"Oh? I'll remember that." He smiled.

Deidre bridled and narrowed her eyes. "And though this isn't a good first impression—"

"Actually, I've never been big on first impressions myself."

Jutting a hip, Deidre sighed as the seconds limped past. She wondered what it would take to come out even with him. And she had to come out even; it was a matter of pride now.

In the tough-lady tone she'd used with the man and his three thousand dollars' worth of aluminum siding—and Nicolas Noreiga, too; she remembered him now!—she said, "Look, mister, if it's any of your business, which, by the way it is not—"

"You're not demented or intoxicated and this has neve happened to you before." Laughing, he extended his arm and let her know that he wasn't buying the tough-lady act. "I know that. Now, are you going to come here, or are you going to let the sun fry you like an egg?"

Stymied, Deidre wryly considered the invitation of his arm. Going to him suddenly seemed the most necessary thing in all the world. Sighing and pulling a what-the-heck face, she let him circle her waist and draw her close so that she stood for a moment in his safe, sheltering silence.

Presently he draped her arm around his neck, and she was aware of the texture of strange, exhilarating male flesh beneath her fingertips. "Please see that my body is shipped back to the States," she murmured huskily.

Francis didn't reply. He was finding it more and more difficult to do anything for fear he might wake up and realize she was nothing but a dream. Enjoy it while it lasts, old man. When she comes to herself, she won't look at you twice.

He made an effort not to tighten his arms around her back and said to a curl that snagged coyly on his eyelash, "Around here they call it green hell."

Leaning back, she braced her hands on his chest and measured him with blinking suspicion. "Green what?"

"The heat factor's about a hundred and twenty-five." He considered wiping away a droplet of sweat that slid down the bridge of her nose and shimmered precariously on its tip.

"That's hell, all right," she agreed and laughingly blew the drop away and nestled her face into his shoulder again.

"You learn to respect it."

"I'm sure that's true."

"And you don't ever make the mistake of thinking it can't kill you, because it can."

"I'll remember."

"Relax."

She stiffened. "How can I relax with half the world watching?"

"My men?" He grinned at the tempting whiteness of her ear. "Their discretion costs me a lot of money."

"Sir?"

The strange voice requesting instructions made Deidre grow stiff in the man's arms. His voice rumbled like thunder in his chest. "Why don't you men just go on back to the ranch. I'll see you there."

A hesitation was laced with polite protests. "Are you sure that's advisable, sir? We don't know how close they are."

"Well, you and Moody stay, then. Send the others on."

Footsteps crunched unenthusiastically in the gravel and melted into other sounds.

How close *who* was? Deidre wanted to ask, but she let out her breath against the lapel of his bush jacket. For the moment, she supposed she was safe. She had to be, didn't she? With his Adam's apple a mere six inches from her nose?

She let it fill the landscape of her entire vision. Flecks of gray were sprinkled in his five o'clock shadow. On one side of his neck was a tiny scar where he had nicked himself shaving. She pictured him stripped to the waist, standing before a mirror with his feet spread and his hips straining against his pants—not as a boy would cockily spread-eagle in his sexy Levi's but as a man of experience would stand, unimpressed with his own virility, having no sexual points to prove and being vastly more appealing because of it.

A seismic thrill jolted her. Stepping breathlessly back, she lifted her hand to her head. "Ah, you've been very kind," she said with polite finality.

"You're welcome."

Moments continued to tick with nuclear precision. She gestured erratically and looked at the Jeep behind them. "Uh . . . what I mean to say is . . . you've been very kind."

"You said that."

"Well—" she reddened "—you have been."

"I'm never kind."

Oh, Lord! "You know—" Deidre shifted her weight as her temper rose several degrees closer to the boiling point "—I realize this whole thing is bizarre, but every time I open my mouth to explain—"

"Does it matter what I think?"

No woman could have been the recipient of such a question and not have looked straight into the eyes of the man who asked it. And if Deidre had been subconsciously hoping he would dodge such a confrontation, she was wrong. He didn't blink, and he didn't flinch.

The truth was, it did matter what he thought, and Deidre didn't know any reason why it should. An incredible emotional momentum was building between the two of them—

too quickly—containing the potential for destruction that all sudden momentum contains. Her memory groped inside its darkened chamber. She sensed she'd felt the same momentum before.

"Well, I have to say something," she said lamely. "I feel like an idiot standing here. I feel . . ."

She looked helplessly at the waterfall exploding off the rocks in the distance. Sighing, she let her shoulders slump. "Oh, damn."

Francis tried to suppress a smile but couldn't do it. Quite apart from her physical charm, to him she was a strange and intriguing woman, full of sudden, improbable passions, and she made him feel like that headstrong young hellion again.

Laughter burst from him, and he realized he had many things he wanted to tell her. "Exactly," he said.

Before she could stop herself or think how hysterical it made her look, Deidre matched his laughter with a giggle— not a smile or a chuckle but a silly, undignified giggle, as if she were on a glue-sniffing high. Then she laughed. She laughed until the tears ran down her face. They laughed together, like children letting their balloons go and cheering them on and on until they were out of sight.

Then they stood quietly looking at each other until the smiles ebbed away. Now was the time, Deidre thought, if he had a grain of tact, for him to gently explain how she came to be here on the road with him. She expected it. She regained her poise and sorted through possible replies.

He did nothing except remove his hat and, with a backhand flick, sent it skimming back to the seat of the Land Rover like a Frisbee. Wild, gray-streaked black curls sprang out from his head—the kind of hair that babies could bury chubby fists in and buttons on ladies' silk blouses could snag upon. Deidre drew in a sharp, surprised breath.

"If you'll forgive me for saying so," she said and awkwardly tied his handkerchief into a knot, "I'm not feeling too well. I really would like to be about my business now."

"Then you're in the right place. I *am* your business, Deidre Miles."

She blinked at him. "Then let's get it on. Business, I mean. Not..."

Deidre promised herself that if he laughed, she'd slap his charismatic face. The sunburst of lines at his temples crinkled, then swiftly disappeared.

"You want to talk about the money I owe you?" he said with proper businesslike gravity. "Right here in the middle of the road? Well, all right, I guess we can do that."

Deidre nearly dropped the handkerchief. "Money?"

"Ah, the magic word." He blandly plucked his handkerchief from her hand, picked out the knots, folded it and slipped it into his hip pocket as if it were a sacred ceremony. "You'd be surprised how often that clarifies the issue."

For the life of her, Deidre couldn't remember that he owed her money. She kept her eyes fastened tenaciously to his big, rough hands. "Ah, I hope you have the check with you."

"Of course." He patted the left front pocket of his bush jacket.

"Then hand it over."

"Not so fast." Folding his arms across his chest, he threw his weight lankily to one hip, wincing slightly. "There's our contractual agreement to be considered."

Deidre didn't know anything about a contract. Perhaps it was a test. Blotting her forehead with the back of her hand, she studied him shrewdly. "You're not trying to weasel out of the deal, are you?"

He leaned so dangerously close that Deidre glimpsed a fascinating chip in one of his front teeth. "You don't have an idea in the world who I am, do you?"

"Of course I do." She threw back her head in one of her most reliable bluffs at hauteur.

"Tell me, then."

Hesitating, she wished she'd never begun the silly contest. She wished she had never come to this place for whatever reason, and she wished desperately that she knew what that reason was. But suddenly she did know! She had sold the *Albatross*!

"I don't have to tell you anything," she mumbled. What else did she know? What else, what else?

"You're fighting the wrong person, Deidre," he said as if that small conciliation satisfied him. "You know, you struck your head pretty hard. It's my guess you have a slight concussion."

She'd struck her head? Yes. She remembered now. She wiped a line of perspiration from her upper lip and plucked at the collar of her jump suit. "I did strike my head, didn't I?"

"Think of the positive side." His grin had to be one of the cardinal sins. "No matter what you do, I'll forgive you."

Momentarily forgetting the contest, Deidre tipped her head to the side and tried not to smile. "You certainly are generous for a jungle man."

Laughter rolled easily out of him. "I'm sure you'll remember everything in a few minutes. And now that we've got that settled—" he reached out a hand for hers "—are you coming with me?"

Deidre studied the rows of calluses and the hard, toughened skin of his palm. A person had to respect a hand like that. "Where?"

"The hospital would be my suggestion."

She shook her head. She might have forgotten a few details of the last hour or so, but she knew with a healthy certainty that if she turned up as a patient in some hospital, Jonathan Miles would be her first visitor. She was returning to normal. She dreaded seeing her father.

"I'll be all right." She waved his suggestion away. "You're right. I did take a hard lick, but I'm feeling much better now. In fact, I think I—"

It hit her then—the treacherous heat of green hell. It struck her violently in the back of the neck and in the center of her chest, against the drums of her ears and deep in the pit of her stomach. She swayed on her feet from the impact.

"Maybe I do need just one tiny minute," she whispered and struggled frantically for each breath.

He was moving so quickly she could scarcely keep up. Swiveling to the Land Rover, he swiftly slipped his rifle from its case and dragged it over his shoulder by the strap.

"Wait here!" he shouted to the men in the jeep. Grasping her wrist with a circle of fingers, he began drawing her off the road. "You can't stand out here any longer."

The sight of his gun brought every distorted, hysterical two-o'clock-in-the-morning nightmare rushing to Deidre's surface. "What's that for?" she wailed.

"I promise to be quick when I murder you. Look, you're going to have to walk because I left my Tarzan suit at home. Okay?"

Somewhere inside Deidre's brain, a key turned unexpectedly in a lock. She strained back on his grip, for she suddenly remembered setting down the plane. She remembered the gunfire and remembered hitting her head and being dragged out of the plane by men's hands.

"I remember now," she mumbled to his back as she stumbled along in his wake. "I remember—"

"Remembering won't help much if you pass out," he said. "Then I'll have to take you to the hospital whether you want to go or not. Will you stop fighting me?"

But Deidre tried clumsily to free herself of his grip. Bushes snagged on her jump suit and switched her arms. "I remember I was trying to land on your crummy airstrip."

Stopping, not releasing her, he turned with a half-teasing growl. "What d'you mean, crummy?"

"I damn well nearly killed myself!" she cried fiercely.

With a mildly self-deprecating grimace, he shrugged and resumed the trek. Over his shoulder, he said, "You don't seem to have hurt your mouth very much."

Deidre made a face at his back. "You don't seem to have hurt your mouth very much," she mimicked in a sassy singsong taunt.

But the sight of his back as he led the way, the command in his arms, and his stride with its subtle, fascinating limp, kept awakening impressions in Deidre's imagination. Time had no shape where he was concerned. It was like a new sisal rope that kept uncoiling into an endless, perfectly uninterrupted length. She could have known him forever. She felt she could say anything to him.

But she couldn't. He was a stranger. She wasn't herself.

To the brim of his hat, she asked wonderingly, "You helped me, didn't you?"

"That's me, the Good Samaritan. I'm also kind to dumb animals, and I make a great cup of coffee."

Deidre missed her step and nearly went crashing down on top of him. "Do you have a smart answer for everything? I'm telling you, I remember who you are."

"That's a relief."

"You're Francis MacIntire. Hey!"

This time Deidre jerked back with so much strength that she brought him swinging around to loom high above her like a monument before which human sacrifices were offered.

"What is it this time, darling?" he growled.

Tipping up her chin, Deidre pasted a bright smile on her face. She gave him the full force of all she'd learned at the feet of mechanic gurus and clerks and bankers and landlords and salesmen.

"You owe me a hundred and seventy-five thousand dollars, Mr. MacIntire," she said sweetly and thrust out her hand. "Pay up."

Francis guessed he would never forget Deidre as she was at this exact moment—captured innocently against the latticed shadows of the trees so that sunlight danced across her lovely, smiling face and glinted off the dishevelled silk of her hair.

The dappled light made her lift her hand to shade her face like a woman standing high on a ledge and staring across the world. It turned the tiny fuzz at the nape of her neck to gold, and accentuated the little pulse beating there until his own pulse began to do crazy things.

He supposed she considered herself to be unbeautiful with her working woman's hands and her lack of feminine artifice that came in bottles and tubes and plastic packets. In a short space of time he'd seen the best and the worst of her. Her artlessness was her charm, the thing that kept her from being like any other woman he knew. She was extraordinary, rare, totally unspoiled, a little cheeky but asking nothing of anyone and the rest of the world be hanged.

Startled, she stepped swiftly away and swallowed. She looked around them, idly at first, then in earnest.

"What's the matter?" he prompted hoarsely.

They were in another world here. The rain forest was so dense that the air was ten degrees cooler but very humid. The trees dripped as if rain were falling, and the air whispered with it. Blossoms were so weighted with moisture that their stalks bent low to the ground like miniature ballerinas in révérence.

Deidre knew that if she became lost in this place, she would stay lost forever. "Where are we?" she demanded breathlessly.

Francis tore his fantasies free of their delirium. "There's a pool just a few more yards through the trees."

She shivered. "That's a long way."

"It's cool."

She indicated she would follow, but once he had resumed his lead, she said to the back of his head, "I feel funny. Really... weird."

Not half as weird as he did! "You should've gotten off the plane into a nice, air-conditioned limousine instead of standing out in the sun arguing with Candido. It's a wonder you don't have sunstroke on top of the concussion."

"Candido?"

"You don't remember Candido?"

She trudged along in such silence that Francis knew she didn't remember as much as he'd thought. He couldn't take advantage of that, could he?

At length, she said, "I don't think I like your green hell, Mr. MacIntire."

"That's all right," he said and willed himself not to turn back and see her smallness or her vulnerability because it would make him start imagining pale gold thighs again, and he would forget all the lessons life had taught. "It likes you very much."

The sound of the waterfall soon grew deafening, and then Deidre saw it, a great, wide ribbon of white cascading off the cliff to strike huge rocks midway down so that it broke into several smaller falls—big atoms of wet and light dancing frenziedly on their way down to become the river.

Some feet below the falls was a pool, deep and as crystal clear as glass, wrapped about by an incredibly beautiful curtain of mist and carpeted with pebbles that glistened like misplaced jewels.

Deidre glimpsed the flash of birds in the trees. And butterflies glinting over the tops of the flowers. She didn't know what to do with herself, and she let Francis MacIntire draw her to a wide slab of rock at the bank and push her down to sit.

Removing his rifle and leaning it against the trunk of a tree, he stooped, leaning over her so that his mouth was pressed to her ear and she could feel the straining urgency of his legs.

He spoke over the thunder of the falls. "One of your problems, my dear, is that you came to the party overdressed."

Deidre smiled, but before she could summon the presence of mind to stop him, he knelt at her feet and began unlacing her shoes. She reached down a hand in protest, but instead of touching his shoulder as she intended, instead of erecting the one barrier that would save them, she had the most terrible need to bend her head to his, to touch foreheads like lovers and ask, "What's happening to me?"

The need left her weak and drifting. She murmured in a daze, "You don't have to do that."

His voice carried up to her, low and strong. "I know that."

"But it's not right."

"What's not right?" Pausing, he looked up.

Drawn into his aura of honesty, she shrugged. "I'm not used to being touched."

The lines beside his mouth softened in a smile. He finished unlacing her shoes. "I know that, too."

"Then, why..."

"Because you need touching."

His simple words brought a rush of warmth and energy spreading over her again—the chemical reaction that made no sense, the one that she couldn't articulate, even in the spaces of her own mind.

Say something to break the connection before it's too late, her logic demanded. She was capable of it. She could pull herself back in such a way that he wouldn't dare to press the issue. But she sat staring at her own hand as if she didn't know whose it was.

Quickly, before she could change her mind, she blurted, "Are you married?"

At first she thought he would refuse to answer. Then, without looking at her, he said, "I was."

Her silence seemed to urge him to continue. "She's dead now."

"You loved her very much."

He shrugged sadly. "I hurt her very much."

"I'm sorry."

"It was a long time ago. Our son is about your age."

"What's his name?"

"Why are you asking me all this?"

Deidre boldly lifted a finger and brought it quite near the sharp angle of his cheekbone. Smiling up at her, he touched the tip of her own finger and chanted in unison with her, "Because you need asking."

They laughed. He placed her shoes side by side on the rock. "I wasn't a good husband," he said with more ease. "I was an angry young man. After my wife died, I became an angry father. Sean and I...well, he'll understand, I suppose, when he stockpiles as many regrets as I have."

Deidre couldn't resist teasing him. "You sound like an old man, with your 'stockpile of regrets.'"

Chuckling, he unfolded himself and grasped one of her hands and pulled her up. For a moment he stood with a hand resting upon her waist. "Did you think I was going to say, 'But I *am* an old man'?"

"Maybe." Laughing, she dipped her head away, then eyed him from an angle. "Why aren't you saying it?"

"What if I had?"

"I would've said that you wanted me to argue the point."

Screwing up his face, he buried a hand in his curls and scratched his head. "God almighty, girl, what a tongue you've got in that head of yours."

Deidre flushed. "And you, Mr. MacIntire, are skirting the issue."

He laughed. "That's not what I'm skirting at all."

"What, then?"

"I'm skirting the fact that I want very much to kiss you."

How long did it take the human brain to reprogram a person? Scientists could have calculated the time for a computer down to a millisecond. She wasn't a computer, yet in less time than it would have taken her to say the words, "But I don't know you that well," Deidre had relived the feelings she had once cherished for John Desmond. Then she'd called it love, but now she knew it had been nothing but chemistry. Her generation confused chemistry with love. Especially women, for they'd been denied the freedom to fly for so long that they overreacted to sex until the whole world seemed stuffed full of it. Sated. Glutted. Strangling. Until one day a woman woke up and asked of the Cinderella dream she'd always believed in, "Is this all there is?"

Then there was the woman's real world, all those crushing responsibilities, the demands of doing too many things at once and most of them going unnoticed and unappreciated. To say nothing of the terrible prices to be paid for loving the wrong man these days—cruel diseases. To love a man was a risk of life, literally.

Sex, chemistry, was in danger of burnout. Disenchantment was settling in until it often seemed more desirable to find a friend than a lover.

So embarrassed that she could no longer meet the honesty glinting in his eyes, Deidre nibbled her lip. "I think I'm not the only one with a tongue in my head, Mr. MacIntire."

He released her solemnly, and Deidre watched him step to the edge of the slab. Without looking at her, he said, "You've been married?"

"I wouldn't exactly call it that. More of a disaster, really."

She had no wish to discuss it with him. Intuitively understanding, he gazed about at the grandeur thrusting upward to the sky. "Do you know," he said presently, "that men work their whole lives in this country and wind up with less than they started with?"

It wasn't really a question, but if it had been, she couldn't have found the words to answer him.

He went on. "Life is a bitch, you know. We live in bits and pieces. We fight for superfluous things, then fight wars to hold on to them. We've turned away from the morals of our forefathers and debased what little remains." He shook his head. "I live too well down here. I've grown accustomed to my cattle and my fences and my rain forest. There are nights when I wake up and wonder if I'm not living on borrowed time, if this wonderland isn't going to turn into a nightmare of assassins..."

The poetry in him moved Deidre deeply. Even if he never kissed her, if they never acknowledged the so-called chemistry, she wanted Francis MacIntire for her friend. He was a good man, a man of vision. The world had too few good men of vision.

Swiveling, he flicked a button loose on one of her sleeves. That done, he began on the other. Deidre leaned breathlessly nearer. "Things will change between you and your son, Mr. MacIntire."

The tips of his fingers played magically over her skin, and their work-roughened calluses opened secret doors in her mind. "You're sure of that, are you?"

She smiled. "One day he'll see what he has in you."

He didn't agree or disagree. Deidre wished she hadn't said anything about his son. It was presumptuous. They didn't even know each other.

"Why are we really here?" she asked him, looking up at the mist of the falls.

He left her sleeves hanging loosely about her wrists. "Why are you trembling?"

Deidre couldn't tell him that—about how she was two women and one of them was growing hopelessly infatuated with him. "I don't know."

"And neither do I know why we're here."

As he uttered the words he took hold of the tab of her zipper and, with a single downward jerk, bared her from her neck to her navel.

Deidre had neither the wit nor the reflexes to grab her suit and jerk it closed. He stripped her sleeves from her arms, and the top fell about the bottom hem of her camisole. Before it could slither below her hips, however, he bent and, closing his arms about her knees, lifted her easily in his arms and stepped off the edge of the rock into the cold crystal pool.

Gasping, flinging her arms about his neck, she thought he would at least remove his boots before he waded out into the water, but he walked boldly into the current and anchored his feet upon the bottom.

"What if someone comes?" she blurted illogically.

It was the kind of compromising remark a lover would make. He stopped where he was, and Deidre could feel his thighs, hard and implacable against her legs. Her breast was grazing his jaw.

Leaning back, he considered the proximity of her bosom and said without flourish, "Candido or his men are the only ones who would count, and he wouldn't follow us here."

"But your men."

He grinned. "Even if they saw, they would never tell."

The fact was no comfort. He moved deeper into the water so that it reached her waist, and the shock of it made Deidre slide lower in his arms and tighten her arms about his neck.

"This Candido?" she yelped. "Who is he?"

"A barracuda."

"A barracuda?" She sniffed with mock disdain as the coolness swirled refreshingly around her.

The water turned her camisole into something more revealing than naked flesh, and Deidre saw that her breasts had become as wanton as a temptress's against the silk. He was taking a lazy interest in the impression of her nipples, and Deidre could no more stop looking at them than he could.

If she spoke, she told herself, she could break the spell. "What kind of an answer is 'A barracuda'?"

"A barracuda has a large mouth with many dangerous sharp teeth," he said and lifted his eyes to hers as if he had no idea that he was even speaking.

The falls drowned out Deidre's fragile reply. Like some victim caught in a web, she was paralyzed by the enormity of what they were doing. She couldn't move. She couldn't pull away. She could only stare at the wide slant of his mouth and wonder if he still wanted to kiss her.

"Sometimes he's been known to have actually attacked swimmers," he said dully.

"Remind me to stay out of his way."

"You may not be able to."

He tilted his head such an infinitesimal amount that Deidre was more intuitively aware of it than having seen it. No magnet could have held their eyes so unbreakably, and she wouldn't have been surprised if she had heard the crash of her own heartbeat over the thunder of the falls.

Yet, as he dipped that small amount toward her lips, something made him jerk up his head and blink himself free of the trance.

"Why?" she gasped.

Misunderstanding, he thought she was talking about Candido. He let out his breath in a heavy sigh. "Because he hates me."

Deidre swiftly turned her head away. "But that has nothing to do with me."

"It has everything to do with you."

"I don't see—"

So successful was she in regaining her composure—outwardly, at least—that Deidre was totally unprepared for him to shift her in his arms until he was no longer balancing her but embracing her. Now her waist was clasped firmly to his, her thighs to his thighs. She had been wrong, Deidre saw immediately, to think that he had changed his mind about his male desires, for he was tautly urgent, and he made no pretense otherwise.

Her eyes widened, and he looked at her with a gaze full of deep, discomfiting insights. "Because," he said raspily, "Candido believes I'm going to fall in love with you."

Chapter Five

If Deidre hadn't been out of focus from the blow to her head, if she had not been prey to the debilitating lethargy of the jungle, plus jet lag and a weariness like none she'd ever known, she would have given Francis MacIntire a smile for such outrageous words.

She would have brushed them aside with an assumed naïveté that was anything but naive and said, "Well now, that just goes to show you how wrong men can be, doesn't it, Mr. MacIntire?"

And if Frances hadn't been at the end of a long list of trials, least of which was his crushing disappointment over his son and Francisco Araujo and something much more defeating that had to do with the making of a world alone, the empty words and tired images, the private rivalries and petty jealousies that seemed to constitute the entirety of each day's existence, he would never have uttered such an insane thing in the first place.

But Deidre was out of focus, and he was at the end of a rope. She was also in his arms, clinging and sweet, and there was something strangely virginal about her, some part of her that was frightened at what he was doing and the words he was saying. He found that enormously appealing.

At the same time, in her smile, was something that was not at all virginal. She was two different people, and at least one of them was more fastidiously honest than he would ever be in the area of sexuality. That sophisticated woman would force him to see his desire more nakedly than he had ever seen it before. And he found *that* enormously frightening.

It also made his sexual excitement rise, and he felt as if someone were leading him blindfolded to the edge of a precipice.

Releasing her, except for a hold on her elbow, he let her drift out into the depths where the water was over her head. She was unwilling to be so brave. She returned to clasp the front of his bush jacket with one hand and to splash her face greedily with the other.

Dousing her head until her hair swirled on the surface like spilled paint, she came up sputtering and bubbling and rinsing and spitting. She made a face and squeezed her eyes tightly shut, baring her teeth so that the water made them sparkle and hurt with the cold as she dunked her head again.

When she emerged she slicked back her hair and laughed. "Isn't it wonderful?" she cried.

Not as wonderful as she was, he could have said. Her eyelashes glistened in tiny wet clumps that stole his breath, as did the beautiful protrusions of her body, her bones and breasts and dark, secret hollows.

But she was battling with her jump suit now. The weight of the water was dragging it lower and lower about her hips. She tugged on one side and hitched it up, then switched hands and tugged on the other. No sooner had she caught one part of it than it was down somewhere else.

"Help me," she pleaded.

Did she think he was insane?

Francis dipped his own face into the cold to quell the desire that plagued him. But it seemed to have no beginning and no end, and as he emerged he saw his mouth filling with her flesh and drawing in the sweet-tasting whiteness of her shoulder, her arm, her breast, then her mouth in a way he had never done before. He wanted to be inside the center of her very being. He wanted to be drawn in and feel her shudder with the thrill of it.

He was out of his mind. The legs of her suit were finally caught by the current. The suit disappeared, then reappeared in the swirling foam, snagging on a rock some yards away.

Deidre turned to him with amazement.

"It won't go too far," he said with a grin he felt clear to his spine.

But she stared at her clothes as if the garment were some handwriting upon a wall that only she could read. When she finally did speak, he had to lean forward to hear.

Her voice was rough and deep. "I think it already has, Mr. MacIntire."

Clasping her jaw in a palm, Francis slowly turned her face toward him. "What does that mean?" he gently questioned, hoping, praying.

For one second he thought she would lift her face to be kissed, but she blinked and seemed to shake off the seductive spell. "It means," she said with a whimsical half smile, "that I can't swim."

She had afforded him the way out. Francis knew he should take the hint, but with a trembling deep in his bones he lifted a wet strand of hair from her cheek and placed it behind her ear. He watched for the slightest sign of repulsion. He waited for her expression to grow hard and stiff.

But all he saw was wonder. Stooping, he clasped his arms about her knees and lifted her out of the water.

"And what if you flew over the ocean one day, Miss Lindbergh?" he teased, adoring the dimple of her navel near his nose. "What if you had to bail out? What would you do then, hmm?"

"Pray?" she gasped, folding herself so that her knees were braced against his muscled waist.

The sight of her dripping body kindled an inferno in Francis's own as she groped for balance. He knew a moment of panic and saw her lips trembling, the small lines around her eyes questioning him: So, what do we do now?

Slowly, with the roar of the falls drawing closer and closer around them, he balanced her and reached up to draw a strap off her shoulder. She didn't try to stop him as he dreaded she would, and he cursed his hand for shaking.

"I think you'd better start praying now," he said thickly as he struggled to keep the focus of his interest on her face, not the greed of his own hands.

She cloaked her own nervousness with teasing. "You mean I'm not safe with you, Mr. MacIntire?"

"If you can ask that," he said solemnly as the other strap slid slowly off her shoulder, nearly baring her breasts, "you're more of a fool than I give you credit for, Deidre Miles."

Sobriety claimed them both. As Deidre clung to his arms, suspended between the blue of the sky and the crystal of the water, time holding its breath while the drumroll of the falls heralded some moment of truth, she started to speak. But she was so enthralled by him that she simply gaped.

"What?" he said.

She turned her head from side to side, unable to think. "I don't know. You aren't..."

"Aren't what?"

"You're not..."

"Say it."

Was it the blow to her head? she wondered. Was it the beautifully wicked isolation of this place? Her mirror image that was in some way a stranger's?

"You're not what I expected," she whispered, and she suddenly wanted to hide her face.

He let her go limp and slide low in his arms again until he could have laid his head in the hollow of her neck. He curled his lips in a grimace. "Am I that much of a disappointment?"

Deidre's heart threatened to stop beating. The strength in his arms flexed in warning. "I expected an opportunist and found a poet," she said.

He hesitated, touched by what she'd said. "Perhaps you are the real poet," he murmured.

She shook her head. "Blacks and whites," she whispered. "I see the world in blacks and whites, Mr. Mac-Intire."

Deidre didn't think he really heard her. He was staring between them where the water swirled and twirled and teased her waist. Disbelief was on his face as he finally confronted her with the vastness of his need.

Did she say yes with a look, a movement of her head? He was suddenly letting her drop backward and was bending with her and over her and was trapping her arms to her sides so hard that his hands brought pain. The straps of her camisole were cutting into her elbows, and her hair was swinging free and her head was going back, so far back that her throat was an arc and she was looking up into the blue pit of the sky as the falls drummed against the bones of the earth and into the feet of the man who held her.

"Oh, God!" she heard herself groaning as his mouth sought her naked breast, found it and closed over it.

In those swift, lightning moments her breasts seemed conductors to every other part of her body, and she hurt so far inside that nothing could soothe it. He pulled her close to him then and captured her lips, kissing her fiercely, trying to sate an all-consuming hunger.

Then she was being hurled free. For timeless moments she was simply woman, and she lifted herself in his arms, burying her fingernails in the muscles that bound her. Her half-spoken words fell about his head. She kissed his throat and touched his ear, crooned to his cheeks. He filled his hands with her curves and angles that seemed to bring him as much pain as pleasure, and his kisses became so devouring that she gave up trying to please him and simply received. They were like dancers without a choreographer in an unplanned expression of wonder.

Yet Francis knew—he knew when she wrapped her legs around his waist and he reached between them for the hard, primal source of his ache, meaning to find ease no matter what—that there were prices to pay for such moments. Slowly, in agony, he lifted his head and gazed sadly down at her.

In a rough, hoarse, grating voice, he said, "Sweetheart, we're ahead of ourselves."

"Shh," she whispered and bit her lip. "Don't say no."

"Ahh, Deidre." He drew her dripping head gently beneath his chin. He tightened his embrace to make her stop shivering, but she was so small he felt he was holding a dream. Then, to his horror, she began to cry.

Feeling like Cain, he whispered against her ear, "What do I say to you?"

"I'm not crying because I'm sad."

"Then why?"

She tried to smile up at him through her tears. "Because."

"Because?"

She nodded. "Because."

Francis supposed it was as good an answer as any. He didn't know the words to say, either. If he had known them he would have told her that he hadn't wanted to stop, that he could have done terrible things.

But she drew away and primly pulled her straps into place and arranged herself. Then she looked up and smiled. "I'm getting cold, Mr. MacIntire."

An incredible sadness tightened in Francis's gut—the pain of time resuming normalcy and making him twice her age again, making her the young goddess he would never have.

He smiled. "Please call me something besides Mr. MacIntire. You make me feel damnably much like Jonathan."

It was strange, Francis thought, only seconds after it happened, how life could turn around. In less time than it took the heart to beat.

Her smile began its slow, puzzled disappearance and sent a chill nibbling at the base of his skull. She braced her hands on his arms and cocked her head with the charming curiosity of a pup.

With unfeigned wonder, she said, "Why didn't you tell me that you know my father?"

It was true: a man was his own worst enemy. Years before, many years before he had sent Joaquim to buy the *Albatross*, Francis had known that Deidre Miles was Jonathan's daughter. In a foreign country men of the same nationality tended to drift together—birds of a feather, or something along those lines.

Except that in this case it was probably more like misery loving company. There was all the political unrest in those years. His life-style wasn't particularly low-key. The U.S. officials didn't like his friends. Jonathan didn't like the extra work he caused. Still, they were two men alienated from their children—Jonathan from Deidre, himself from Sean. They'd shared occasional photographs, sometimes a tender memory.

Only too well could he remember now the years when Jonathan had sat beside the fire in his own house and stared at brandy swirling in a snifter and recalled falling in love with Deidre's mother. They had been delirious with pride when Deidre was born, and Jonathan was horrified when he realized he had lost his daughter for a fleeting affair with a woman half his age.

He could see himself slumped low in a chair, holding photographs of Deidre year by year and thinking what a lovely young woman she was growing to be. In a very real sense, he and Joaquim had watched Deidre grow up. Deidre had never really forgiven her father. Alice's pride had had a lot to do with that, he supposed, but hardship played its part; Alice had lost everything in order to keep from asking her ex-husband for money. When she died, Deidre had waited tables and taken her GED exam to get through high school. At eighteen, she'd moved to Dallas, Texas, and taken a job at Bell Helicopter.

So how did a man explain to a woman that he'd come to think a certain way about a girl in a photograph? Only to meet her and be shocked into realizing that she wasn't a girl anymore? That a real, fully grown woman was looking up at him with dazed yearning in her eyes?

Francis shivered. Yes, he'd meant to tell her, right from the beginning; he relished the connection of a past between them in a way he did not yet totally understand. But not to have told before she asked made him a keeper of secrets.

Tightening his arms around her, he lowered his face into the hollow beneath her ear and searched for an answer that wouldn't sever the delicate thread holding them together. Even as he hesitated, she mistook it for reluctance and was detaching herself.

"I should have known that you'd figure out who I was," she said with quelling coolness.

Already she was leaving him, and a sense of loneliness like none he'd ever known washed over Francis. It made his words sound sharp in a way he hadn't intended. "Was it a secret?"

"It was my business." Carefully, inoffensively, she slipped free of his embrace.

He said, "And your business is your business?"

"Isn't yours?"

Until now, it always had been. He was a self-made man. Isolation came with the territory. "I didn't guess who you were, Deidre," he admitted, choosing his words as he stared at the tons of water crashing down upon the rocks. "I already knew. I've always known."

She was balancing herself lightly on his hands and had automatically followed to see where he looked. As she turned back to him and he turned back to her, the beat that hung between them was as thunderous as the falls.

"You'll have to explain that," she said distantly.

Francis hadn't explained himself in twenty years, not even to Araujo. "Jonathan is the U.S. ambassador to this country," he said edgily. "How could I live in Santiago and not know him?"

She thoughtfully pulled her straps higher onto her shoulders, turning almost away but not quite. "A lot of people live—"

"It's a small country."

Deidre was always on guard for hidden motives; she'd had to be in order to survive—reading people's moods and catching intonations, the changes in their mouths and eyes—and now she stiffened at the one she imagined in him.

As one would scoop up a sword to do battle, she flicked her sharp little "on guard" in his face. "Just how close is this friendship between the two of you, anyway?" she demanded.

"You're making too much of this, Deidre."

"Don't tell me what I'm doing!" she lashed out in sudden anger. "I know what I'm doing!"

"I don't think," he said much more quietly, "that either of us knew what we were doing a few minutes ago."

Had she not been desperate with self-protectiveness, had she not been delirious to convince herself that she hadn't made a colossal mistake in wanting him, Deidre could have accepted his boyish irony. His words were even more true in her case than his, for in the passion of the moment she had ludicrously equated his act with some kind of permanency.

Oh, how stupid, Deidre! Do grow up! The man has spent years with your father. He knows things about you that you don't know about him. He's had the luxury of making judgments when you haven't been there to defend yourself.

She felt stripped naked in a brutal way she wasn't prepared for, much more naked than she had just been. She felt as if he had walked in upon the privacy of her bath or had caught her standing before a mirror, studying herself.

Violated, she wanted to go ashore, but she couldn't get there on her own. She stared at the trees on the bank. With unforgivable cruelty, she said, "I suppose he put you up to it, didn't he?"

"Stop it."

"All this business between us—" she made the wound deeper "—sending Joaquim and the check and having me make delivery for the balance...it was all contrived, wasn't it? You and my father got together and decided to make a charity case out of me."

"Damn it, Deidre—"

"'Poor Deidre, she's in such financial straits, we should do her this little favor.'"

Deidre knew as she mocked him that what she said wasn't true, but she was determined to hurt him because she saw now that she'd made an awful mistake. To him, she was a kid, nothing but a sexually liberated kid.

He gripped her by the shoulders. He would break her now if he could, Deidre knew. He was a proud man, and he wanted to drive her to her knees.

"I don't discuss my private affairs with anyone," he told her as his eyes ruthlessly pillaged her face. "Least of all your father."

"You knew about my mother, didn't you?" she cried, demanding proof that she was right.

His lip curled. "I knew."

"And Lily? Did you know about her?"

Now his face was a stone-cold mask. His fingers were bruising her arms, and his thighs were not seducing hers but were hard and implacable.

Deidre buried her nails deeply into her palms and met his anger with a look as cold as his. "You're not saying anything, Mr. MacIntire."

"Don't ever call me Mr. MacIntire again," he said and abruptly started carrying her ashore.

So it was done, Deidre thought as frustrated tears welled in her eyes. He'd done what she hoped he would do. He'd made her hate him.

She shoved herself away and attempted to touch her feet to the bottom. The water closed over her head, and, thrashing her way back up, she gasped and strangled and grabbed at straws. He caught her arm and pushed her to shore like a barge.

He waited in stony silence while she found a foothold. When she finally stood, coughing and pounding at her own chest, he said, "I apologize. I didn't realize that you harbored such a grudge against Jonathan after all these years."

She threw back tendrils of dripping hair. "Don't lay that psychological hang-up on me, Francis MacIntire. I don't hold a grudge against my father. I simply don't have any desire to see him. Surely you, as a father, can understand that."

The meanness of such words was horrible. Deidre wished she could call them back. *Slap my face,* she thought. *Do anything, but don't be hurt.*

"I see," he said with pained dignity.

She hung her head. "You don't see anything."

He didn't reply.

Deidre felt like a hysterical witch. "Well, why should I care about him?" she demanded hotly. "He was the one who walked out on us, not me."

He was looking over his shoulder to find her suit. He had to raise his voice for her to hear. "Maybe he had his reasons."

"Look at me!" she yelled at him.

When he did, she drooped in defeat. She tried to make her voice reasonable. "Do you think it was easy accepting the fact that I was no more than the result of biological processes that Jonathan and my mother were involved in? But I worked hard at that, Francis, and I did it."

He was preparing to dive for her suit.

"My father promised to love my mother forever," she hurled at him. "And then he ran off with a woman twice his junior."

If it was possible to make a disaster worse, she'd just done it. Tasting the most hideous disappointment, Deidre jerked herself around and stomped out of the pool. He was staring at her wet panties. She stood shivering on the rock and thought it would have been easier to be stark naked. Then she could have crossed her arms in front of her like any other human being.

Now he walked toward her as if he were considering taking her for real this time, furiously, on the grass.

"I want someone to take me to Las Tablas," she demanded. "I'm returning to the States immediately."

"No."

She gritted her teeth. "It was never my intention to be here, you know."

"Things happen sometimes. It was never my intention to seduce you."

"You didn't seduce me."

"Well, somehow it didn't seem appropriate to say 'make love.'"

But it could have been, she thought with a wretched twist of her heart. It could have been very appropriate if he . . . if she . . .

"Surely you see that I can't possibly remain in Rio Tepuí overnight," she said more reasonably. "If you'll just give me what you owe me, Francis—"

"No one calls me Francis but my mother."

"If you'll just give me what you owe me, *Francis*," she nastily retorted.

His smile could have cut glass. "You'll get your money, my darling, when the terms of delivery are met."

Confusion rang a bell inside Deidre's head. Was there something else she didn't remember? "But I met the terms," she declared, hoping it was true.

"Indeed?"

"I delivered the plane."

"You mean, you wrecked the plane."

Deidre almost flew at him, claws bared. "What do you mean, I wrecked your plane?"

"Wrecked," he said aridly. "As in two feet of bent props and a broken landing gear. Or did you think I hadn't noticed?"

Not often did Francis despise himself as much as he did now. Yet he couldn't be honest, for if he told her of how he was in a death grip with his own desire to have her, he would have to admit that he was merely inventing excuses to keep her here. He would have to confess that he could repair the plane himself or hire someone else to do it.

Since he couldn't say all that, he did what he did best: he behaved like a supercilious son-of-a-bitch. Turning, he walked back into the water and disappeared beneath the surface.

When he burst up from the pool, Deidre was filled with the passion of the unjustly wounded. She could have attacked him when he sloshed ashore like an ill-tempered Neptune having been summoned from the deep.

He flung the wadded jump suit at her feet with a *splat*, and she swooped to pick it up. Then she stopped where she was, suspended between heaven and earth. She *had* bent the props into pretzels. She *had* damaged the landing gear.

She felt like a fool. Slowly straightening, recovering a portion of her anger, she said guardedly, "If you were there, you realize that it wasn't my fault the plane was damaged."

"Well, it wasn't *my* fault," he said ungraciously.

Longevity, Deidre, longevity. She blinked back tears as she snatched up the suit and shoved a foot into one leg. She wobbled until she got the other foot into the other leg. Gritting her teeth, she shimmied down into the adhesive thing, and after much wriggling to get it straightened, made her final, furious commentary on the entire incident with the zipper's rasp.

Narrowing her eyes, she snapped, "I hope you enjoyed that."

He didn't move a muscle. "We're not that backward down here."

"I suppose now you'll tell me you've seen better."

"I have."

Oh, she hated him for that. "At least I'll be spared the guilt of knowing I caused you discomfort!"

"Well, I wouldn't go so far as to say that," he quipped as he bent for her shoes.

Before she could stop herself, Deidre looked directly at his crotch. The skirt of his bush jacket modestly covered everything.

"Trust me," he said with an evil smile.

Bastard!

Deidre snatched her shoes from his hands and crammed her feet into them. Leaving them unlaced and feeling like the biggest idiot of all time, she began squishing and stomping toward the road.

Yet deep inside, she could still feel the warm, feminine desire he'd aroused. It would take a long time for those ashes to turn cold, but when they did, she knew she would find beneath them the cinders of a dream that could have put Cinderella's to shame. How sad, a woman who still believed in fairy tales.

Of all the people Captain Candido Malta disliked, he

hated only two: President Francisco Villas Araujo and Francis MacIntire.

To one, Araujo, he disguised his hatred by yielding fawning loyalty until the man could be removed from office, which, in his opinion, would not be much longer now, for the rebels were gaining in strength every day. It was only a matter of time until he was put before a firing squad.

Francis MacIntire was another matter entirely. For nearly twenty years now he'd been waging a cold war with the investor from Boston, Massachusetts, who'd come to Santiago like God himself. Oh, MacIntire had been good for the country, yes. His companies created jobs that were badly needed. His crops were viable on the world market, and his interests were blue-chip in some parts of the world.

But he'd also attracted the attention of speculators who now saw the Amazon valley as some last lucrative frontier. Santiago could do without so much attention, and he personally had consoled himself that when Araujo was brought down, MacIntire would be brought down with him.

During the past year, however, something had happened to the friendship between the two men. Now a definite hurdle lay between himself and a goal he had worked toward with infinite patience for as long as he could remember. That goal was to hold the highest position of power in Santiago.

Actually, his desires were very simple. He didn't have much use for money, even less for approval. Power, that was all, and not the kind of power Araujo flaunted, the kind that eventually destroyed a man. His own speciality was working behind the scenes, the Great Puppeteer controlling the political reins. So close was he to achieving it, just thinking about it acted upon him the same as being with a woman.

But it all stood to be ruined because of one man who wasn't even a citizen. There had been a time when he thought MacIntire could be corrupted with money, but the more money MacIntire got, the less he seemed to care about it. That left only one avenue to the man's soul: sex.

It wouldn't be easy. He had made several attempts in that area already. Once he'd thought that Cidinha, Araujo's sister, would steal the black Irish heart. When that no longer held promise, he had hired women to tempt the man. He had planted little girls in the man's own household. He had even been tempted to try little boys.

Nothing had worked, and over the years he had come to believe that the only weapon against MacIntire was his son. Sean MacIntire, however, was as slippery to deal with as his father, even if they were to men at opposite poles.

But then a gift had fallen from heaven. As he watched MacIntire's unbelievable assault upon Juan Geisel, he knew he'd stumbled upon the key. Never before, to his knowledge, had MacIntire ever looked at a woman as he had looked at Deidre Miles. The man was due. Despite the gossip to the contrary, he lived like a monk at his ranch on the hill.

So he must now see to it that the young woman didn't leave the country just yet. He must detain her on whatever trumped-up charges were necessary. In the meantime, he would wave her beneath the elite Irish nose and see what happened.

Fortunately, she was a perfect counterpart to MacIntire: strong-willed, gritty, full of fire. And she was young. MacIntire was at a dangerous point in his life. No man, fifty or otherwise, who retained a grain of manhood could help but be attracted to such a woman. He himself found her greatly desirable.

Yes, it would all work out. The rebels would rid him of Araujo, and between Sean and Deidre Miles, he would rid himself of Francis MacIntire.

He felt better than he had in weeks. Before leaving the airstrip, he made a final inspection of the sentries. Finding them to his satisfaction, he returned to his jeep and had his communications man radio his office at Las Tablas.

He asked his aide about the poachers he had hired to make another foray into MacIntire's precious jungle reserves. To his dismay, the man told him the poachers had been captured.

"What do you mean, captured?" he demanded.

"All four of them, *Capitán*," the aide's voice crackled over the radio receiver. "They were spotted by a helicopter and outnumbered five to one."

Before today this would have been a galling irritation, but now he simply must cope. It wasn't the last straw. "Where are they now?"

"It is my understanding that they're being held at MacIntire's ranch until he returns."

Candido gazed out at the squad of men who awaited orders. He lifted the transmitter and pushed the button. "How many trucks of timber got through?"

"We're not sure, *Capitán*. Maybe none of them."

"Keep on top of it, and alert Panama City to be on the lookout for a 210 Centurion. If you hear anything before I get back in, do not send it over the radio."

"Is that all, *Capitán*?"

As he handed the transmitter to the communications man, Candido stood tapping the side of his leg with his quirt. Presently he motioned for Juan to step nearer.

"How're you feeling, corporal?" he asked.

Juan was sick to his stomach, but he kept his head erect, his chest out. "I feel fine, Captain Malta."

"Very good." Candido walked around to the passenger side of the vehicle and placed his foot up on the step. He laid his hands across the back of the seat. "I want to know every move that Francis MacIntire makes. I want to know what he says and to whom. Do you know what I'm saying?''

Juan didn't ask how he was to accomplish this feat. He had performed such services before. "I understand.''

"I'm sure you do.'' Candido kept his voice low, for though he hand-picked all his men, it didn't hurt to be careful. "And I want to know about the bomber that landed here today. Tell your contact to get word that I want information quickly. Arrange a meeting.''

Juan Geisel snapped to a more brisk stance. "Yes, Captain Malta. Do you want the meeting the same as before?''

Signaling his driver that he was ready to leave the airstrip, Candido shook his head and adjusted the visor of his cap. "No. Have her come to me. She will know.''

"Is there anything else, Captain Malta?''

As the key was turned in the ignition, and the engine fired, Candido shook his head. A rare smile drifted across his face. "Nothing I can't handle myself,'' he said. "You're a good man. Drive on, Private.''

Chapter Six

The eight-nation Amazon basin, of which Santiago was the smallest of small countries, was larger than the whole United States combined. To Deidre's way of thinking, two million square miles should have been plenty to go around.

Unfortunately, no one else agreed. Over the years many of Santiago's settlers had found themselves in a grueling and bloody battle for space, not only against the hostile jungle but against ruthless ranchers and multinational giants who came to the country bent on reaping the Amazon's spectacular treasure.

With grudging respect, Deidre saw that Francis hadn't raped his land with greedy machinery. On one hand he had a functional, working town in Rio Tepuí with a hospital and schools and churches, modern shops and services, clean streets of residences and nice, respectable town houses.

Yet, on the other hand, he had the foresight to preserve vast sanctuaries where thousands of acres of primary forest were left uncut and undeveloped. Here existed more than two hundred species of birds and innumerable varieties of trees that grew nowhere else in the world.

He was pondering his ranch from a long way off. Deidre watched him survey some twenty acres of scattered buildings where the main house—huge, red-bricked and one-storied—was like a ruby dropped into the center of lesser jewels, sparkling in the glow of the setting sun. Its roof was thatch and interrupted by four chimneys thrusting up like sentinels, also of red brick.

The ranch had looked big from the ground. On earth, it was even bigger, encompassing an office building, a white-fenced stable amid small paddocks where sleek horses grazed, a sooty blacksmith's shop, a boathouse, a small chapel, the homes of his brothers and their families and the bungalows of the house servants that formed a perimeter to fend off the ever-encroaching jungle.

Lights were twinkling to life over the grounds, a chain of them along the roofs and high atop poles and at the edges of the drive and from recessed places in the landscape. A group of people were moving about on the lawn.

"Damnation!" Francis said with a venom that made Deidre glance at him with surprise, then curiosity. He sought the rearview mirror for the vehicle following them.

Not understanding his concern, she looked at the people and spiked her reply with mockery. "Personally, I think Telemann should be playing. I mean, bring out the trumpets, the king is returning. Hail, hail the king."

A menacing flame kindled briefly in his eyes. "Maybe I should warn you that I've been known to thrash people who bring me bad news."

She rolled her eyes drolly to the ceiling of the Land Rover. "Case in point, ladies and gentlemen, Juan Geisel brought down in his prime by one fell blow. Very impressive, Francis—much like Errol Flynn in his swashbuckling days.''

"It was two blows, and keep on, my sweet. You're going to get yours.''

"Hah! You don't scare me." Deidre tucked a grudging smile behind a wind-tossed lock of hair.

The engine whined up the last long climb to the compound, and their trail dissipated into the purple-black dusk. The headlights danced a ghostly ballet through the trees. The stars were coming out, Deidre saw as they reached the crest of the rise. They looked oddly different from Texas stars—closer, warmer. The tires took a healthy bite of driveway gravel and skidded to a stop behind a Mercedes coupe.

Deidre craned to see. People had faces now, and voices, and when she turned to remark upon the crowd, she was amazed to find Francis gripping the steering wheel with powerful fists, his eyes drilling straight ahead, his face grooved and lined like a brown leaf, but stealthy, calculating. He was tensed as if he was considering spinning back out again and roaring away.

She shifted nervously in her seat.

Sighing, flicking her a look, he slipped from beneath the wheel to swivel on the seat. He reached into the back for her things and promptly bumped his head against the ceiling. His hat fell into her lap.

"Damn!" he growled with even more vehemence than before. "Damn, damn."

With sympathy knotting in her throat, Deidre turned in her own seat so that she knelt alongside him. At the rear bumper, the men were climbing out of the jeep, and as they hesitated about what to do, she asked them with a telling look to please give them privacy.

Not understanding but accepting her authority, they walked discreetly to the edge of the drive and positioned themselves.

"Francis," she said gently. She placed her hand on his arm, their quarrel at the falls unimportant now. "What's the matter? Tell me."

He picked up the rifle that had been left out of its case and did not reply.

"Don't treat me like this." She wasn't sure if he would tolerate being spoken to in such a tone by a stranger. She repeated her demand more tenderly. "A little while ago, you treated me like a woman. Don't treat me like a child now."

A debate took place in his eyes for a moment, then he said, "Do you mean, what's wrong besides a friend who wants my soul and peasants who want my land and an army officer who wants my hide and a really great woman who wants my head on a platter?"

She rebuked him with a chiding laugh. "I do not want your head. A few curls, maybe, but not your head. And you're fencing with me."

Gratitude flashed briefly on his face. "I know these cars," he admitted dourly as he double-checked the safety latch and poked the rifle into its case. "They belong to members of our great and mighty press. I see a television station, two radios and a newspaper."

"Is that bad?"

"Well, it ain't good."

"You're a famous person, obviously."

"I'm afraid I can't take the credit for this one."

Deidre looked down at herself, then back to him. "You don't mean me?"

When he reached for his hat, Deidre clapped it upon her own head. "Francis," she declared, planting a fist on her hip, "you're the only *old* man I know whose silences can be death threats."

He narrowed his eyes. "Yes, well . . . you're not the first to tell me something like that, *young* whippersnapper."

She smiled, but her chin lost some of its challenge. Francis MacIntire was an important man in this country. She'd understood that much when she landed. Anything that happened to him was news, and today, on his land, had occurred shooting, an airplane crash, and a confrontation with a military authority. Had she thought no one would notice?

He busied himself with the rifle case again. "What I said before—all that about your staying here and fixing the plane?"

An unseen hand plucked one of Deidre's nerves like a rubber band. She caught a quick breath from the sting of it. "What about it?"

"I've changed my mind."

For several moments Deidre didn't move. Presently she leaned back upon her heels and dragged his hat from her head, leaving her hair wildly dishevelled.

"What do you mean?" she asked softly.

"Changed my mind, bonnie lass, as in deciding you were right about the damages." He shook his head. "It wasn't your fault at the airstrip, Deidre. I'll assume complete financial responsibility and write you a check. Then I'm putting you on the first plane back to the States."

Behind them, trees cast gargantuan silhouettes against the sky. To an outsider, the scene on the lawn would look more like a party than a press conference. Glasses clinked. Jokes were batted back and forth—all the synthetic veneer and plastic gossip of people trying to make everyone else think they were doing something important for the world, while, a few miles away, nineteen-year-old boys were getting shot or blown up by antiquated military equipment.

Lunging up on her knees so that she was nose to nose with him, the rifle a barrier between, Deidre stabbed a finger into a curl that lay an inch above the top button on his bush jacket. "*You're* putting *me* on a plane for the States?"

"I thought I just said that."

"Oh, shut up, Francis," she threw back at him. "You and ten like you couldn't put me on a plane."

Propping the rifle outside against the fender of the Land Rover, he scooped up her flight bag and her attaché case. "Look, I was wrong," he argued. "Okay? I made a mistake."

"That's a novel admission after making a federal case about it."

"I was angry when I said it," he admitted a little less grudgingly. "I wanted you, and I let my heart get in the way of my head."

Deidre was caught too off-guard to think straight at such a statement. It was one thing for a man to tease a woman about desire and quite another to talk about it being right or wrong, making it all so irrevocably real.

But he was making decisions that affected her, as if her own wishes were a negligible factor—an I'm-doing-this-for-your-own-good sort of thing. She jammed his hat into his chest and crushed it into a wad of crumpled felt.

"Hey!" he growled.

He promptly dropped her bags and began to repair the damage to his hat. The sight of his big round hands indulging in such uncloaked male vanity turned Deidre in yet another direction. All the fascination she had felt for him before was culminating in something much more dangerous. One didn't fall in love in a single afternoon, but one could do an awful lot of considering it, especially when a man has known about you for years. And when a woman could see a man's faults and still find him lovable...

Now she saw that she'd been thinking of him in terms of "Could he be the one?" from the outset. Even when she was arguing, she'd been angry not because he'd befriended her unfaithful father but because that friendship might jeopardize the interpretation she was placing on his smiles and his kisses.

He replaced his hat on his head, lovingly arranged the crown and repaired the slant of its brim.

Deidre was still immersed in her self-examination. "I've changed my mind, Francis."

The moment radiated between them like dry heat.

He pinned her with a look. "What do you mean, changed your mind?"

"I mean that it won't be necessary to take me to Las Tablas. I'm staying here."

"No way," he said as the lines about his eyes tightened. "Anyway, an hour ago you were charging me with all kinds of vile things because I wouldn't take you."

"I'm a woman." She drew her mouth into a stubborn line.

With a look that flicked over the appropriate curves, he threw back his head in silent laughter. "No comment."

Deidre's blush was lost in the darkness. "I mean, Francis, that I've changed my mind. I've decided to fix the plane. I did agree to deliver an aircraft in perfect working order. I'm going to meet my obligations, and that's the end of the discussion."

The pause between them lasted only long enough to confuse Deidre about his true reactions. Without warning, he gripped her jaw in his palms.

"You're hurting me," she gasped.

Sighing at his fierceness, Francis dropped his hands to her shoulders. He guessed that if he was truly honest, he was glad she'd rebelled, but he couldn't explain to her why his reaction was so violent. He wasn't sure he knew how.

"Not nearly as much as those reporters up there will hurt you," he muttered, anger aching in every feature, but not *at* her, *for* her. "Do you have any idea why they're here? Do you know what's about to happen to me?"

"I know that your son has done something terrible."

"My son? Oh, my son has really committed the ultimate crime. He saves people's lives, no matter what their politics are."

"Francis, don't you think you're taking too much credit for yourself?"

"You don't believe in the sins of the fathers being visited upon the children, et cetera, et cetera?"

"One more et cetera, and that's not fair."

"I don't know why not. I have it coming, don't you see? If Sean too easily takes sides, my sin is in refusing to do it altogether. People don't like it when you don't choose sides, Deidre. My son doesn't like it because I won't side with the rebels. President Araujo doesn't like it because he's afraid I'm going to pull out on him, which I am. The United States doesn't like it because I won't support Carlos Navarro. And Candido... hell, why should he be different? I'm on everyone's bloody bad list, and that's okay—I did what I wanted to do. But anyone who's with me gets dragged along for the ride. Are you getting the picture now? Do you understand why I'm putting you on the first plane out of here?"

Wanting to say something to comfort him but not having any idea what that would be, she circled the wrists of the hands that gripped her. "Why did you ever buy the *Albatross* to begin with if all this is true?"

"Things weren't like this when I bought the plane. And I certainly never planned on my son getting himself attacked by the Scourge of Santiago at the very moment you were landing!"

In disbelief, Deidre struck his hands from her. "*That* was your son? That—"

"Madman?"

He looked straight into her soul, and Deidre thought she had never witnessed the cruelty of love as she was seeing it now. Life, through his son, had changed on him; nothing was balanced anymore, and his big body was slumping with the weariness of fighting.

She wanted to hold him. She laced her fingers tightly and shook her head. "I'm sorry, Francis. I know you're in an awful position here."

"That's the understatement of all time." Scorn was in his heavy sigh, and he laughed bitterly. "You know, I really thought it would be easier. I thought I could wean myself away from Francisco Araujo like tapering off cigarettes. I thought I could be true to myself and not take an open stand. I thought, 'I'll do for Araujo what he doesn't have the character to do for himself. I'll give him this plane as a gift, but it won't really be for him, it'll be for the people. He'll be forced to accept it on their behalf, and it'll pacify them for a little while. The rebels will get off his back, and it'll pay my debts. I won't owe him anything anymore. And I won't have to feel guilty about the rebels. And besides, maybe a miracle will happen in the meantime.'"

His fingers were struggling with themselves. "Miracles don't happen, Deidre. People can stand only so much. Now, I suggest you help me get your things together and take them into the house. While you get something to eat, I'll deal with the piranhas of the press. Then . . . we'll say goodbye pleasantly, more decently, civilized . . . something."

Deidre felt as if she were drowning in a swirl of mixed emotions. Kiss me again, she wanted to say. Just kiss me so I'll know I'm not a fool for wanting you.

But he slowly turned away and, bumping her hip with his, found his gloves and stuffed them into a rear pocket. Through a dazed film of frustration, Deidre located her attaché case. She took her flight bag out of his hands and drew the strap of it over her shoulder. When she glanced up, he was measuring her in the darkness.

"Deidre?"

"Leave me alone," she said and swore that if she shed so much as a tear she would never forgive herself.

"Look at me."

"No."

"Look at me, I said."

She peered up at him. She wanted to hit him. She wanted to hold him. Lord, she didn't know what she wanted!

"About what happened this afternoon..." he muttered.

"I don't want to hear that." She shook her head. "I understand."

"No, you don't."

"Then I don't understand, but I'm as much to blame for what happened, Francis, or what nearly happened." The fight drained out of her. "I'm sorry, too."

"That it happened?" he questioned more gently.

"I—"

"The truth, darling. I have to know that much."

The urgency in his voice made Deidre feel as if he had landed a blow to her stomach. Truth? The truth was, despite all her purist resolutions about going for broke and marriage or nothing, that she wished he had made love to her back at the falls. Now the chance was past, and who was to say that life would ever grant another? The truth was, she wished he wanted more of her than he did, even now. She wished he would say that he was desperate to have her stay and stand beside him through all the trouble that was about to crash down upon him. She wished that he wanted to start all over again with her. *That* was the truth!

But he had grown abruptly private again, engrossed with his immediate problems, and she thought he had shut her out. All her instincts warned that life would be much simpler if she just got out of the car and did exactly as he'd said.

"You didn't tell me how he was doing," she said softly.

His voice was thick with emotion when he replied. "He misses you. He understands. Really, he does, but he misses you, and he wishes that things weren't like they are. He wishes..."

Swallowing, knowing in the way that women always know that somewhere in the communication they were no longer talking about her father, Deidre closed her eyes. Keeping her head down so that her hair was a cloud between them, she whispered softly, "He wishes what, Francis?"

"Hey, Mac!" a voice shouted from a distance.

With a harsh, indrawn breath, he compelled her to ignore for one more moment the world that pressed hard upon them. "Deidre, sweetheart..."

She obediently lifted eyes that were brimming with need and wished she dared hold his face between her hands.

"He wishes you would ignore all that talk about leaving. He wishes you would stay," he said.

Her heart jerked with a thrill, but she wanted more. "And what do *you* wish, Francis MacIntire?"

Sighing, Francis looked first one way, then another, then back at her. After living through a war and coming to this place, after surviving twenty years and working miracles he would have said were not possible, he looked into the depths of this young woman's eyes and saw himself dying. He saw himself dragging her down into the seat of this car and tearing off her clothes. He saw a man—surely not himself—driving wildly into her, driving, driving, driving....

He was caught in the backwash of a generation that was out of step with the world, and he was smart enough to know that he couldn't keep up with Deidre Miles.

"You have to tell me," she said.

But he was too old, and she was too young. "Don't push me, Deidre," he said grittily.

Angry now, for reasons he didn't articulate, he rubbed his mouth and jaw. He mustn't touch her. To touch her would drive him beyond his limits.

"Coward," she muttered.

"All right," he said recklessly through his teeth. "I'll say it. I wanted you this afternoon more than anything I've wanted in a long time. Yes, we could have something between us. For either of us to deny that would be stupid, and I'll go further than that, Deidre. In the snap of a finger, I could say, 'Fall in love with me, and I will worship at your feet.' I could say, 'Let's be mad and forget where we came from or where we're going.' But I'm old enough to be your father, and I have people hanging all over me. Every one of them needs more than I can give, and I don't have anything left anymore. Do you understand that? I don't have anything left, and I wake up so flaming tired that sometimes I think I could head off into this jungle and never be heard of or seen again. So you listen good to me, my darling girl. I want you to stay. It gets worse. I want to fall so deeply in love with you that it makes me blind. I want to do things I never had the courage or the sense to do before. But I can't, and don't you even think about doing it, because if you do, you'll wind up with nothing. If you haven't learned that much from Jonathan Miles, I have, by God!"

For a long time, Deidre held herself like a bow bent back upon itself. Finally spent, he dropped his hands to his sides.

Moaning softly, she folded to her knees and hugged her bags to her chest. Her pulse was slamming at her wrists, and she felt sick to her stomach. What kind of masochist was she that she wanted to take him to her breast and just hold him? To rock him in her arms like a tired man come home at last? Every day she rubbed shoulders with men—smart men, men who knew their way around in the world, tough men, men she had to admire. But he was the first man she could ever remember respecting.

So, where was her ability to reach out and take what she wanted? Was she going to be like the eons of women before her and think she could change this man's mind? She would never change anything about him. And that only made her want him more than ever.

When she finally gathered the courage to look up, she saw disappointment engraved upon his face. Ever so gently he extended his hand and drew the edge of his thumb along the curve of her lip.

Bending her head, trying to breathe over the sudden storm in her chest, she grazed her mouth over the rough crest of his knuckle, then another knuckle, over the strong, tanned span of his hand, her eyes closed, nipping the skin with her teeth, touching with the tip of her tongue and moaning because it was only a parody of what she really wanted to do.

"Mac?" The man's voice was much closer now, more urgent.

Deidre heard Francis's breath catch. "I'm coming," he called in a deep, strangling voice as he took her own hand in his and tremblingly aligned their fingers.

"It's all right, darling," he whispered as he plundered her eyes. "I understand."

But he didn't understand at all. Deidre watched him transforming as he assumed the responsibilities he had spoken of, his big shoulders settling with a ruthless display of willpower as he prepared to do what must be done. His jaw became a stone fortress, and she wanted to kiss away the hard slant of his mouth and the lines that stamped his face with power.

"So," he said as he forced a false edge into his voice, "at least we're blood brothers, aren't we?"

Deidre could hardly speak. She forced herself to smile, knowing that he would break her heart. "But you're not bleeding," she accused in a small faraway voice and dropped her hand.

Laughing bitterly, he twisted around and stepped lightly to the ground. Reaching up, he helped her out and picked up an armload of items. He started walking with her toward the twinkling lights.

"That's what you think," he said.

Except for faded jeans that were stained with dirt and a shirt that had one sleeve torn out, plus a cheek that was turning blue and an arm that was draped with a sling, he looked exactly like Francis. Minus ten years, give or take a day.

He called out as he sauntered toward them, "Are you in for it, Mac! We've been looking everywhere for you. Where the hell have you been?"

Before Francis could do more than make a noncommittal growl, his younger replica stepped up to Deidre and poked his right hand out of the sling.

"Well, hel-l-lo, beautiful," he purred. "Welcome to paradise." Too late, he remembered his wound and substituted his left hand.

Laughing, Deidre uncertainly accepted the handshake. He was Francis's brother, naturally, curls and all. What charmers they were, these bold, good-looking Irishmen.

"Hello, yourself," she said and stared back while his gaze traversed her length. Yes, definitely a MacIntire.

"Who's in for it?" Francis demanded with a scowl for his brother. "What happened to you, and who are they?"

"Poachers." The man jerked his head in the direction of the stables. "Would you believe I captured them single-handedly?"

Beyond his head, Deidre was perceiving dozens of things at once. The house and grounds, which from a distance had appeared merely spacious and sprawling, now gave the appearance of more meticulous care. The impression she'd gotten of gracious informality was not accidental; it was, in fact, carefully and artistically planned to appear informal.

The verandas of the house were probably the most clever feature of all, for it was difficult to tell where house left off and landscape began with the exotic tropical plants strategically arranged with gently massed shrubs. Fragrant flowers spilled off the railings and into the rambling gardens. Wicker furniture and hospitable tables had been placed along their reaches, with hot, steamy afternoons in mind.

In fact, in almost every direction she glimpsed places where one could take respite from the daily rains: a gazebo here, a cluster of trees there, a hidden nook beyond a slope and a wayward path veering off from the stables and ending in a sinfully private arbor.

Now that night was falling, rectangles of golden light streamed out of the windows and leaped across the railings onto the grass. The guests relaxed—or had been relaxing before Francis's arrival—on the wicker furniture or were strolling about on the lawn. A number of barefooted, aproned girls came in and out the doors carrying trays laden with frosty glasses and platters of hors d'oeuvres.

But everyone looked out to the darker spaces near the stables where three men sat slumped upon a bench. Between their legs dangled hands that were bound, and they looked up from beneath battered hats when Deidre and Francis emerged from the congestion of the driveway.

"No, I wouldn't believe it," Francis said.

The brother laughed affably and indicated his sling. "The truth is, there was a little mishap with one of the log trucks. They cut your fences again, Mac, and there's no telling how much timber they pulled out before we caught them."

"Where?"

"Up by the dam."

"Great." Francis shifted his weight and unwittingly pondered Deidre as he talked. "If they've damaged the university's experiments, I'll have their heads."

"I couldn't tell. I don't know that stuff like you do. Who's she?"

"My wife," Francis said dryly and ignored Deidre's small protest by slipping an arm around her waist and drawing her to his side. "Darling, meet my youngest brother, Travis. When I can keep his hands off pretty women, he handles the shipping end of the business. This is Jonathan's daughter, Blackbeard—Deidre Miles, and I think she outgrew your kind several years ago."

"I'll arsenic your Geritol for that." Travis laughed as both his black brows rose wickedly. "Deidre Miles? The one with the braids?" He chuckled. "You've changed a little since yonder year, Miss Miles."

"Braids?" Deidre browsed through her memory. She hadn't realized that her father was a friend of the entire family.

"Your picture." Travis pinched the curls at his temples and pursed his mouth into an effeminate bee sting as he made his voice a falsetto. "Fourteenish. Cute little butterfly pins? Mother's had it on the mantel for years."

With a groan, Deidre recalled her graduation picture from junior high school. "I can say without qualification that my change is for the better, Mr. MacIntire."

"Trav. Call me Trav."

"If you'll call me Deidre."

"Call you Deidre? Why, if you hadn't already married my brother, I'd propose on the spot."

Flushing, Deidre eyed his wedding ring, and he sighed. "Yeah, sorry about that. I've got three kiddos, too. Oh well, I guess marriage is out of the question, huh?"

"If you two don't mind getting on with this," Francis dourly reminded them, "perhaps we might—"

"Where've you been?" another male voice demanded out of the shadows as a second MacIntire replica moved between parked cars and confronted them. "We've been looking everywhere."

"So I heard," Francis said.

"Who's she?"

To prevent Francis from making another flagrant announcement about her being his wife, Deidre blurted, "Deidre Miles."

A smile threatened to turn up the sides of Francis's mouth. "Meet Eric, sweetheart," he murmured.

"Jonathan's daughter." Travis happily filled in the missing pieces.

"The one with the braids?" Eric lifted sooty black brows. "You've changed."

Laughing, Deidre obligingly shook hands with a bright, brisk scholar whose horn-rimmed glasses were perched at half-mast on his nose. He was more slender than his brothers, more tensely wired.

"They descended upon us," said a third MacIntire man as he walked up wearing the same face but with slightly fewer curls and a few more pounds than his fraternal look-alikes. "Like hordes of pagans."

Francis made quick work of his duties as host with a jabbing thumb and indicative looks. "Deidre, meet Chris. This is Jonathan's daughter, Chris."

"The one with the braids," Deidre quickly informed him.

A wide MacIntire smile approved. "You've changed, Miss Miles."

She laughed. "I know."

Francis was quick to return to the problems at hand. "Okay, who's the most hostile, and what do they want?"

Without fanfare, Joaquim ambled up to complete the phalanx of five. He nodded politely to Deidre, then promptly dismissed her. All the men stood in a close huddle that excluded her, their shoulders nearly touching, their heads bent in conference.

"Keep your voices down," Joaquim told them in a low warning. "This thing's turned into a virus, Mac. The newspaper in town got an 'anonymous' tip about the incident on the airstrip this afternoon. In some greatly mysterious manner, the radio just happened to pick it up."

Chris added, "From what I can tell, everyone in town is about to go crazy. The Foundation is upset. Dad says our stock is slipping on the European market already. Mother just keeps giving me those looks."

"There've been a lot of questions about the plane," Eric reported in a somber way, "and they're very curious about Miss Miles. After they started talking about the CIA, I shut up and handed them over to Isabella and took off."

"Well, hell." Francis tugged at the brim of his hat as he glanced over the faces staring at them from the vicinity of the verandas. "What's Isabella been doing?" He remembered Deidre and, over his shoulder, explained from the corner of his mouth, "Isabella's my secretary."

"A live-in maid, he means," Travis said with a high-pitched laugh that brought him a series of glares from them all. Instantly, his smile turned to solemnity. He shrugged at Deidre. "Sorry. She's wonderful, really. Works miracles, walks on water—the whole bit."

"Cut it out, Trav," mumbled Chris.

As Deidre followed the men's glances, she caught sight of the miracle worker. Isabella was the kind of woman other women hated on sight—the kind who could make a man forget Monday night football. Her sleek black slacks and flowing white blouse were lovely but not overdone; her heels were expensive and smart. Her jet-black hair coiled in a tasteful twist on the back of her head, but wearing it up didn't diminish her feminine allure; it only made a person wonder what it would look like falling down to honey-colored shoulders and framing one of the most beautiful faces Deidre had ever seen.

Had Francis slept with her? she wondered. Of course, she decided. No man whose pulse is still beating could resist her.

Isabella was moving among Francis's guests, a clipboard in the crook of her arm. Pausing, she gave an order to one of the maids, who instantly departed to obey it. She signaled a butler from across the veranda, and he, too, moved to respond. Then she hesitated before one of the screen doors and reached to hold it open. From the shaft of light emerged a wheelchair bearing a slender, balding man with an afghan covering his legs.

Except for more of his scalp showing, he very much resembled the four men who waited in a half circle at the edge of the grass. In his wide shoulders was written a saga of pain. Behind him walked a tall woman who, even at seventy or so, was still magnificently erect and graceful. She wore a prim pink shirtwaist, and a lace-trimmed collar fitted high about her throat. She didn't look much like the men, except for the coloring, for her face was quite thin and finely boned.

Deidre was reminded of small Victorian girls who were never allowed to lean back in their chairs. Nodding to Isabella, she pushed the wheelchair out onto the veranda and immediately noticed that her oldest son had returned. Leaving it there, she descended the steps and glided toward the small group while the guests hushed their talking and waited.

Deidre moved imperceptibly closer to Francis.

"Isabella just finished talking to the president's press secretary," Joaquim was saying. "Araujo's flaming mad because he wasn't told about the plane coming into the country. He's reported to have said that Captain Malta should have retained Miss Miles in custody until an investigation was made, and if you want my opinion, Mac, you'll do yourself a giant favor if you simply make a statement here and now."

The creases deepened across Francis's forehead and beside his mouth. Deidre laid her hand upon his arm. "Francis?"

"I want those poachers over there released," he said tersely. "Immediately."

"Just like that?" Chris exclaimed. "They were stealing us blind, Mac."

"Have them work it out then. Something, but don't turn them over to the authorities."

"He's right," Joaquim said.

Deidre pressed the muscle beneath her fingertips and murmured again, "Francis."

"Francis?" The echo passed fleetingly between the brothers, and they all shot her leering grins. "Francis?"

The look of warning that Francis turned upon them brought instant silence. To Deidre, he explained with a chagrined grimace, "Some of them carry scars from calling me that."

Deidre blushed, and he was momentarily distracted, engulfing her with one of his surprising smiles.

She thought, with dismay, that he would have given away their recent intimacy had not someone innocently pressed, "So, what're you going to do then, Mac? About the press?"

With a visible effect to return to the matters at hand, Francis threw his weight to one hip. His sigh was long and contemplative. "Give 'em what they want, I guess."

"That's suicide," Eric snapped. "There're a dozen ways Ramon Mendenez can trip you up."

"Mac really doesn't have a choice, Eric," Joaquim blandly observed. "The question has already been raised."

"No, he doesn't," Francis's mother softly agreed as she walked up with a discreet whisper of silk. "I gave them my word that you'd hold an informal press meeting when you returned, Francis. The phones have been ringing off the wall."

"Hello, Mother," Francis said with a kiss for her cheek.

Mavis MacIntire was exactly the kind of woman Deidre had always planned on being but never would be. Silverhaired, yet proud and beautiful, Mavis's strength lay in what had come before. Her past was in the grace of her long, ivory neck. The way she moved her hands and carried her head showed great discipline. Had she been born a century earlier, one of her sons would have explored the Rocky Mountains or formed a state. Mavis was the genuine article. Her sons would have died for her.

"We were told by the reporters," Mavis said graciously as she extended her hands to Deidre without the formalities of an introduction, "that a woman had delivered the plane. But, of course, they didn't tell us who…" She hesitated and looked toward Francis. "Why, she's Jonathan's—"

"Deidre Miles, Mother," Francis said with a tired smile. "In the flesh. No braids, no butterfly pins."

The older woman lifted her brows in elegant censure. "And you've kept her standing out here in the dark?" Mavis appeared puzzled at the state of Deidre's clothes but was too well-bred to mention it. "Where are your manners, Francis? Goodness, child." She pressed Deidre's hand. "I can hardly believe it—Jonathan's daughter. I must apologize for my son's—"

"Oh, brother, here we go," Eric groaned as Joaquim cleared his throat in a polite reminder of the impatient guests.

"Mother," Chris said, "can this wait?"

"It most certainly cannot," Mavis declared and circled Deidre with a long, slender arm.

As she drew in the consolation of the older woman's embrace, Deidre had to remind herself that Mavis saw her as a child. Not only was she Jonathan's daughter, she was also the age of Mavis's grandson.

Mavis reached up to brush the hair from Deidre's face. She saw the wound. "Good Lord, child!"

Deidre had almost forgotten the crash landing. That was a lifetime ago. "It's nothing, really. I hit my head when I landed the plane. Carelessness on my part. I'm fine."

"Then it was true," Mavis said. "Oh, dear."

Francis was armored now, calculating, and dangerous in a way that Deidre didn't understand. He straightened his bush jacket and arranged his trousers. Smoothing back his hair, he squared his shoulders and prepared to approach the reporters as the king protecting his kingdom.

Deidre didn't think she could bear to see him face the reporters alone. It hadn't been his fault that his son was an idiot. It hadn't been her fault, either, but she would rather take a beating from the press herself than see him take one.

"Wait!" she whispered and gripped his jacket and rose on her toes so that her face was just beneath his.

Unfortunately, they all waited. They all stared at her as if she had made a threat against the president's life.

Feeling like a fool, she flushed and dropped her hands to her waist. She mumbled, "Let me."

"Let you what?" Francis said as he looked at her with barely veiled intimacy.

Hesitating, she looked uncertainly at the people waiting. "Let me go with you."

"To talk to them? It's going to be nasty, Deidre."

"Well, I can be nasty."

His teeth flashed in a smile, and the waiting brothers shuffled impatiently.

Lifting her hand to cover her mouth, Deidre muttered hotly from behind it, "Will you just let me talk to them?"

"Are you crazy? They'd eat you alive."

"Listen to me," Deidre insisted, thinking on her feet but thinking with a shrewd know-how that had kept her alive in a world of man-eating sharks for years. "I'm the cute lady pilot from Texas, right?"

Francis cleared his throat, then laughed silently. "Sweet-heart—"

How many looks like that one had she gotten in her life? "Look, Francis," she said with rough-voiced intensity, "cut the bull, okay? I know these types. Believe me, I know what to say. Now, I can't get you off the hate list, but I can buy you some time. Do you want it or not?"

They all looked at her in disbelief, except for Francis, who was plundering her thoughts as he'd done once already today. Deidre could hardly believe what she'd just said. Who did she think she was? She would make a laughingstock of herself. She would ruin everything.

"Cute lady pilot?" Francis wiped a hand over his face and looked down at her with the most infuriating wink she'd ever witnessed.

"Cute enough." She began twisting up her hair.

What crazy things a woman did when she wanted a man, she marveled.

She smoothed her jump suit from bosom to waist and drew her sweating palms over her cheeks. Straightening her collar, she lifted her chin and flashed Francis a dazzling, bluffing smile she'd worked years to perfect. Six pairs of eyes watched her.

"Well," she said brightly, "how do I look?"

Chapter Seven

The desperado in Francis had always known the score—that to trust life was one of the most colossal mistakes a man could make. Like trusting a jungle afternoon, which, as any native child knew, could change in seconds from a sky propped magnificently on high shafts of sunlight to one of roaring winds that carried away the cries of birds and tore the world into dripping rags.

The natives knew exactly when to head for cover. Yet here he stood, out in the open, with his heart laid bare and the lightning singeing his hair.

It had started with such innocent things. By no means did he object to his mother summoning Dr. Perez from Rio Tepuí in the middle of the night. On the contrary, he would have gotten ten physicians before he let a molecule of Deidre's body suffer. But the quack had the unmitigated gall to put Deidre to bed for two days. Under no circumstances should she become excited, he said.

Idiot! Didn't he know that Deidre had already made a miraculous landing of an A-26, had come within an inch of falling into a torrid love affair and had pulled off a small coup with two of the most vicious reporters in the country? Of course not. Visitors should be kept to an absolute minimum, Perez said, which meant that to pick up the events that had his own brain in a sexual tailspin was a no-no.

Sol Perez shuffled around like one of his geriatric cases and did a lot of sniffling and wiggling of eyebrows. But his heart was as big as an army tank, and Francis had always cherished a fondness for him. Until he found himself collared by the old coot and asked what in hell he'd meant by not taking the ambassador's daughter straight to the hospital after the incident at the airstrip.

And to drag her into a press conference with those baboons, Mendenez and Oropesa? Perez snorted. That bordered on the criminal.

Francis mentally cursed Perez, reserving a few choice epithets for himself. He sourly congratulated himself for having the foresight to place Deidre in the room adjoining his own on the west veranda. At least he could steal a few moments alone with her after things had settled down.

Wrong. Mavis approached the task of nursing Deidre as if the family owed Jonathan a debt of honor for befriending Francis over the years. Not for a moment did her vigilance slacken, and every time Francis did more than poke his head into the room to ask Deidre how she was doing—she was irresistibly sexy in the little lacy affair Mavis had lent her to wear—Mavis turned upon him one of her disappointed looks that could always make Francis feel like going out and hanging himself from the tallest tree.

Even Cleary dragged himself away from his computers and wheeled himself all over the house, dedicated to running special errands and mentioning things like, "Do you remember when the President of the United States wrote to Jonathan about you, Mac?'' Or, "If it hadn't been for Jonathan, boy, the CIA would have hauled in your boots years ago.''

To complicate his life even further, Jonathan, upon seeing the headline, "U.S. Ambassador's Daughter Questioned,'' telephoned from a diplomatic summit and said he would be arriving at the ranch the moment he returned to Santiago.

Francis was frayed raw. Getting Deidre became an obsession. Every waking moment he thought about her, and his nights were a battlefield of frustrations that left him hard and aching.

Because the truth was too exhausting, he lied to Jonathan. He said that his business with Deidre happened accidentally, and she seemed eager to see her father again after so many years. Yes, yes, she was resting. No, her ordeal with the commander of Araujo's Special Task Forces didn't appear to be having any adverse effects. She was fine. Just fine.

His brothers, thankfully, had turned the poaching incident into something of an advantage, publicity-wise, but they adamantly refused to deal with the press, who were being fed rumors by Candido Malta on a daily basis. Left to him were the tedious meetings with officials in Rio Tepuí and an almost daily flight into Las Tablas in an effort to circumvent a tragic showdown with Araujo.

"I've ordered my personal military deployments increased by ten percent,'' the president informed him the day after Deidre arrived. "I need your public support, my friend. Things are less than ideal here at the capitol. I receive daily threats upon my life. Every bastard in Congress is threatening me with an investigation. Yesterday I received a cable from the United States.''

How could he give Araujo his support any longer? Francis wanted to shout. Every day the man was more of a threat to Francis's own son.

But Sean was a subject he and Araujo never discussed. Only through the grapevine did he hear about Francisco's raging tantrums and violent threats to strip the MacIntires of their holdings and expel them from the country.

"Mac, you can't straddle the fence any longer," Chris said from his end of the dining table while Luiz refilled glasses with rich claret and dished up dessert. "You've got to come out strongly in support of Navarro."

"No," Francis said.

"If you want my advice, Mac," Eric added as he, too, stopped eating and pushed his glasses higher onto his nose, "make a clean break. Have Miss Miles fix the plane as soon as possible and take the thing back home. Forget about Araujo. Let nature take its course."

Francis leaned forward over the table, his weight on his elbows, and said with a nastiness that raised all their brows, "Eric, even as a child your head was in your back pocket. I didn't like it then, and I don't like it now."

After a fuse-lit silence, Travis announced, "Yes, well, if you don't do something, Mac, *el Presidente* is going to fly into one of his teensy weensy rages and send us all packing with just the clothes on our backs. And he may well get himself killed before he's through. While Miss Miles is at it, have her fly Mom and Dad and all the women and children out of here at the same time."

"Just a minute." Cleary MacIntire pushed his wheelchair back from the table. "Mom and Dad make their own decisions around here."

The dining room in Francis's house was so large that one of the peasant bungalows could have been placed in it. Lying in the exact center of the house, its walls were windowless, which was compensated for by white, twelve-foot ceilings and two Italian chandeliers.

On ordinary days, the table seated twelve. When all the grandchildren were home from school, plus Isabella and Joaquim, who always attended family meetings of importance, nineteen of the chairs were filled. Over the years, the room had become a meeting place at the end of the day—the oasis, the watering hole.

Mavis despised quarrels at the dinner table with the same dignified fervor that she despised business talk there. They would all end up dyspeptics, she said. But the MacIntire men possessed fiery natures, and life moved too quickly sometimes to allow for idle pleasantries.

Only the adults were present tonight. A tray had been taken to Deidre's room. During the soup course and well into the entrée the subject of conversation had been the possibility of a coup by Carlos Navarro versus a military takeover by the rebels versus another political fiasco by Francisco Araujo.

Amanda, Eric's wife, was so nervous that she lit a cigarette. "Nothing doing, Chris," she said to his suggestion. "I didn't want to come to this country in the first place, if you remember. But now I've taken root and borne acorns. Right, Meg? Pat, isn't that what you say? That we stay here and tough it out? We have to, Mac. We're not quitters."

"What Mac ought to do," Travis said, "is start a few rumors. You don't have to do anything about them, Mac, just let the word get around that you're considering having a talk with Navarro."

"That would be like signing Francisco's death warrant, Trav," Francis argued, "and you know it."

"And sitting here, letting the rebels think we're behind Araujo, is like signing our own," Chris protested.

"We wouldn't even be sitting here if it weren't for Araujo," Francis hotly declared. "Where's your loyalty, man?"

"He's not fit to be a president any longer."

"That doesn't mean we have to throw him to the wolves," Francis hurled back. "There are discreet ways of doing things."

Eric smirked. "Well, do you think helping Miss Miles here in the house is one of them? All that CIA gossip? We're lucky the rebels haven't burned us out already."

Francis lowered his head. "That's enough."

"Hell, I like her, too, but at least send her to her father."

As voices rose in argument, pro and con, Francis's mind seethed. Deidre wasn't going anywhere, not if he had anything to do with it. And his family owed her more than they knew. No one could have handled Ramon Mendenez and Jose Oropesa with as little bloodshed as she had that night.

The reports had been particularly nasty, which was surprising; Ramon's forte was an innuendo in the back, not a pickax. Why had Francis bought the *Albatross*? he'd immediately demanded. Was it for the rebels? Or was he planning to wage his own private war? Was there any truth to the rumor that he and the president were squabbling? Was he going to leave Santiago? Or had he just wanted another toy to play with?

If Francis hadn't been in love with Deidre already, watching her would have cinched it. With no fanfare whatsoever, almost shyly, actually, she prettily mentioned that she was the pilot Candido Malta had held for questioning.

Of course, there was no controlling them, then. The newsmongers bombarded her with the same CIA line of attack Candido had used. No one knew better than he did how reluctant Deidre was to use her connection to Jonathan, but no, she said, she was not with the CIA. It was quite simple, really; she was paying a visit to her father, the *United States ambassador*, whom she hadn't seen in some years, and she was conducting a little business at the same time. Was there something wrong with that? *The United States ambassador?*

Shocked, what could they say? She glowed with innocence. The more they pried and poked, the more she came alive, running the gamut from shy femininity to hard, fierce competitiveness, and then she went off on a brilliant tangent about the merits of the A-26 Invader.

No one could get in a word. On and on she rambled about how the two Pratt & Whitney R-2800 engines gave the plane a maximum speed of three hundred and sixty miles an hour, which was nearly eight miles an hour faster than the B-25s and the B-26s had been. And did they know why the A-26 was such a superior design? Because monocoque construction had eliminated the maze of wires and pipes inherent in the older welded tube types, of course, and the repair and maintenance was much easier. Why, the engines were so perfectly interchangeable and fitted together so beautifully that she could do a complete change herself in only one day. Once, gentlemen, when Lieutenant Mikesh was with the 17th Group at the Pusan Airfield in Korea... And had they heard the one about "Sweet Susie" of the 452nd?

No one had the nerve to tell her to shut up. "Why, it's a mechanic's dream," she declared with a winsome smile and a sweet Texas drawl that not only stole his own heart but took the firepower completely out of Ramon's innuendoes.

"And guess what, Señor Mendenez? They added double slotted, electrically operated flaps. That gave us the drag we needed, of course. Oh, I know what you're thinking. The drag, you see..."

And on and on and on. Even cranky José Oropesa had found himself caught up in her spell, and by the time she'd brought the plane through World War II and into Korea, then into Vietnam and on to Chile, everyone was so dead on their feet that it was a simple matter to play them with a bit more booze and send them packing with a promise to do it again right away.

Now Francis stared at the unappetizing plate of cold fruit. He was wondering if he had the nerve to tell Deidre that he wanted to take back all that silly talk he'd spouted out in the driveway about not wanting to fall in love. To tell her that he was in love with her already.

Not if he really cared about what happened to her, he couldn't. He looked up. "For the last time, Eric," he said tersely as he lifted a piece of mango to his mouth and returned it to his plate, "I am not going to support Carlos Navarro. Give the man four years, and he'll put Araujo to shame."

"You don't have to support him, Mac," Chris said wearily, "just pretend to."

"Don't you find that a bit dishonest, Chris?"

Chris mumbled, "And I suppose giving a plane to Araujo isn't?"

"And all that wining and dining of Cidinha Araujo is all in good fun?" Eric added.

A deadly hush fell upon the room. Even Luiz let Isabella's dollop of whipped cream slough off the silver ladle to the floor.

Cidinha Araujo was her brother's secretary of interior. A good, decent woman, she'd been in love with Francis for years. Much of the MacIntire wealth was due to the advice Cidinha had given them over the years, and though Francis hadn't capitalized on that, he hadn't gone out of his way to refuse her favors out of guilt for not loving her in return. Of course, if he had loved her, most of their problems with Araujo wouldn't exist to begin with.

"Look," Francis said with a growl as Luiz bent and furiously scrubbed at the cream, "I have to take that kind of garbage from Candido, but not from you two."

"And speaking of the devil," Travis interjected, "you don't take that vermin seriously enough, Mac. One of these days you're going to wish you had."

"Travis," Mavis scolded with a maternal sigh. "Not at the table, if you don't mind."

"Sorry, Mother." Travis glared at his older brother.

"I don't underestimate the man," Francis argued in his own behalf. "I never have. But what can he really do except talk? If you backed the man against a wall, the worst he could do would be to hit you with that damned quirt of his."

"Yeah," Eric sullenly said, "back him against a wall. That was one smart move, Mac, slapping a man. The country's about to have a civil war, the family is in danger of being expelled in poverty, and you go around slapping enlisted men!"

"That's enough, Eric," Cleary MacIntire warned from his wheelchair.

"Sean's the one who should have his face slapped," one of the women whispered.

Francis's chair scraped harshly on the floor, and his silver struck his plate with a clutter. His glass of claret tipped, and an ugly stain spread upon the starched linen.

Luiz immediately rushed from damage to damage, and Pat MacIntire closed her eyes in apology to her brother-in-law. Everyone knew the rule: Sean MacIntire's name was never to be made dinner table conversation.

Stretching out her hand, Mavis attempted to prevent Francis from leaving the table. "Son—"

"She didn't mean it, Mac," Eric murmured softly in defense of his wife.

But Pat had meant it. She was only saying what they all felt, that they could not forgive Sean for jeopardizing their own children.

"If you'll excuse me," Francis said angrily as he brushed crumbs from his cream-colored linen slacks, "I've had a long day. Isabella, in the morning I want you to start a whispering campaign about the damnedest party Rio Tepuí has ever thrown for the president. Make sure the right people get it back to the capitol. Pull in some markers from our good friends, the press. You, Trav, get the bomber into the hangar. And, Joaquim, I want parts for that plane this week if we have to buy every A-26 McDonnell Douglas ever made."

The handsome man lifted a finger of acknowledgment as Isabella scribbled herself a series of notes.

"Hell, Mac!" Trav blurted. "You want it in the hangar tonight?"

"Yes, tonight, damn it!" Francis ordered. "Get a bulldozer out there."

"Mac," Eric said solemnly, "if you don't mind my saying so—"

"Well, I do mind!" Francis thundered.

When Francis was in this frame of mind, everyone knew better than to argue. He had built the MacIntire empire almost single-handedly, and if it went down, he would be the one who would suffer the most.

Rising, Mavis followed her son as he stormed out of the dining room and slammed the door until the glass of the chandeliers chattered like the gossip that would sweep from Rio Tepuí to the capitol the next day.

Whispers followed Mavis to the door, about how stroking Francisco Araujo at this late date would do little good. And if Sean had any conscience at all, he would at least lie to the president and pretend to mend his ways and come down out of the hills.

"Mac's walking too fine a line here."

"Our lives are at stake in this, too."

With her hand upon the doorknob, Mavis faced her family. "I'm ashamed of you," she said simply. "The man has given everything for us. No one could have done what he's done." With tears in her eyes, she hurried through the door.

Francis knew his mother was following but hoped that this once she would accept his rudeness and simply let him go sulk in peace. He walked swiftly to the west wing of the house, and when he paused outside Deidre's door, he saw Mavis step into the corridor.

Sighing, he leaned against the wall and slumped with weary frustration. Reaching up, he pinched the bridge of his nose. He had to see Deidre. Things inside him were changing too quickly, and he didn't know who he was anymore. Was he the brash young hellion who'd been born swinging both fists? Fighting for what he wanted even though he wasn't quite sure what that was?

Or was he the older, used-up man who had nothing left inside him and who could head off into the jungle and never be heard of again? Older, yes, and very tired, but feeling a rush of fire melting his veins, a new, possessive energy for Deidre Miles, and knowing it was crazy but still wanting to go blind with love for her and carry *her* off into the jungle like some love-crazed Tarzan!

It was the wrong time, the wrong place, but he had to see her—he had to.

"Francis," Mavis whispered as she stepped near enough that she could smooth the collar of the freshly starched white shirt he wore. "They didn't mean all that."

"Yes, they did."

"But they love you dearly. And they respect you."

"I know they do."

"What are you going to do?"

He shook his head, feeling as if he were in a bad dream and couldn't wake up. "I don't know. What am I going to do with Sean, Mother? He won't listen, and I understand his need to do something good and decent. I applaud it, I admire it, but damn it—"

"Don't swear, darling. Listen to me. You can bear children, and you can love them, but they grow up, Francis. You can't live a grown man's life for him. You simply can't. You let go. You let him make his own way, make his own mistakes."

"I can't let him ru'n his life."

"You don't really have a choice, do you?"

Francis wiped a hand over his mouth and shook his head. She was right: he didn't have a choice. About a whole lot of things.

"It's late, Mother," he said gently. "Go to bed."

"Are you going to bed?"

It was a gentle rebuke. He knew Mavis had made the connection between his erratic behavior of the last few days and Deidre Miles. But she could not accept his presence at Deidre's door and his need to go inside and hold her in his arms through the night. She would never approve the primitive forces that drove him, but surely she had to understand them. Someday, when he was feeling very brave, he wanted to ask her, "Mother, did you ever once want someone so badly you thought you would die?"

As if she read his thoughts, she closed her eyes briefly and laced her fingers as if prepared to pray. "Do you think this is wise?" she asked in a soft attempt to dissuade him.

"I, too, am a grown man, Mother. Please stay out of it."

"I can't, my darling. She's just a girl."

"She's a woman."

"She's Jonathan's daughter."

God, didn't he know that? If Jonathan Miles were thinking about a daughter of Francis's what he himself was thinking about Deidre, he would have killed the man on the spot with his bare hands.

"Then why don't you call Jonathan?" he urged her gently. "Talk to him. No one can play the diplomat like you, Mother. Make him feel better."

"What happened between you two, Francis? You were always so close."

"Nothing happened," he said, sighing.

Standing on tiptoe, Mavis curved her palm about her son's stubborn jaw. She smiled sadly. "Always fighting. Always taking on your own demons and everyone else's, too."

Francis came away from the wall. Lifting her hands, which had worked hard for seventy years, he kissed her creped cheek. Gently then, he turned her by the shoulders and pointed her in the direction from which she'd come.

"I'll see you in the morning, Mother. It's late."

Mavis dropped her hands to her sides in resignation. "I only hope you know how late it really is."

At least she hadn't said she'd pray for him. It always killed him when she said that.

Not until her steps were no longer audible did Francis place his hand upon the knob of the door to Deidre's room and grimly twist it. He stepped into the darkness where she lay sleeping. Though he half hoped she would awaken, he moved silently and shut the door without a sound.

The room was Spartan, with its tall, undraped windows and the stark white of its walls and ceiling. The four-poster bed was polished ebony and was draped with sheer white netting, now tied to the posts so that the hems were caught by the breeze and thrown out in a sail.

Yet, even without the frills, the room was still a feminine one. The bath, completely white, twinkled with shiny brass fixtures, and in the cupboards were every item imaginable for a lady's toilette, even to the batiste gown Deidre was wearing.

She hadn't given herself a great deal of freedom in the room, for little of her was visible. Her bag and her case were neatly out of sight, and her survival basics could have been placed in one small drawer of the bureau. He's started to have Isabella outfit her with a complete wardrobe, but spending money on her was one thing Deidre would not accept. He'd almost begun a war when he cabled payment in full to Aero Classics before the repairs were made.

Deidre lay on her left side, her legs bent, one arm angled alongside her head so that her armpit was a perfectly sensual line. Her body seemed much smaller in slumber, somehow. Her hair spilled over her pillow. Her face was so girlish and beautiful that Francis was filled with a kind of despair.

He'd been smiling, he realized, and as his smile waned, he studied the drape of the sheet along her waist, the shadows of her breasts beneath the gown. With growing arousal, he followed the line of her hip, the little angling jut of her pelvic bone, the low, muted nest of hair.

There it was again, the sexual, animal drive. Maybe all he needed to purge himself of this infatuation was a woman—any woman. How long had it been? He couldn't remember. He couldn't remember who the woman had been...a party at the capitol...

But this was hardly an infatuation, was it? How much simpler it would be if it were. This closeness of mind, this shared intuition, the empathy even when he wasn't near her—if they never made love, he would still feel unfaithful if he had sex with someone else.

Bending his head and closing his eyes, he found himself praying—not the repetitive words he had recited all his life from a book, but an anguished plea like the one he'd groaned as he stood over Mary Beth's body and watched her life slip away. *Please, don't let anything happen to those I love. Don't let anything happen to Deidre.*

The breeze stirred her hair, and she roused slightly, turning so that her face was near his knee. Wanting badly to touch her, he crouched so that his hips rested on his heels.

The ache inside him was unbearable. He couldn't keep doing this to himself. Oh, he could delude himself for a short time that he could take a child bride and live in his castle happily ever after, but even the talk at the table had shattered that fantasy to a thousand pieces. Soon all the women would have to leave. Unless he did something.

What? Betray the integrity he had always prided himself on? Remain loyal to Araujo? Support Navarro? Pull out of everything and let Araujo pay for his sins?

Rising, he moved into the shadows and waited beside the door until all his senses were whirling with the rhythm that lifted her breasts so sweetly.

"I love you," he whispered. "Don't hate me for what I have to do."

As he shut the door, Francis didn't think he'd ever been so unhappy in his life. Francisco Araujo wasn't the only one who had sold his soul; now he would end up making Deidre despise what he was, as Mary Beth had despised it, as Sean despised it.

But maybe that was best, the least painful way for her to survive this. He would push her so gently away that she wouldn't feel it. She would go home grateful that she hadn't wasted her affections on a man who no longer belonged to himself.

Going to his room, he shut the door and, without turning on a light, poured himself a glass of potent Irish whiskey. Then he proceeded, systematically, to get very, very drunk.

Deidre had her speech all made up. During the long hours when she had been tended by Mavis MacIntire, she had little to do except plan exactly what she would say.

"Francis, it's this way," she saw herself explaining. "The fact that you're nearly fifty and I'm not yet thirty is outdated thinking. The fact that you're Catholic and I'm not doesn't disturb me. The fact that you're rich and important and I'm up to my neck in hock to Consolidated Savings and Loan is unimportant. Well, kind of unimportant. So what that you're beautifully educated and I barely made it through high school? So what if you built a town with your bare hands? I'm very clever, Francis. I can build a plane. I can remodel a room. I can overhaul your car. I can do anything—even be a lady. So what that I have to first scrub the grease from under my fingernails..."

It was at this point that she invariably faltered. What did she think he needed, another mechanic, for pity's sake?

She gave up on the speech. Life moved at a too-hectic pace in Rio Tepuí. She couldn't get close enough to Francis to say a dozen words, much less really talk to him.

Seeing him wasn't the hard part. A dozen times a day she watched him come out of his office, his head bent in conference with Isabella. Sometimes he stood at the gazebo with his thumbs hooked in his back pockets as he consulted with Joaquim or his brothers about matters of shipping and harvesting. Sometimes he met dark-suited men who climbed out of Audis and Mercedes at all hours of the day and night.

"Hurry!" the servants would whisper. "It's the ambassador."

"The Colombian Secretary..."

"...diplomatic envoy from Chile."

At other times she glimpsed Francis in the living room or the kitchen with a telephone pinched between his jaw and shoulder. He would smile at her and signal her with the lift of a brow or the wave of a finger. She saw him in his bush clothes and old hat, dark suits, casual linens and once a tuxedo with a brilliant crimson cummerbund.

With his parents, he took her to dinner at Hedary's and Maxim's in Rio Tepuí. He was charming and gallant. He introduced her to people whose names she couldn't remember. The next day he instructed Joaquim to take her riding, and Isabella helped her with insurance forms for the *Albatross* and put through phone calls to Phillip Magaskin in Dallas.

The sisters-in-law insisted on lending her dresses and showing her their homes. In the Rolls-Royce, they took her on a tour of the schools in Rio Tepuí. Mavis invited her to mass, and she, in turn, took Cleary MacIntire flying in the Cessna. Whenever guests arrived in the evening, she was always invited for cocktails. She made them laugh with her jokes about Texas.

All in all, a very familiar affair. But whenever she tried to talk to Francis, fifteen other people were always in the room. The amazing thing was, Deidre didn't know why it took her so long to figure out the truth. She wasn't usually so dense. Francis Collins MacIntire, the irascible, curly-headed Irishman she'd fallen head-over-heels in love with, was giving her the brush-off!

She didn't believe she would ever really forgive him for it. Who did he think she was, a child to be weaned? Oil and water cannot mix, he was telling her. *Do you see now, Deidre? Can you understand what I tried to tell you? How loving me isn't fair to you?*

It wasn't fair—that was just the point. She wasn't a child. She was a woman, and she was hurt and angry.

"I'm trapped here," she fumed. "I can't stay, and I can't go. All I can do is watch him coming and going with all his important business."

In Dallas, she would have worked herself into a stupor until she got over him. But here, in this country where she didn't even speak the language, she was doomed to wait for some vague shipping company to send parts for a plane that wasn't even produced anymore.

Waiting, waiting. And even then she couldn't be sure the parts would come. There was only one thing she was sure of....

On Tuesday Francis bounded out of the Land Rover and slammed the back door until the frame rattled. He strode through the house with his usual long-legged energy and found his mother in the kitchen calmly planning the day's menu with the butler, Luiz.

"They've struck gold up at Cockcrow," he said enthusiastically. "I want Deidre to come and see the carnival."

"Why, dear," Mavis said as she looked up and smoothed her hair back with both hands, "I think Deidre's out with the vaqueros today. I'm not positive, of course, but I do believe I heard her talking to Joaquim about it. Luiz, didn't I hear them talking?"

Francis frowned. "Vaqueros? She's out with the vaqueros?"

"Well, I thought so, dear. Why don't you let me check—"

Jamming his hat on his head, Francis stormed out of the house before she could finish. Vaqueros? His wife? But she wasn't his wife, was she?

For an hour he tried to locate Joaquim, only to discover that the man was handling some shipping matter at Rio Tepuí and the vaqueros wouldn't be back until dark.

"She's lost her mind," he simmered under his breath. "That's what she's done. She's gone crazy."

Heads would roll for this, he consoled himself. All his men knew better than to take a woman out in the hills without a guard. And Deidre, of all people!

On Wednesday, just as he was planning to get to the root of the trouble, he stalked through the house to Deidre's room, only to learn from the maids that she had gone to the rice paddies. Some of the young women took their children to the fields rather than opt for day care and sitters as they would have had to do in the city.

The rice fields! Damn it! What was going on here?

On Thursday she flew Cleary to the Cuna headwater, and on Friday she attended the funeral of one of the vaquero's relatives. After a week of finding himself one step behind her, Francis grew more and more angry. Who did she think he was?

To Deidre's amazement, she found herself looking forward to sitting at the end of the day with the tired vaqueros. She liked listening to them talk as they smoked their last cigarette and watched the sun set. Sometimes she sat in the kitchen with the cooks and helped them peel potatoes while they prepared for the coming morning. They taught her words of Spanish and chattered in broken English about how different life was since the MacIntires had come to Santiago.

"Oh, Señor Mac, he don't allow none of his girls to wear those short skirts and go into the city to peddle themselves. He makes 'em go to school. When one of the mens die, he sees th' money don't stop comin'. Someone gets sick, Señor

Mac pays the hospital bill. He take care of his people, Señor Mac does."

Yes, Deidre thought. Señor Mac did almost everything. He worked to preserve the ecology of the rain forest. He kept the few remaining tribes of natives from being driven off their land to extinction. He did what could not be done, but he didn't know one penny's worth about loving a woman!

"I want to talk to you," Francis said gruffly as he finally caught up with Deidre at the dinner table the evening Chris's sons came home from the academy.

The dining room was filled with people. All the grandchildren were swarming about, and the brothers were talking shop. The maids weaved through them with platters of food.

Deidre smiled innocently up at Francis while her pulse picked up its pace. "Of course, Francis," she murmured sweetly. "What's on your mind?"

"Privately, if you don't mind."

She lifted her brows. "Dear me."

Luiz filled her glass with water. "How pretty you look this evening, Señorita Miles," he said politely.

"Why, thank you, Luiz. *Gracias*." Deidre laughed charmingly at the butler as she prepared to take her seat, then explained to Francis, "Luiz is helping me with my Spanish."

"Really?" Francis said between his teeth.

"Does the garbage disposal work better now, Luiz?" Deidre asked.

"Perfectly, *señorita*." He made a circle of forefinger and thumb. *"Perfecto."*

A strong shade of red stained the sides of Francis's neck as he narrowed his eyes at his trusted butler. So Luiz had joined the conspiracy.

Placing a hand upon Deidre's shoulder, he literally pushed her into her chair. "Garbage disposal?" he growled through a menacing smile as his fingers tightened.

Deidre pretended equanimity as she removed his hand and managed a smile. She had wanted to rankle him, and she had. But now she wasn't quite sure what to do with herself or him.

She took a deep breath and folded her hands primly in her lap. "Do sit down, Francis. You look like a bullfighter. Or maybe it's the bull. And I think you'd better plan on replacing the disposal. The bearings are bad. I'd do it myself, but I've already started taking the props off the *Albatross*."

The color of Francis's blue eyes turned to steel gray as he loomed over her. Deidre felt the palms of her hands growing damp as he ran the tip of his tongue threateningly along the inside of his cheek, then said with warning softness, "So you went to the hangar today?"

"Of course," she said demurely. "Didn't you know?"

"Without a guard?" he added with even more menacing tranquility.

Deidre had not forgotten the scene with Juan Geisel, and she didn't trust Francis when he grew so nice. She tipped the edges of her mouth in what she hoped was a bright smile and lifted her glass of water.

She sipped. "Of course."

"How did you get there?"

"In the Land Rover, naturally. I drove myself. I wasn't sure which key belonged to it, but Isabella said—"

"After dinner," Francis snapped as Cleary wheeled in to the table and everyone began taking their places. "On the veranda. Be there. I mean it."

Deidre didn't think she tasted a single bite of her meal. Once dinner was over, she marched straight to Cleary MacIntire and asked if he wouldn't like her to wheel him out onto the veranda so he could enjoy his cigarette without one of his wife's reprimanding glances.

"So you noticed those, did you?" he said, laughing as he gave her hand a fond pat. "Full steam ahead, Miss Miles, and we'll drink to bad habits."

"Deidre," she reminded him as she laughed and gripped the chair and pushed him out of the room while Francis followed her with piercing eyes.

When Francis found them, they were deep in conversation about Chrysler's performance on the stock market. Francis parked himself on the rail and crossed his legs while Cleary earnestly explained to her the genius of Iacocca.

The chitchat seemed endless, and when Cleary lit his third cigarette, Francis gently removed it from his nicotine-stained fingers with a warning worthy of the surgeon general.

"I came to invite you to the concert in Rio Tepuí," Francis told Deidre with quiet formality. "Of course, it's just a community thing, and Shostakovich is a little out of their league. We're the baser sort down here, but it should prove...interesting."

Deidre carefully avoided Francis's eyes. Part of her wanted to look at him with the love that was growing inside her more every day, and part of her wanted to punch him for squandering the precious time they could have had.

He laced his fingers and steepled them under his chin. She fidgeted unnecessarily with a metal catch on Cleary's chair.

"I'd love to, Francis," she said with matching formality, "but, honestly, I wouldn't be comfortable at the concert. You know I didn't bring any clothes with me, and I—"

As if to prove her point, she glanced down at her brown slacks and an inexpensive top that one of the maids had insisted she accept as a gift.

"Then we'll go shopping," he said, smiling.

"But—"

"My treat."

"I couldn't. I—"

He was making the effort to reach across the breach that had developed, Deidre knew. She also knew he loved her. Then why were they facing each other down like this?

"We'll make a day of it," he added with husky persuasion, "and meet everyone for dinner before the concert."

Suddenly overcome by an accumulation of frustration and irrational rage, Deidre threw back her head, leading with her chin. Her voice had the cutting edge of a machete.

"And it'll be just a *wonderful* day," she sneered, "right, Francis?"

Between them, Cleary froze and let the smoke drizzle past his lips. Flushing furiously in the darkness, Francis glanced down at his father, then back to her as if she had just leaned over and bitten him.

More softly he muttered, "What's the matter with you?"

"What's the matter?" she practically shrieked. "You say the words *shopping* and *Shostakovich* and expect me to turn all soft and sweet, Francis? Why, I get to go to the hair dresser and spend a lot of money, don't I? We'll have lunch at a fancy restaurant, then we'll stroll down the main street and window-shop. Well, thanks but no thanks, Francis MacIntire. My affection can't be bought with a few yards of silk and a bauble! Lord knows, I would have given it to you for free! I can't believe I'm saying this. Damn you, Francis. Damn you, damn you. I'm sorry, Mr. MacIntire. I didn't mean to do this in front of you.''

During her speech—only this one was horribly un-planned—the volume of Deidre's passion had risen until she was hissing her words. Francis was livid, and she was blis-tering with regret. Poor Cleary managed to find his lighter, but the breeze kept extinguishing it.

Taking the lighter, Francis flicked it and held it beneath the trembling white cylinder while he drove Deidre back against the wall with a series of rapacious looks.

Deidre wanted to melt through the floor. She wanted to grovel before Cleary and throw her arms about Francis's neck and say she hadn't meant a word of it.

But he didn't take her aside and give her the chance to do that. He didn't draw her off the veranda into the shadows and hold her and explain why he was treating her like a child. Instead, he looked as if he could have circled her neck with his hands and gladly strangled her.

"I'll arrange with Isabella to take you shopping," he said quietly, as rigid as stone. "I would have done it before now if you'd let me."

Which was not the point at all, and he knew it! Whirling around, delirious to get away from him after she had spent so many days wanting to be with him, Deidre wasn't able to reach her room before the tears pushed through the frail barrier of lashes and streamed down her cheeks in molten rivulets.

Boy, you sure told him, Deidre, she thought as she threw herself face down across the bed. You let him know better than to take you for granted ever again, yessiree, girl. You got his attention, all right.

Sleep played a cruel, elusive game that night. When it fi-nally did come in the depressing wee hours of the morning, Deidre dreamed of waiting for a man in a strange, moonlit garden—a secret rendezvous in a lavish arbor with marble statues of men and women in lewd, erotic poses. Sitting on a bench, she waited and waited until at last she heard his voice. Rising, she went to search. She found him in a crowd of people. A number of women surrounded him, some of whose faces she recognized, but most were strangers. They were flirting outrageously, stroking and caressing him, slipping their hands inside his shirt and along his thigh. From time to time he bent his head to accept a kiss. Looking up, he invited Deidre to come and join them, but she, horrified, refused. Laughing, he grabbed one of the women and kissed her while Deidre watched.

In the dream she was somehow transported much closer, and then she could see where he put his hands upon the women. In the vision she grew unbearably aroused, and it was painful. She was suddenly one of them who waited for his favors. She was fighting to reach him, and all around her were people engaging in sex of every kind. She was crying his name, but the more she fought to reach him, the farther away she was, until she was outside the world and could see everything from a place very high. She gazed down at Francis making love to a woman, and when the woman locked her long, naked legs around him and threw back her head in a cry of pleasure, she saw in her shock that the face belonged to Isabella.

"Now you, Deidre Miles, belong to me," a man's voice said, and she looked up to see Juan Geisel's body lowering upon her own.

In the dream she screamed, and when she awoke, she was sitting up in bed, wringing with sweat, heaving to breathe. Tumbling off the bed, she hurried into the lovely white bathroom and threw cold water on her face. Bracing her hands on the sink, she let the running water wash away the dream.

Twenty-four hours, she vowed to herself. She would give the airplane parts twenty-four more hours to arrive. If they had not come by then, she would ask Joaquim to take her to Las Tablas. She couldn't stand it anymore.

The next day, the new landing gear arrived from the States. While Pat and Amanda were making one of their daily visits to Mavis and Cleary, Deidre asked Isabella for the keys to the Land Rover. She asked Joaquim to find someone to help her.

She worked straight through lunch and late into the afternoon.

Chapter Eight

Paulo!"

Deidre lay stretched, red-eyed and exhausted, along the top of one of the *Albatross*'s engines. Her head, feeling like a cantaloupe, was operating at brain-damaged capacity. Her fingers fumbled like so many thumbs and retained only enough of their involuntary motor responses that they did the right thing in spite of her.

And those were the minor complaints. It was her face! It had stared back at her from the smear of the morning's mirror, and she couldn't believe that one night of weeping could do so much damage. Her nose was swollen beyond recognition and incapable of breathing. Her eyes were surrounded by puffy pink stains that could have competed with Nicolas Noreiga's. She skipped breakfast for fear of running into Francis and giving her heartache away, and now her stomach sounded like a cat whose territory had been invaded.

When Joaquim gave her the keys to the Land Rover, he'd angled her a curious look. She winced and said she must be allergic to some of the plants outside her window.

"Dear, dear," he murmured and lifted his stunning brows. "Francis must be allergic to the same thing. Looks like the devil himself this morning."

She could cheerfully have kicked him.

And now, with conversation to Paulo consisting of a screaming match to be heard over his portable radio, she lay limply on the airplane and tried to decide between dying and finding the energy to yell one more time.

Paulo was only fourteen. In all fairness he'd worked like a trouper helping her get the hydraulic jacks into place beneath the nose of the plane. Between the two of them and a tractor, they'd gotten the bomber's nose propped up on two fifty-five-gallon drums and a cross tie. One propeller was already on, and she hoped to have the second on by noon.

Outside, Candido Malta's sentries paraded haughtily up and down the road, but during the afternoon rains their habit was to migrate en masse to the jeeps to guzzle Cokes. The first time she'd driven onto the airstrip, she'd felt as if she were crossing a picket line. Not once had they bothered her, though, which surprised her; she'd expected harassment, at the very least.

"Where'd you go, Paulo?" she finally yelled over Mick Jagger. Paulo had wheeled off the portable scaffolding and left her stranded atop the engine. "I'm ready to get down."

She laid her throbbing head on her arms while she waited. Damn Francis. Why was he so hung up on the age thing, the father-daughter thing, that it never occurred to him that she could love him no matter how old he was or who he was or what he looked like, simply because he was worth loving more than any man she'd ever known? Sometimes he made her feel as if *she* were the older one and he was a kid.

She was tired of waiting. "Paulo!"

"Comin', *señorita*," the boy bellowed.

At least it was rock and roll, Deidre consoled herself as she dourly gathered up her tools in both hands.

When Paulo came shuffling up in perfect time to the music, never missing a beat as he pushed the scaffolding in front of him like a clumsy four-footed dancing partner, he peered up from beneath a shock of slack black hair. Deidre prepared to shinny down on her stomach so she would drop onto the sheet of plywood mounted on the scaffold.

"Another couple of days like this," she told him without looking around, "and we'll have this monster in the air."

"*¿Qué?*"

"I said . . ." Here she was, screaming again. "Forget it, Paulo."

Reaching with her toes for the plywood, Deidre found it, dropped the wrenches into the tool box and stood on her toes for the end of a bright orange cable that was draped over the nacelle. She pulled it down.

Before she could turn, the rollers abruptly swept her away from the plane. Tools clattered across the cement floor in all directions.

"Hey!" she cried as the radio went instantly silent, and she clung to the rails for dear life. "What're you—"

Her words trailed off to a feeble whisper as she spied Paulo a distance away with an uncertain grin on his face. Twisting, she found Francis bringing the rollaway to a stop with one booted toe.

"...doing?" She trailed off on a deflated sigh as she took note of Francis's scowl. Had his expression been a double-barrelled shotgun, it would have had her picking buckshot out of her behind for a week. "Oh-boy-oh-boy."

"My sentiments exactly," Francis said with a satyr's smile as he tipped back his head. "I want you to know, my precious, that I hate doing this as much as you do."

Her perch above him didn't diminish the illusion of his size in the slightest. If anything he was taller and his shoulders spanned a greater width. Even his tan seemed darker and the angles of his cheekbones more dangerous.

His jeans were starched and creased today, his white shirt was spotless, and his sleeves were rolled up crisply to the middle of his forearms. But he hadn't shaved, and there was a suspicious red cast to his eyes that hinted at an overdose of potent Irish whisky.

"You don't know the first thing about hate, Francis MacIntire," she snapped.

"Probably not." He tapped his boot impatiently. "Are you going to stay up there all day?"

She glanced down at her soiled jeans and the now greasy shirt she'd borrowed from Joaquim. Not once had Francis seen her looking pretty, and she could be pretty, dadgummit; she could be lovely and hold her own, given the right circumstances.

"Well, are you?"

"It depends," she said, feeling like a bag lady.

"You sound as if you're catching a cold."

"I'm fine. Really, fine."

"Then perhaps you should come down before you catch one," he murmured more suggestively.

Oh, no, Deidre promised herself. Not this time. She absolutely would not let him wheedle her into being congenial and sweet. He always did that, and she ended up forgiving him all his antiquated ideas, and nothing ever got settled.

"Francis," she began and carefully moistened her lips, "about what we..."

"What we what?" he prompted.

She turned up a palm. "Well, what I'm trying to say is..." She felt as if she were that rattled stranger standing out in the road again, unable to remember. She moved her palm in another direction, as if to take a fresh attack. "Have you...uh..."

He flashed his teeth at her and made Deidre feel so much worse that she wanted to lean down and grab a handful of his curls and pull them out by the roots. Instead, she tried to imitate his smile and failed.

She said bleakly, "I suppose you enjoyed Shostakovich?"

His brows snapped down. "What?"

"Your evening out. Surely you haven't forgotten it so soon."

He squinted. "The second violins were out of tune."

This conversation wasn't going to end well at all. Deidre turned down the corners of her mouth in a threatening way.

"And the brass section was horrendous," he added cheerfully.

Deidre slammed her foot hotly on the plywood, and the scaffold rattled while several more wrenches went scuttling to the floor. "Well, wonderful, Francis! That's just wonderful! Peachy-keen wonderful!"

Laughing, he gave the scaffold a jerk, and Deidre, blistering with anger, gripped the metal bars until her knuckles turned white. Closing her eyes, she let her shoulders drop. What she should be saying was that he should have known better than to try to do anything without her; he would never enjoy life half as much again unless he shared it with her. Didn't he know that by now?

He took three steps closer until his head was in direct line with the toe of her left sneaker. Without warning, he circled her ankle with a thumb and forefinger and pulled it until she grabbed the rails.

"Don't do that!" she cried.

"Deidre Miles—" his voice was husky with intent "—did anyone ever mention the fact that you have a nasty mean streak running through you?"

One of the first memories of him washed over her with aching sweetness: *Did anyone ever mention the fact that you're a little cross when you first wake up?*

I don't wake up with people.

Indeed.

But she wanted to wake up with him. For the rest of her life. "Almost everyone!" she yelled.

Grinning, Francis called to poor Paulo, who still waited apprehensively by the rollback door of the hangar. "That's all for a while, Paulo. In fact, why don't you take the Rover and head on back to the ranch? Miss Miles and I have a slight business matter to discuss. Hey, and Paulo, don't ride the clutch." To himself, he grumblingly complained, "The damn thing's got to be overhauled again and I just—"

"You stay exactly where you are, Paulo!" Deidre shrilly countered just in time to see the little coward slipping behind the tail of the *Albatross* and disappearing.

Outmaneuvered, Deidre swiped at her face with the back of her hand and pushed away the hair that had sneaked free of the knot twisted high on her crown. She spread her feet like a boxer preparing to get decked.

"All right, Francis MacIntire," she declared, "we're going to have this out, right now. Once and for all."

He chuckled, and Deidre lost a fraction of her hauteur. He stared. She inspected her zipper. "What?" she demanded.

"Nothing, you just have a greasy streak running down your face now. No, that only makes it worse. Never mind, I like it. It brings out the gray of your eyes. Are you going to stay up there all day?"

"Yes, damn it!"

"Stop swearing."

"I'll say anything I damn well please, Francis! Do you know something? You just can't go around telling people what they can do with their lives. There just happen to be a few people in this world who don't depend on you for every breath they draw. And they enjoy making their own decisions, thank you, even if they're wrong. Frankly, Francis, it's a mystery to me how you've lived to be so old and haven't learned anything."

No sooner was the word *old* out of her mouth than an evil gleam flashed in his expression and the scaffolding whipped wildly around the cement expanse like a whirling chair she'd once ridden at a state fair.

"Stop it, Francis!" she yelped. "I mean it."

Anchoring his long legs, he brought the thing to a screeching halt, and when he threw back his head he looked exactly like what he was—a mature man who has played the game long enough. He knew what he wanted, and he wanted her. This time, Deidre knew he didn't intend to let anything stand in his way, not even his own rules.

"Get down," he ordered in a low, rough voice.

"I'm not one of your peasants who thinks you're God."

"Get down, or by heaven I'll drag you down."

Deidre felt ridiculously like an ill-tempered child going from room to room, slamming doors and kicking carpets. He was the strongest man she'd ever known. She wanted him madly.

When he held up his hands and took hold of her own, she didn't dare refuse him. Trembling, she let him slide his hands beneath her arms and swing her down. When she was clasped fiercely against the length of him, she wrapped her arms about his neck and closed her eyes.

"I hated you," she confessed against the strength of his jaw.

"I know," he said and kept her tight against him, not allowing her toes to touch the floor. "I know."

"But where will this end up?"

"Only where we want it to."

No, it would not. She wanted to be his wife. "That's no answer."

The guttural protest was deep in his throat even as he tightened his arms and dipped his mouth hungrily for hers. He kissed as if he could never get enough of her taste, then finally, when they could hardly speak, he lifted his head to say, "I can give you my love, Deidre, and my life. But don't ask me for tomorrow. It's the one thing I don't have to give."

But love, to Deidre, was inseparable from tomorrow, and the kiss, when he took it from her again, couldn't help but be one of those half angry, half desperate kisses that had no future.

Francis truly welcomed the hurt of Deidre's hands reaching for his hair. The keen pain she brought him as she tightened her fingers made him more needful of her than ever. He kissed her endlessly, but the more they searched for satisfaction with their mouths, the more insatiable was the need.

He lifted her beneath her hips and started walking, refusing to relinquish her mouth long enough for her feet to move and her eyes to see.

Deidre realized that he meant to have her here, in this place, now. But she was too aware of the men outside—Candido's men, his own men. Any one of the sentries could trespass and spy. His own men could feel driven to interrupt.

The taste of Francis was like a drug, but she fought herself free with heavy arms and clumsy, pushing hands. "No," she choked as she dragged her mouth from his. "This is crazy. You can't do this here."

He stepped behind a partition of tin where parts and electrical equipment were stored. Here, the dusty mellow light hung like lace curtains across the morning, and the air was musty and close. Lowering her slowly so she could find her footing, he released her and stepped back, passing his hand over his face as if he were trying to clear his head of desire.

Deidre's own desire heightened as he sought to capture her eyes in a mesh. "We have to," he said simply.

"But I have to know about tomorrow."

"Why? I won't stop loving you. Ever. Is that what you need to hear?"

Deidre covered her face with her hands. A dozen times she'd imagined herself saying this, yet now that the time was right, it felt wrong. "I think I need to hear..." she heaved a sigh "...a proposal of marriage, Francis."

The silence took root until their minds filled with the sounds outside, the men's voices and their occasional shouts.

Gently Francis pulled her hands from her face and stood watching her clasp them in front of her waist in a pose of despair. Only a moment ago they had been one person. Now they were two again, and they were far apart.

"And I—" he measured his words carefully "—in another time, would never have dared touch you in this way without marriage."

"A different age, Francis."

"No. People don't change that much."

"But you're managing quite well, aren't you?"

Deidre despised herself for that. Her anger deepened, as did her love, because she knew why he would not ask her to marry him, and that was what she loved most in him. He wasn't like any other man in her life. He could not be bought or sold. He could not be broken.

But they had both come to the end of something invisible. She thought she was as tired of her own history as he was of his. Swallowing, she gazed unhappily up at him.

"I didn't know I was such an old-fashioned girl, Francis," she whispered and began, with shaking fingers, to unbutton the shirt she wore.

Francis felt as if someone had hit him between the eyes as he watched her slip the buttons, one by one, from their holes. For one brief second she flicked a look at the window high above their heads, and he wanted to tell her that she had nothing to fear from the men outside, but he didn't know if words would come to his lips.

Her breasts, when she discarded the shirt and stood in just her jeans and shoes, were as he remembered—small and full, pebbly tipped and very white, and they quivered as she stood watching him with dazed wonder.

Smiling, he slowly pulled the tails of his own shirt free, but he wasn't as graceful with the buttons as she. It seemed forever until his shirt lay in the dusty clutter with her own.

She stared at his chest and the sprinkle of black and gray curls. She tried to smile but couldn't. When he reached for the button of his jeans, she mirrored his move. He slipped the button free, and she followed suit. As he unzipped the zipper, she did the same until, with his pants loose about his middle and her own having slipped low beneath her navel, he growled, "To hell with this."

They were encapsulated in deep shadows as he grasped her by the hand and pulled her deeper into a niche of stacked boxes where the air was hot. Quickly he stripped the jeans off her legs. He thought she took off her own panties, but he wasn't sure, knowing only that she refused to wait until he was undressed before she leaned back against the wall and pulled him against her.

There wasn't even a place to make her comfortable, and for that he apologized with a wretched groan as he got his clothes loose enough to touch her burning flesh with his. Ablaze with urgency, his mouth found her throat and her sweet cheekbones and the shell of her ear and her mouth again as she slipped her hand between them and closed her hand about him.

Oh, God! Her hands were cool, and he was on fire. "It was all my fault," he whispered thickly as he kissed her and tried to touch her everywhere at once. "I thought I could stop this from happening, then I thought I could make it happen slower."

"Keep what from happening?" she asked in a voice that didn't want to know.

Through his glazed desire he stared down at her. "I want you to stay here with me, Deidre. I don't have the right to ask. I don't know what's going to happen. I don't know what's going to happen to this country. I don't know anything. I just don't want you to go home."

Deidre felt the little stitch of fear that exposing herself always brought. She was afraid that if she spoke any more he would know the speeches she had concocted in her mind. She felt tears stinging her eyes.

"It doesn't matter," she whispered and averted her face, tears drizzling down her cheeks. "I love you, Francis."

Francis laid his hand on her waist as he took her lips swiftly in a kiss. He glided between her legs, and she instinctively tightened against him, but he coaxed her with his mouth, showing her gently what he intended, then mirroring it with his touch, knowing intuitively where to stroke, where to press.

She did not resist his caress now but found a place for her foot and, bracing herself, arched into his touch, placing her hands on his hips and drawing him to meet her halfway.

He entered her with one stroke that slammed her against the wall. Immediately he regretted it, but she refused him the time or the luxury; with her eyes closed and her concentration fiercely fixed on what they were doing, she moved with him and against him.

It was the nature of such encounters to be a search, and they were both searchers. Deidre guessed that they tried to learn as much for each other as for themselves. Francis was the same kind of man in his love as he was in his life—bold, brash, taking hold of things and making them work with the force of his drive and energy. There were moments when she thought she must do something, but she could only cling tightly to his arms, to his shoulders and his back. She felt his flexing muscles and the fullness inside her, and she felt the cessation of aloneness, the satisfaction of being "part of" that made her wish it would not end.

But she did not go into the paroxysms of blind release that she knew he would want. As he drove to his man's finish, she felt him protesting.

"Tell me." He grated the words in her ear as he struggled to hold back. "Teach me what you want."

"Just do it," she gasped and took everything he could give. "Please."

He did, and when the moment was over and the despair of his embrace began slowly to lessen, Deidre dropped her head into the curve of his neck and prayed he would not speak.

Inevitably his raspy, love-hoarsened whisper grated at her ear. "Deidre, I want more from you than that."

He was still joined to her. She basked in the sweetness of knowing that. "I love you. I don't want more."

"Yes."

"No."

"Damn it." His lips grazed her cheek and found the corner of her eye and kissed her lashes. "It's not right."

"Shh. Lean against me. I love your weight. No, don't leave me."

"I feel terrible."

"And don't look at me like that. To answer your questions, yes, I can do it. The first times are throwaways, Francis—you know that."

"Such vast experience you have, my dear."

"Will you stop that?"

"Tonight? In a bed?"

"I don't feel right in the same house with your mother."

"It's my house. It's my bed."

"I'll wait for you."

"I want to marry you, Deidre."

It was the irony of humankind to want what it could not have and to lose interest in what came easily. Not that Francis's proposal had come all that easily, but there was a vast difference in getting something because one asked for it and getting it because it was inconceivable that it could be withheld.

Deidre knew that Cinderella would not have gotten a proposal the way she had, and she wanted to laugh at her old-fashioned ideas. But they weren't funny somehow. And it wasn't as if Francis had been right in holding out and had now shown her that marriage wasn't necessarily the answer to what she wanted.

Then, what was? Was doing what was best for the other the most important thing? And knowing that the best wasn't necessarily the ability to reach out and know that the other would always be there physically?

She felt lost, purposeless, when she should have been exultant. She wondered if he wanted an immediate answer, and she also wondered why she didn't say, "Yes, yes. When?"

He drove her back to the ranch in a pickup, and Deidre mistrusted herself as she leaned her head against the seat and tried to imagine living out her days in a country other than the United States. When he pulled into the garage and parked, walking around to open her door, he braced both gloved hands on the opening and leaned inside.

"You surely are taking a long time in giving me an answer, my love," he softly accused as he found her face and brushed a feathery kiss across her lips. "You're not thinking about giving me the old one-two, are you?"

In his eyes, Deidre could see her own reflection. She felt less sure of herself than ever. "The old one-two," she lightly scoffed and kissed him back. "You know my answer already, jungle man."

Smiling, he placed another lazy kiss upon her mouth. The passion had not died between them as much as she thought—the coals had only been banked. Groaning softly, he pushed her back in the seat and stretched himself on top so that he lay between her gently splayed legs.

"How do you do this to me?" he asked, and his breath came raggedly when she lifted herself to move against him. "I'm a sane man, don't you know? I don't make moves on women in garages."

"That's not sanity, you stubborn Irishman," she teased as her heart began its race with time. "That's plain old male egotism."

Positioning his weight so that he could watch his own hands, he pulled off his gloves with his teeth and dropped them to the floorboard. He watched his finger poking between the buttons of her shirt and grazing the space between her breasts.

He smiled. "Are you punishing me?"

"For what?"

"Because of what I said before. About not wanting to fall in love with you."

"Why did you ask me to marry you?"

"Because I fell in love with you."

"And it's that simple?"

"It was until two seconds ago. Why haven't you said yes?"

"That's not the point. Do you get everything you want to?"

"Damn it, Deidre."

Deidre slipped her own hands beneath the waist of his jeans and over the hard, muscular hips. Her fingers found a ragged scar. "How did you get that?" she quizzed.

"In an A-26 in Korea. Don't hide behind words. Answer my question."

"I want to know all about it."

"About the scar? We have the rest of our lives."

"Do we really, Francis?"

When he dragged her shirt from between them, Deidre was painfully aware of their proximity to the house. She resisted him in silence, fighting the rising warmth of her own body. He knew her now, and he knew how to use her body against her and was doing it.

She floated out into space and grew slippery with heat. He was pressing against her, crushing her, and his face was blurring in her vision. She lifted her arms behind her head, found the handle to his door and closed her hands upon it. He lowered his head slowly and took her breast into his mouth. His teeth sent shivers chasing down her spine.

"I want to make you come," he whispered thickly.

The words both excited and alarmed her. She shook her head. "I can't. Not here."

"No one would see us." He was claiming her with his mouth and his hands. He found her silkily wet beneath her clothes.

Deidre moaned softly and placed her hand tenderly upon his hair. "Yes they would."

Sighing, he rose onto his elbows and gazed down at her with the flush of frustration. For some moments he waited for his breathing to level off, and when it finally did he closed her shirt and said, "I once saw a movie with Gary Cooper where he fell in love with his daughter's roommate."

Deidre smiled unhappily. "And now, I suppose, you're going to make some point about our ages again."

"People mistook him for her father, Deidre. In the end, they stopped seeing each other."

He slid off the seat and took several steps toward one of the other parked vehicles. Buttoning her shirt, Deidre followed him and looked enthusiastically around the garage. It was more organized than many people's houses.

"As I recall, Francis," she said, "Gary Cooper was the one who ended it, not her. He drank himself to death."

"That's not the point."

"Then what is the point? Do you want to take back your proposal?"

He swore a terrible oath, and the sound of it exploded in Deidre's ears. He straightened. He brought his fist up to his mouth and made a whistling sound through it.

"I didn't say that to be difficult, honestly," she said glumly as she moved up behind him and wrapped her arms around his waist. She laid her cheek against the firmness of his back.

When her arms came around him and held him, as if asking forgiveness for things she didn't understand, Francis reached behind him and pulled her so close that her breasts melded to his back. Of all the things they had done together this day, this one moment was the most intimate of all, going deeper than he had been able to penetrate her, uniting them more totally than any physical coupling or any pronouncement of marriage. The light pressure of her lips against his spine, the fragile brush of her hair, her legs straining against his—he would do anything to preserve this moment.

But as the sound of an approaching car jarred him to his senses, he stiffened and looked back. Anger spread swiftly over him. Without a word, she felt it, and she intuitively mirrored his movement and followed the direction of his look.

Together they watched as a tall, distinguished, graying gentleman of fifty-plus years climbed out of a chauffeured Mercedes.

"Who is it?" she whispered, stepping away from him.

But not soon enough, Francis thought belatedly, for the passenger to miss seeing them. He had walked around the front of the car and glanced quite naturally to the open garage before him.

A less mannered man might have said something, but the visitor drew himself as erect as a prince and, with his head held at a regal angle, walked away from the scene toward the wide front steps of the house.

"You mean you don't know?" Francis asked her.

Deidre stared a moment longer and squinted, tilting her head to the side like a child trying to decipher a word it should know.

"It's your father, Deidre," Francis told her grimly. "And now, God help us, he knows."

Chapter Nine

He's in love with her, Cleary."

"Mavis, you're jumping to conclusions."

"Then how do you explain all that's been going on ever since Francis brought Deidre Miles into this house? Tell me that. You said yourself that the quarrel they had was completely out of character for Francis. I haven't forgotten his temper in the past, but I haven't known our son to lose control of himself like that since Mary Beth died."

"Maybe it's better that he did. Francis carries too many burdens, Mave. God knows, I'm one of them."

"Now, don't start that."

"I'm not starting anything. I just say a man has to let go sometimes."

"Don't you tell me about my own son, Cleary MacIntire. I know that man better than any human alive, and I'm telling you that he's about to do something very stupid, if not dangerous."

"Love gets stupid sometimes. Look what happened to me when I fell in love with you."

"Don't change the subject. You know, of all the surprises today, Jonathan was the real one. I don't believe I remember when the man wasn't eloquent, but today he could hardly put two words together. He just sat there like a zombie. And I sat there, and you sat there, and Francis looked as if he could spring up and knock down a wall."

"Oh, I don't know, Mave. I thought the meeting went pretty well."

"That's because you have the sensitivity of an Irishman, Cleary MacIntire. Why, when Jonathan put his arms around Deidre, I thought the child would faint. Did you see the looks that passed between Francis and her? Every time anyone said a word it was as if they had to consult with each other. And Jonathan—crossing and uncrossing his legs, and Francis pacing back and forth like a caged tiger when Jonathan suggested pulling strings with the president and getting Deidre flown out of the country. I haven't seen Francis so defensive since we lived on Berry Street, and that's the truth. And when Deidre spilled her tea—goodness, Cleary, the least you could have done was let it pass. Instead you try to clean it up yourself."

"It gave everyone something to do besides let their imagination run wild, honey."

"Was it my imagination that Jonathan kept referring to old favors and how a man is beholden to his past? You know what he was talking about. I'm telling you, Jonathan suspects that our son has designs on his daughter."

"You talk as if they were fresh out of high school. And besides, you don't know that."

"Cleary, sometimes I can't believe you."

"And what if he has designs?"

"She's twenty years younger than he is, Cleary."

"Young man's slave, old man's sweetheart."

"You say that because every man, deep down in his heart, wants to go out and find himself a young darling in the hope that he'll stay young forever."

"Mavis, honey, I love you. You're a knockout of a woman and always have been."

"I am not. I'm old."

"Of course you're old. I'm old. But sometimes you're dumb, Mavis. Did it ever occur to you that Francis wants Deidre because she's nice? And she's smart? She's interested in something more than her fingernails?"

"There's no talking to you, Cleary MacIntire."

"Let's face it, Mother, what's really troubling you is not whether Francis is getting himself involved with a young woman but whether we're going to have to leave this place."

"I don't need to hear that."

"It won't be the first time you had to accept something you didn't want, honey. You didn't want to come here when Francis first invited us, if you remember."

"I remember perfectly well. Oh, it's so uncalled for. It's so fixable. If Francis and Cidinha would only—"

"Mavis, wars aren't fixable. Now, I love you, and I respect your opinions, but Francis and Cidinha Araujo are none of your business. You leave it alone, do you hear me?"

"Cidinha's always loved him. She's a good woman. She's an intelligent woman."

"That is not the point."

"Then what is? It makes as much sense for Francis to accept kindness from a woman who loves him as it does to refuse everything because of pride. Or lose his head over a woman half his age. Why doesn't he take a look at Jonathan and realize how hopeless it is?"

"I'm sure Francis has faced the pros and cons in his own mind."

"Do you know what I heard him saying when he was picking up the broken pieces of her cup?"

"You shouldn't have been listening."

"He said, 'I want my answer.' He's meeting her, Cleary. In this very house."

"It's his house."

"Don't give me that. You know perfectly well what I mean. It's not fair. It's just not fair."

"It wasn't fair for me to fall off a roof when I was thirty, Mother. It's not fair that Francis has had to carry a cripple all these years and have no life of his own—even worse, to have no privacy, no freedom. No, it's damn well not fair—"

"Hush, hush, now, my darling. I'm sorry. No, don't do that. It's all my fault. Me and my mouth. Never once has Francis begrudged you anything, my sweet, darling man. Why, you've carried your weight and spared him all that tedious book work that he despises so. You've given him more freedom than you've ever taken away, Cleary MacIntire. You're a source of strength to this family, and I don't want to hear any more of that talk."

"I'm an old fool, Mavis."

"And you're married to an old fool."

"What do you suppose two old fools ought to do at eleven o'clock at night?"

"Go to bed and try not to worry about tomorrow."

"Then it's settled."

"Let me take off your shoes."

"I hate for you to have to take my shoes off every night."

"And you can't possibly know how sad I would be if I didn't have you here to take them off of. I get scared, Cleary."

"Of dying?"

"Don't you get scared?"

"No."

"There. Button your pajama top and let me help you onto the bed."

"Are you ready for the lights to go out?"

"Yes."

"Goodnight, Mother."

"Goodnight, Cleary. Cleary?"

"What?"

"Do you think that they've done it?"

"Who?"

"Francis and Deidre Miles, of course."

"Done what?"

"Oh, Cleary, you know."

"Go to sleep, Mavis. Try to remember how it was with us when we were first in love."

"Oh, Lord, Cleary. Why did you have to say a thing like that?"

Lying on her back in the darkness, it seemed impossible to Deidre that she had slept. After the appalling scene with her father, she would have said that she would never sleep again the rest of her life.

There was no forgiveness in her heart for Jonathan. He'd known she was following him up the walk, but he'd refused to stop or look back. And now she lay in the dark womb of the night, shivering, feeling as if she were still plunging toward it—that thing she'd done wrong but didn't know what it was. She had failed some crucial test.

She sat up in the darkness. Where was Francis? He hadn't been immune to Jonathan's dignified martyrdom, either. If Jonathan had simply burst out in a rage and yelled at him, "What do you mean, playing fast and loose with my daughter, you damn fool!" it would have been cleansing.

Everyone could have gotten in their licks and come away feeling better.

But to so pointedly ignore it, to insult her by giving her no chance to rage back and throw Lily in his face, to treat her like a child, was unconscionable.

The silence of the room was a wasteland. She sat very still and listened for the step outside that would herald Francis's coming. She began to count the seconds until they grew interminable.

After a time—it couldn't have been more than two or three minutes, at most—she rose and stood before the window. She inhaled the fragrance of flowers and the smell of the wax on the cool floor. What now?

She slipped into her jeans and pulled on a shirt. She listed reasons for not going to search for Francis, but the door had an irresistible power to draw her, and she moved soundlessly toward it, opened it and stepped through it into the dark corridor.

Every floorboard announced her the moment she placed her foot on it. She went first to Francis's room. She didn't knock but quietly opened the door. The room was empty. The bed had not been slept in. Less certain than ever, she shut it.

The floors seemed to groan beneath the weight of her steps as she moved along the corridor, and she wouldn't have been surprised had the whole house come crashing furiously down upon her head so that everyone knew her disgrace.

As she reached the living room, not so much as a nightlight had been left on. The pieces of furniture were unfamiliar landmarks as she carefully threaded her way past them. Once she was out on the veranda, she heard a baby wailing softly for its mother. Then she heard voices, men's voices, and she recognized one of them as Francis's.

One of the stable doors was widely ajar, and the light streamed out in a golden shaft that attracted huge, fluttery moths and fretting insects. With a sudden twitch of her nerves, Deidre slipped into a splash of shadow and held her breath.

"I'm through begging you," she heard Francis say with a thick weariness in his voice that broke her heart. "You're a grown man. I can't force you to listen."

"Then maybe you'll listen to *me*, for once," the other man replied.

"Sean, I heard you before you even spoke. Do you think I'm some kind of monster that I do not know you? You're my son."

Sean! Deidre knew she shouldn't be hearing this. She should return to her room. In due time, Francis would come.

"Must you be so stubborn, then?" Sean insisted. "Is it a matter of ego? Must you be dragged down simply because you can't admit that you put your trust in a man who could betray his own people? Rob them? Murder them?"

"You never knew the Francisco I knew," Francis said.

"Ah! So you admit that he's changed."

"We all change, Sean. Even you've changed."

"The president is a dead man."

"Stop it!"

"There're men out there right now who would stop at nothing to free this country of the tyrant."

"Francisco isn't a tyrant."

"He's worse. He's a seducer."

"Are you one of the men who would kill him?"

"Don't be ridiculous."

"Who, then?"

A long, desperate silence filled the night, during which Deidre could hear the mad sawing of the insects and the fearful pounding of her own heart.

"Don't do it to me, Father," Sean snarled. "Don't try to pump me."

"And don't you talk to me as if I were an idiot. Who do you think you are that you can league yourself with those outside the law? You want to get rid of Francisco? Elect a new president."

"Oh, that's been tried so many times it's ridiculous. You know how the man operates. By fear, by bribery."

"So now you turn to murder?"

"I save lives; I don't take them."

Even from where Deidre waited, shivering in the shadows, she could feel the intensity of the son's fury for the father. Not even her love for Francis could bear the pain of such a conversation. She lifted her chin in preparation to walk away.

"I can't talk to you," came the sullen mumble, followed by a scrape of furniture.

"That's a shortcoming of fathers," Francis said. "We make bad listeners when our sons are about to get themselves killed. You're a fool, Sean."

"I was born of a fool, Father."

Stopping her ears to such pain, Deidre hurried through the darkness, but behind her she could hear the crunch of footsteps. Walking swiftly, she ducked behind the first tall shrub she came to.

When the footsteps passed she hurried to the veranda on the opposite side of the house from her own, the one near the servants' bungalows. Reaching it, she slumped against the wall to catch her breath. If she were caught here, eavesdropping, they really would believe she was working for the CIA!

For ten minutes she waited, standing so still the insects forgot about her. The darkness here was made thicker by heavy masses of shrubbery. When she moved on, she had to feel her way. Finally she reached the bottom step of the veranda and placed her foot upon it.

A rough hand came down heavily on her shoulder. In disbelief, she found herself caught in a man's violent embrace.

"Oh, no!" she gasped.

She was spun around so that one of his hands caught both of her own behind her back. Deidre didn't have time to scream as she was crushed in his arms and his mouth closed hotly upon her own.

She guessed she writhed more than she fought. But fighting was difficult when a person couldn't breathe and her bare feet were lifted off the ground. His free hand had threaded through her hair and closed about her neck. His chest was a span of straining, rigid bands, and his breath tasted strongly of brandy. He wasn't a large man—not as tall as Francis and more slender—but he was powerfully constructed, and his body, pressed tightly against her own, was as hard as iron.

When she finally had the presence of mind to go limp in his arms, the same hand that had imprisoned her head found its way across her shoulders and skimmed the length of her spine to rest upon her hip.

Moaning softly, Deidre shook her head and haphazardly kicked at his legs with a bare foot. As suddenly as he had grabbed her, he released her. His hands jerked back as if they'd been burned.

"My God!" he said aloud and took such a quick step back that Deidre toppled onto him.

Groaning, she put up both her hands and looked up to see the sleek black beard, the flash of pearl-like teeth. It was Sean. "Please..."

As her trembling registered upon his shocked brain, he stood her swiftly upon her feet. "Hey, I am sorry. I mean, my Lord, lady, I mistook you for someone else. I'm so sorry."

"Oh, dear..." Deidre stood hugging herself, looking at the ground, at the railing of the veranda, then at his heartfelt shock. She swallowed. "It's all right. I mean, there're no hard feelings."

"Speak for yourself," he said with a short laugh, and then grew penitent and grave. "Sorry. Really. I feel like a first-class jerk. Please, accept my most profound apologies so I won't have to run out and commit hara-kiri on my sword or something."

Deidre's laughter was too weak to be heard.

He grasped her by both shoulders and gave her a little shake. "Are you okay? You are okay, aren't you? Please say you're okay. Shall I lie down here in the grass? You can grind your heel in my temple so I'll carry the scar forever. You can kick me in the thorax so I'll never be able to speak again."

Bubbling over with giggles, Deidre gasped helplessly. "Will you stop it? It's okay. You're forgiven. Absolved. Completely."

"I knew you'd see it my way." He smiled sheepishly. "Say, who are you, anyway? You must be one of the new girls. Believe me, I'd remember if we had met. Speaking of meeting, allow me to introduce myself."

His dark, wicked eyes danced as he bowed low. He grasped her hand and placed a kiss on it. "I'm Sean Mac-Intire. Fleet of foot and quick of brain. At your service, mademoiselle."

"I'm Deidre."

"Deidre what?"

"Miles."

"Well, if you're shaking because you're afraid that the master's son will be making this mistake again, Deidre Miles, don't."

"I'm not afraid of you, Sean MacIntire," she retorted with a jut of her chin.

He laughed. "They didn't warn you about me?"

"Should they have?"

He rubbed a hand along his jaw, then dropped his hands to his side and clicked his heels. "Well, I see I can't trip you up. It's been real nice chatting with you, Deidre Miles. I'll be leaving you here if I can't walk you to your room or become engaged to you or something. I don't suppose you'd consider telling me why you're here at the ranch."

"I delivered a plane to Mr. MacIntire."

The pause throbbed with his mental process of taking the information, examining it and cross-referencing it with the terrible day on the airstrip. "Ah," he said eventually, all teasing gone and a respectful wonder taking its place. "So that was you. I see."

"That doesn't tell me very much." She'd expected him to say that he was the pilot of the Centurion. He didn't.

Lifting a fingertip to his lips, Sean kissed it and gallantly transferred to kiss her lips. "May our next meeting be under much different circumstances, Miss Miles. And on that note, I bid you adieu."

Lingering, as much to regain her equilibrium as anything else, she watched Sean MacIntire saunter off into the darkness toward one of the other buildings.

The air was quite still. She heard his feet crunching softly after she could no longer see him. High above her head a few of the warmest stars were out, but very little moon. Why she stood looking at them for so long was not clear.

Very low, then, and not as faraway as she imagined him to be, she heard Sean say, "You witch, you took your sweet time. I damn near ran off with someone else."

A woman's voice murmured softly in retort, but Deidre couldn't distinguish the words. She heard the soft rasp of a door opening, footsteps, then a low chuckle.

Deidre turned to go, and as she stepped away, the lyrical laughter of a woman reached her ears. Spinning around, she strained to see through the opaque night. Nothing. And no more sounds.

Trembling, Deidre remembered her dream, her night-mare when she had seen the woman's face. The face and the laughter were the same—they were both Isabella's. Was Sean MacIntire sleeping with Francis's secretary? Lord, had they both slept with her?

The light in the stable was gone now. As she drifted in a tide of unreality, Deidre's first thought was that Francis had left while she was being mistaken for a waiting lover—or, worse still, he had seen and misinterpreted.

Anyone with a grain of sense would have returned to her room and leaned against the door in gratitude that no more harm was done. But love had never been known for common sense. After hesitating at the door, Deidre stepped into the stable.

Stalls lined both sides. Near the entrance was an office, or perhaps the tack room. From beneath the door panel shone a pale, muted light. Pushing it open, she moved cautiously through the portal.

At one side, a desk spilled papers and books and telephones. At the other an old stuffed chair was spitting out its insides. Upon its back was draped a new saddle blanket, and over one arm lay two bridles and a pair of chaps.

Francis was seated on a high cobbler's stool beside a wooden bookcase, his back toward her and his legs stretched out before him. The familiar work pants made her smile, but his bush jacket had been replaced with a terry pullover, soft and touchable. Its tail was pulling free of his belt.

Longing rose painfully in her breast. His curls lay so sweetly at the back of his neck, she thought that not to kiss them would break her heart. She considered retreating without speaking, but when his hand lifted and covered his face, when his shoulders bowed with a sorrow so deep that even sound could not express it, she stood motionless.

Presently he sensed that he was not alone. He straightened and made repairs to his composure. When he turned and focused upon her with reddened eyes, she knew he hadn't been expecting her but Sean to be standing there.

"It's late," she whispered. "I came looking."

"Come here," he said with hoarse gratitude and opened his arms.

Slipping into the wedge of his legs, Deidre stood on her toes and circled him with her arms. She drew his head gently into the curve of her neck.

"Let me take the hurt away," she whispered tenderly and cupped her hand about the back of his head.

His only reply was to clasp her fiercely to his body as if he must drain her strength and make it his. "He breaks my heart," he said. "I love him, and he breaks my heart."

"But it's a strong heart," she said as she placed soft, butterfly kisses upon his ear and the frost of his sideburn and his rough, stubbled jaw. "A good heart, Francis. It can take it. It can take anything."

"He's going to get himself killed, you know. Now it's some idealistic game he's playing because he thinks he can make a difference. But war can't tell a hero from a criminal."

"Do you think you can stop that? He's not a little boy anymore, Francis."

"He should use his head."

"Did you, Francis? When it came time for you, did you listen?"

Words were useless, Deidre thought. Right now he was a drowning man, and he was holding on to her as if she were a lifeline. Being needed on such a plane was a new experience—humbling, healing, and though she hadn't consciously thought of it before, she recognized now the vast emptiness of her life. She had no man, no children. She wanted both.

She kissed his temple and teased with sweet sadness, "Anyway, it's the job of the child to do the hurting and the job of the parent to take it. A law of nature, Francis. You can't go against nature."

He laughed mirthlessly. "Don't make any bets on that, babe."

What did he mean by that? Deidre forced a smile to her lips as she smoothed back the damp curls she loved so much. "Is that to say you have no plans to repeat your folly?"

"Repeat it?" He stared into some distant part of himself. "Lord, Deidre, the investments you make in children. The heavy dividends you pay. No, never again. No more for me."

She had unintentionally laid a trap, and he had just as unintentionally sprung it. What had she thought?

Releasing him, she stepped away, but he reeled her back into the nest of his body and locked his ankles around her knees and laced his hands at the small of her back. Smiling, he traced the shape of her eyebrows and the curve of her cheek with his nose.

"Do you know what a miracle you are?" he murmured. "Do you have any idea?"

She was no miracle. She was a woman. She had given herself to him, and part of her was even now reaching for him. He'd said finally that he wanted to marry her, but in her heart she knew that was because marriage was what *she* wanted.

She never learned, not even from the disappointment on Jonathan's face when he'd found them holding each other. You couldn't force people to be what they weren't, and she and Francis weren't of the right decades. They had the wrong obsessions, the wrong philosophies for each other. There would be areas of their lives that neither of them could ever totally share with the other. It broke her heart.

She inched backward to the door, beyond which she heard the silence of two o'clock in the morning. There was no other silence quite like it.

Meeting his eyes, she said with a shake of her head, "It would never have worked anyway, Francis. I would always have loved you more than you loved me."

Deidre supposed she knew that he would follow her. Or perhaps she only prayed he would. With her heart aching, she hurried to her room and rushed inside and shut the door, leaning back against the wall and pressing her hands to her breast because she thought her lungs would burst.

Closer and closer she heard Francis's determined steps, and when the door opened and swept back against the wall, she twirled out into the center of the room and stood there, shivering. He looked ten feet tall as he entered. There was no depressed slump to his shoulders now, no grief in his bowed neck. His feet were anchored ruggedly to the floor, and the thrust of his chin had reclaimed its familiar toughness. His hair was a rough, wild tangle of curls, and his chest rose and fell with the fierceness of a man who has been denied what he thinks is his.

He pushed the door shut behind him. His voice was very low, and the Irish accent of his forefathers was in the curl of his tongue. "I find a wee flaw in yer reasoning, lass, and I ha' to tell ye, it pricks at me sorely."

The door had not closed securely, and he turned and kicked it shut with a brutal crash that made the whole house shudder.

She sucked in her breath. "What's wrong with it?"

"I thought we had things settled. This morning I said I wanted to marry you, and you acted as if that's what you wanted, too. You said that was what you wanted."

"Then you thought wrong, Francis."

She could see him puzzling over the day's events, over everything that had happened to them since the beginning. He wet his lips and dragged a hand through his hair. He turned away, then spun back.

"What *do* you want?" she countered in a thin voice.

His Irish brogue was gone now, and he stalked her deeper into the room. "What do I want? Well, we both know I'm the worst sort—one of the lower creatures who lives on the underside of life. What I want, darlin', is what you did not give me before. I want you—all of you this time."

On and on he came. When no more than a dozen inches separated them, Deidre lifted her head with a boldness she didn't feel. When he reached out and curled his hand about her neck and drew her into the wall of his body, she put up her hands to keep him at bay.

He tightened his arms, and in a frustration so savage that it burned her throat, Deidre doubled a fist and swung wildly at him.

"Is that it?" she raged. "You want some... stupid... physical reaction so you can wear it like a medal? Well, let me tell you something, Mr. Macho Irishman, that belongs to me. I belong to me, and I'm not something you take, I'm something I give. I squandered myself for a man once, and I told myself then . . .''

Before she realized it, she hit his chest, then hit him again, over and over, pummeling and pounding until she heard the sound of her own weeping and was horrified, and he was gathering her into his arms, taking her into the center of his heart and was shushing her cries and telling her it was all right.

But it wasn't all right, and she hurt so wretchedly that she wanted to throw up all her grief as she'd thrown up her poor lunch beside the road the first time she'd ever seen him.

"I hated my father today," she wept. "You know all those things I told you at the falls? About how he was nothing except a genetic factor? That's not true. I wanted to kill him for what he did to my mother."

"Sweetheart—"

"He makes everyone believe that he's kind and good, you know, but inside he's vicious and cruel, and I hate him for the way he looked at us. And I hate myself because I didn't have the nerve to tell him he had no right. And I hated you because you didn't tell him that you were proud to have what he'd thrown away. And right this minute I hate myself because I need to hear you say it, and I don't want to have to ask you to say it."

"Ask me what, baby?"

"If all of this matters. If what we feel doesn't count for enough. Can't we make a life together in spite of wars and children and histories and futures? Can't we love each other that much?"

Francis rocked her in his arms, swaying back and forth and kissing her hair and her wet eyes and stroking, caressing away the anger, letting her cry.

Sometimes I feel that if I could just pour it all out, I would be so light that I could fly away."

He sighed heavily, and he could no longer confront the sharp honesty of her stare. He closed his eyes briefly and placed his mouth to her ear.

"Deidre, you've got me turned wrong side out. I can't tell you that you're the first real thing that ever happened to me, because I've made things happen even when they didn't want to. A good woman loved me. She gave me a son. I carved out a life. I made myself a place. But then, just when I think it's all been Solomon's vanity, you come along. You drop right out of heaven, and I look around and see that I didn't have anything to do with it. I'm out of control, Deidre. Things are happening to me, and I can't control them. You're a free gift, my bonnie. I've never been much of a man to trust free gifts."

Detaching herself, Deidre studied him. Very slowly he pulled off his shirt. She chewed her lip as she watched the muscles move beneath the taut, firm flesh of his shoulders. Her heart thundered in her ears.

He took a step toward her, dipped his head. "I'm a man who makes his share of mistakes, my darling, but loving you isn't one of them. I don't know what will happen. I swear to God I don't."

"Francis?" she whimpered as his hand went to her hair, pulling it gently back so that she could not hide from his pillaging eyes.

"I just want you," he whispered as he drew his thumb across her quivering lips. "I don't want anything from you, I just want you."

Francis wondered, even as he swept her up in his arms, how he was supposed to understand the complexities of a woman. He suspected that no man before him had ever understood, and he doubted that any would after him.

Was he ready to make a fool of himself for her? Was he ready to become so vulnerable that he would let her break his heart in a way that Sean would never—not in his whole life—be able to do?

He carried her to the bed, then stood her on her feet. He unzipped her jeans, dragged them off her and flung them into the darkness behind him. Without even bothering to do more than kick at his shoes until they fell haphazardly to the floor, he pushed her back to the pillows.

She lay there with one arm flung back as if she had fainted. He kissed her hands and stroked her face. He wanted her so badly that his body strained against his clothes, and he had to loosen them. He kissed her feet and behind her knees. Her nakedness was white in the darkness, and she had her eyes closed.

He didn't want her eyes closed, and he kissed them until she looked up at him. He captured them and moved lower, lower so that he could kiss her waist, her belly, and he refused her the privilege of turning away. He touched her with his lips, and his fingers, deeply, wanting to do for her what she could do for herself but not the way he could do it.

Deidre knew what he wanted, and he was a skilled and gentle seducer. She felt both ravaged and idolized, raped and adored. The fever burned hotter and hotter. He knew exactly when enough was enough, and then, when he took her on the longest, most arduous journey two people can take together, it was the same selfish act that it always was: two human beings indulging in the search for completion—one plus one equals one. But it didn't matter. She gave him what he wanted so badly, and in doing so took it for herself.

The magic of it was the peace. When the desperation was finally over, in that moment she knew there was nothing she could not tell him. And the knowledge was very, very sweet.

Only later, after he had loved her many times and she was utterly weary, did she admit to herself the one thing she could not tell—that she took no pills or any other precaution to secure her own future. And that she didn't know what she would do if she should ever conceive his child.

Chapter Ten

Jealousy. It came upon Francis with no warning, like ptomaine poisoning or snakebite. In the back of his mind he knew there were names for what he felt as he walked into the solarium for breakfast the next day and saw, with one damning glance, that his son was looking at Deidre with an expression on his face that no man who had ever loved a woman could mistake.

"Can't you find someone besides Deidre?" his mother was asking Sean. "It's such a killing trip. If you're not used to the climate, it can devastate you. And the diseases, Deidre, are terrible up there. Monkeys carry yellow fever, and the mosquitoes carry malaria. Between them and the sand flies that make you itch like poison ivy and the gnats that sting like bees, it can be exceedingly uncomfortable."

Sean straightened from where he'd been leaning over Deidre's shoulder. His body moved with the reluctance of a stubborn machine that doesn't want to go into reverse.

Francis recognized the ritual; any clever boy figured out at the age of fourteen how to peer over a woman so that his jaw brushed her hair, and how to angle his knees so that his groin made a connection with her hip when she began to turn.

He loved them both, yet he wanted to slam Sean against the wall and hit him with an outrage that Juan Geisel, in his wildest dreams, could not imagine. He wanted to shake Deidre until she fainted.

Yet he stood with an equanimity it had taken him thirty years to perfect. He listened to Sean tell his grandmother, "It's a mission of mercy, Nana. I'll give her an injection before we go."

"But her father's having dinner with us tomorrow night. He's bringing a young man from the embassy he wants her to meet."

"She'll be all right. Think of the Indians, Nana."

"Here's your father. Francis, surely there's someone else who could fly Sean up to the Cuna headwater."

Even before Francis looked at his mother presiding so prettily at the silver coffee service, part of his mind made an automatic reconnoiter of the room: Isabella near the window, sipping her coffee and smoking, reserved as usual and looking glamorous and efficient in slacks and dark silk blouse; Luiz systematically checking the covered trays that weighed down the sideboard with smoked salmon, scrambled eggs, fresh mixed fruit and crusty bread. Joaquim was hanging up the telephone extension near the door that gave onto the eastern lawn. Cleary was hunched beneath a lamp near the window, reading an old *Wall Street Journal*.

Deidre. Every time he saw her she was more lovely. Barefoot, like one of the native girls, she stood in a pool of sunlight beside the buffet, wearing an ankle-length peasant skirt he'd never seen before and a soft cotton blouse with a drawstring through the neck so that it draped deeply in the front and back. She had left her hair down so that it billowed about her shoulders in a cloud of glistening waves.

Looking up to see him enter, Deidre all but dropped her plate. Francis saw her try to read his mind. His jealousy made him lock the doors to himself, knowing as he did so that he would hurt her.

"Good morning, Father," Sean said with a flash of smile from behind his handsome beard. "I was just trying to convince Miss Miles that she should fly me up for a quick medical jaunt through Indian territory."

"Was that what you were doing?"

A moment of discomfort throbbed through the solarium. Mavis seemed unaffected as Sean stopped before her coffee table and accepted the fragile china cup she offered him.

"What about Buck?" Francis suggested coldly. "Get him to fly you up."

"Buck's down with a virus," Sean said and looked distractedly at Deidre, smiling. "And he couldn't do it half so pleasantly."

Love had to be a form of insanity, Francis thought. On the outside looking in, it was like watching a drug addict indulging a self-destructive habit, but when it was happening to you, you knew you would take incredible risks for the sake of it. You felt everything except doubt. Love was impossible.

"If it's a good time you're after," he said guardedly to Sean, "I suggest you be more selective in your press-worthy life-style."

From the first moment Francis had walked into the room, Deidre had felt his aching intensity. She wondered if she hadn't felt it even before he entered. Hadn't she sensed it in the floor beneath her feet as he walked down the hall, even though she had not heard him?

She had not told Francis about Sean mistaking her for someone else. It wasn't the kind of thing a person told a lover: Oh, by the way, your son . . .

She knew Sean sensed something in the air, but he had not yet made the connection that it was between herself and his father.

Francis was painfully appealing to her, with his light cotton pants tucked into old leather riding boots. His curls were still damp from his shower, and his thin knit shirt, a dark crimson, was tucked beneath his belt. He could have been a cricket player with his fit, paunchless middle and lean-hipped grace. Or a lumberjack, a cowboy, a builder of fences, a maker of men.

Whatever he was, he was a man of consequence, ready to take on the world. And he was staring at her as if she were an infidel.

"It's all right, Francis," she said quietly, feeling like a wife already as she lowered herself to a chair. "I don't mind flying Sean wherever he wants to go."

Even the lift of Francis's brows seemed to her a criticism.

Sean gave his father a smile and attached himself to the arm of her chair. He leaned over and murmured to her, "I'm incredibly good, Miss Miles. You won't feel a thing. You have my word on it."

Deidre lifted her cup to her lips. The coffee scalded the roof of her mouth. Coughing, spilling some of the hot brew onto her skirt, she waved away Sean's solicitous offers to help.

"I'm fine!" she choked.

Francis wore a pious, it-serves-you-right expression when she looked at him. Deidre could have hurled her cup at his head. But, of course, civilized people didn't do things like that; civilized people carved each other up with a more sophisticated form of cannibalism.

"Well," Mavis was saying with perfect oblivion to the entire incident, "if you're going to fly Sean up north, dear, I'll have to call Jonathan."

"Just when were you planning this little...trip, Sean?" Francis asked murderously.

Sean, looking more like a gaucho than a doctor in his jeans, boots, chaps and a chambray shirt with the sleeves rolled up, thoughtfully scratched his beard. "This morning. Why?"

"I happen to have some business at the headwater," Francis said with a politeness that bordered on bloodletting.

"Ah." Sean smiled a shrewd, knowledgeable smile. "I see."

Francis narrowed his eyes until they were cobalt slits. "I was thinking I might come along."

"Good." Sean lowered his head. "I was just about to invite you. Actually, I wanted to show Deidre the gold fields."

"Those camps are a bit rough for her, don't you think?"

"Oh, I don't know. Deidre's a strong young woman."

Francis flushed. "Youth has nothing to do with it."

"Really? Then perhaps I should have used the word *courageous*."

How had it all gotten so out of hand? To Deidre, the room had been transformed in the space of a few seconds into a torture chamber. Her heartbeat seemed like the ticking of a great clock. Francis was coming away from the wall with blood in his gaze.

She sprang to her feet. Every head in the room turned. She pasted a smile on her face and lifted her shoulders.

"I really don't mind a few mosquitoes," she foundered.
"And, Mrs. MacIntire, tell Daddy—Jonathan, I mean—
let's see...tell him that I'll see him when I return. And...oh,
yes, I think I should start getting ready now, since I don't
know how far it is. There are so many...I'm sure you understand." She stood speechlessly for a long moment, her
face flooded with color. "If you'll excuse me..."

In a strained voice, Francis said, "It's only a hundred and
fifty miles, Deidre. There's no need to be in such a hurry."

"Was I in a hurry?" Deidre felt her cheeks burning
fiercely. "Yes, well..."

"It'll be an overnight trip," Francis added, his mouth
curling downward. "Bring your jammies and everything."

That did it. "Of course," she said with a cold, deadly
smile.

"They have a little hotel up there."

"I understand."

Sean looked at his father. "Shall we say immediately after lunch, then? I can make my rounds with the Indians and
catch a ride on down the river."

A bell sounded. "Shall I get that?" Isabella asked of
Francis.

Nodding, Francis mentioned refueling the Cessna. Deidre was desperate to escape the room. Carrying her chattering cup and saucer to the sideboard, she turned and started
for the door.

Isabella was covering the receiver with her hand. "For
you, Mac."

Francis went to the telephone. Hesitating at the door,
Deidre turned and watched him.

The timbre of his voice had changed, the angle of his big
shoulders. Everyone seemed to be conscious of it. Mavis
stopped talking to Luiz, and even Sean turned to listen.

From where he was wheeling himself across the room, Cleary, too, paused.

"When?" Francis clipped. "How many were hurt?" A pause. "What's the damage?" Another pause. "All right. Get the men organized and ready to leave by car. I'll be flying up within the hour to do what I can while they're driving up. Does the president know? I see. Okay, I'm on my way."

When Francis turned, a dark, angry color had spread over the length of his neck and onto his cheeks. "Your friends, Sean," he said bitterly. "The rebels just blew up the dam at the headwater. I suggest you forget about the gold fields. Half the Indians along the banks will be underwater by nightfall."

The view of the flooded river Tepuí was one of the most destructively spectacular panoramas Deidre had ever seen from the air. As she piloted the small Cessna up the valley where the terrain rolled and rose, climbing to the grandeur of the mountains and falling away to the rice fields, thrusting up in jungle and giving way to humble farmlands cleared by the Indians, she couldn't understand any politics that would destroy it.

During the trip Sean had attempted valiantly to lessen the tension. He was careful not to mention the possibility of civil war. He pointed out things of interest to Deidre that took her breath for beauty. And he looked at his father with the same misery that had to have been on her own face when she'd run after Jonathan.

Francis was morosely withdrawn. Deidre did not see again the fierce emotion she had witnessed from him in the solarium. After she placed Sean safely down on a secluded landing strip over a hundred miles north of the ranch, complete with his backpack and a rifle, she waited awkwardly in the plane.

Walking to the edge of the jungle, Francis shook the hand of a tribal Indian chief resplendent with nose plumes and earlobe disks. *Love your son,* she wanted to call to him. *Put your arms around him before he leaves you.*

But the handshake between them was less warm than that between rancher and tribal chief. In the cold light of day and in the face of such estrangement, Deidre wondered if she had the right to place another barrier between the two men.

She and Francis didn't talk a great deal as she flew him from the Indian camp northward another fifty miles toward the ruptured dam. Francis was on the radio almost continually, having heavy equipment diverted from the highway that was being constructed near the Colombian border.

"If we can erect a breakwater thirty miles south," he told an engineer, "I think we might save some of the rice crops."

When they reached the small village of Sao Costa upriver from the dam, she brought them gently down on a paved landing strip. Darkness was threatening to creep out of the jungle and envelop the little provincial town with its tired main street and its would-be grand hotel of ten rooms. Sao Costa's indolence looked like something out of a Graham Greene novel.

Hardly had she reached the end of the runway when another plane approached. "I think we have company," she told Francis, who glanced up from the maps spread on his lap.

Sighing, he removed his wilted hat and squinted out at the large aircraft circling high and wide. "When it rains," he said dryly.

"Who is it?"

Deidre taxied off the runway, bringing the Cessna to a stop as several of the villagers ran toward them, urgency marking their broad brown faces.

Francis lifted the binoculars he'd been using during their flight over the river. He trained them on the plane as it made its final descent over the treetops.

"Royalty," he succinctly announced.

"Roy who?" Deidre cut the throttles.

"Francisco Araujo," he said with a perturbed pucker of his mouth. "And, unless I'm mistaken, he has the secretary of interior with him."

"Who's that?"

"Cidinha Araujo."

With a sharp, meaningful look that made Deidre feel that she was being thrust into battle without proper orders, he ignored the natives rushing up to the door and closed his hand upon her shoulder.

"Deidre," he said softly as time between them ran out, "whatever you hear about Cidinha and myself—and you're bound to hear something—please don't believe it. We've been friends for a long time. Nothing ever existed between us."

If she hadn't been irrevocably in love with him already, Deidre didn't think she could have accepted the mistakes he kept making with her. How much did she have yet to learn about him?

They shared a moment's silence. A little too circumspectly, she said, "I believe you." Then she narrowed her eyes until they could have penetrated steel. "Like I believe that what passed between you and your son today was the second act of a terrible play."

He huffed a sigh of bafflement. "How in Sam Hill do you expect me to answer a remark like that? Deidre, sweetheart—"

"You look me straight in the eye and say, 'Deidre, I jumped to a silly, stupid conclusion today.' You say, 'Deidre, I behaved like a jerk.' You say, and mean it, 'I will not hurt my son that way again.' "

The doors were being opened, and the Spanish words were intruding into the cabin of the plane. When Francis turned his gaze upon her, Deidre wondered if it would have done her any good to protest that she was feeling the same jealousy he had felt. Cidinha Araujo? One didn't stay in Santiago as long as she had and not learn about the royal affection the secretary of the interior had for Francis MacIntire.

"I didn't want to hurt Sean," Francis was saying with a frankness that made her feel ashamed, "but neither am I blind. He's a charming man, my darling. I should know. Hell, he charms me."

There was something beyond the scope of words that he was telling her, Deidre knew. He smiled, as if he admitted he was being foolish. But his eyes pleaded with her to understand that he couldn't help comparing himself with Sean as a candidate for her affection.

One of the town's officials smiled up at her. *"Señorita?"* His hand stretched upward to help her out of the plane.

Deidre tremblingly took it, but her eyes clung to Francis's.

I love you both, he said without words.

I know.

He's young and beautiful. You're young and beautiful.

Immediately her flight bag was taken out of her hands, as was Francis's. A smiling, bowing young man put it into the back seat of a battered American car.

"Keep close to me," Francis said as they walked from the Cessna back to the airstrip, where they would greet the president of Santiago.

"I don't think I like this," Deidre told him. "I'm not dressed to meet a president."

Her feminine vanity made him smile. "Sweetheart, you're never dressed for anything. An attack by pirates, maybe, or shooting of the rapids. If the cattle stampeded, you'd be dressed for that."

Inside, she smiled, but outside, she assumed a mock irritation. "Shut up, Francis. Isabella's going to take me shopping. The minute we get back I'll blind you with my glory."

"So do it and stop talking about it."

"You have no milk of human kindness, Francis."

Shading his eyes as he peered up at the plane, he chuckled. "Relax. Sao Costa lives in the informal mode."

"Yes, but your hair is curly, Francis. It's different when your hair is curly."

"Darling, it is for your astute powers of observation that I most love you."

They were arguing, Deidre thought happily. Life could go on.

After the larger plane came to a stop, Deidre watched the steps swing to the ground. Ranks of guards, approximately two dozen men, descended them and approached the officials of Sao Costa, who rushed up with much bowing and gesturing. The guards questioned the townspeople, then spoke into two-way radios.

"Just what I like," Deidre murmured from the corner of her mouth. "A trusting president."

"He has no choice."

A new fear needled between Deidre's ribs, and she clutched his arm. "You mean we're not safe? Are they out there?"

"The rebels? Probably. But if I didn't think you were safe—" he gazed abruptly down at her with a tenderness that made the world stop turning ''—you wouldn't be here, my love.''

Dressed in spotless fatigues, Francisco Araujo was as thick as a tree. His mane of hair was the blackest ebony and without a single streak of gray. His face was the color of old wood, and if he had lived in another era, he would have been a conquistador. His short, thick fingers looked very strong. He wore a wristwatch that cost more than everything Deidre owned.

As he descended the steps and stepped forward to shake Francis's hand, Deidre began to perceive what Francis had admired in him. His conversation demonstrated that he was strikingly intelligent, and though he was selfish and indulgent, he cherished a great love for the land. When he smiled at her, Deidre felt the stunning force of his personality.

Finally Araujo turned to the open portal of the plane. In it waited a small, finely boned woman dressed in a two-piece, powder-blue suit. She wore light blue stockings and low-heeled pumps. It was her hair that made her look like a porcelain doll, long and heavy and wound around her head like that of a geisha. Her makeup was tasteful and light. She wore gold-rimmed glasses.

Deidre guessed that to underestimate her, though, would be a terrible mistake. As Francis introduced her to them, she surmised that Cidinha Araujo was probably the strength behind her brother. But good strength, not selfish, for Cidinha had the most open face and honest brown eyes that Deidre could imagine.

''Señorita Miles,'' Cidinha said in perfect, almost unaccented English, ''I have long admired your father. We are so very pleased to have you in our country.''

"It's very beautiful here," Deidre said uneasily and wished, for once, that she looked like Isabella instead of a pilot.

"Yes. We're very distressed about the damage to the dam." The woman glanced at her brother, but Francisco was deep in conversation with Francis.

Not knowing what fine points of protocol might be expected of her, Deidre lifted her shoulders. "It's a waste. But then, I tend to see things too practically."

"Can one be too practical?" the woman asked gently, inviting Deidre's response.

Deidre smiled. "Well, I don't look at every single penny and think, 'This could have gone to feed the poor,' but I do respect the products of human labor, and it took many people many months to build this dam."

"You have a way of going straight to the heart of the matter. Your background, perhaps."

"If you listen to my father."

"He's very proud of you."

"I don't think I inherited a practical head from him, Ms. Secretary. I think I got it from hunger."

Behind the glasses, Cidinha's eyes crinkled with merriment. "That's why we value the presence of Señor MacIntire so highly in our country. Before he offered them alternatives, women of your age with no family turned to prostitution to feed themselves. Our government would not like for Señor MacIntire to feel that he should leave."

Deidre wondered if the woman wished her, Deidre, back in the United States. Was she somehow a threat to Santiago? One that might lure Francis away?

"In the United States," she told Cidinha cautiously, "we hear a lot of gossip about your brother."

Cidinha's smile was sad. "Unfortunately, some of it is true. Francisco is, after all, only a man, and men make mistakes."

"Do you think his mistakes might be his undoing?"

"You mean, will he last out his term?"

"Will he?"

She lifted a hand to her twists of gleaming hair. "I would rather see him leave alive than try to do what cannot be done."

"Of course."

"We heard that you experienced a mishap with the plane you landed at Señor MacIntire's ranch."

What was her point? Deidre wondered.

She moistened her lips, and Cidinha gently prodded her. "My only reason for asking is that I wanted to know if it had been repaired."

"It's flyable," Deidre reluctantly replied. "Of course, cosmetically, there's still a good deal of work to be done."

"I wasn't speaking cosmetically."

The men were walking toward them, and behind her, Deidre sensed a flurry at the plane. She swiftly addressed the older woman. "Might you have use for the plane, Ms. Secretary?"

With a smile of relief, Cidinha inclined her head. "It's possible. I want very much to keep him alive. But I don't want to put anyone, you especially, in an awkward position."

"I understand," Deidre said. Though she didn't understand the entirety of the situation, she knew that Cidinha was sending out a feeler in case her brother should need a quick means of getting out of the country.

"I thought you would," Cidinha said.

"But the plane doesn't belong to me. It belongs to Francis."

"I'm sure that could be worked out." Which meant, in the unspoken language between women, *I know him that well, for you see, I love him, too.* A smile played around her lips as she extended her hand again.

"I think we'll be good friends, Señorita Miles."

Accepting the woman's hand and closing her own around it, Deidre smiled. "I'm sure we will."

But the smile had not faded from Deidre's lips when she glanced up and saw Candido Malta descending the steps of the plane and pausing to speak with the guards. She was sure that he took one look at her and regretted that he hadn't thrown her into jail the moment he'd set eyes on her.

"Señorita Miles," he purred in his good English as he walked toward her and positioned himself, snapping his heels together and formally bending his head. "I regret that we continue to meet under such adverse circumstances."

"I've been wondering who the trouble is following, Captain," she said with brittle courtesy, "you or me."

"Neither, perhaps." His reply was lofty, and he added with malicious amusement, "I understand that Señor MacIntire had a surprise visit from his son. I think *he* must be the culprit."

Deidre's heart slammed shut like a drawer. "How did you know that?"

The captain's smile turned Deidre's blood to ice water. "Don't you realize by now, *señorita*, that I know everything?"

"I think the creep really does know everything," Deidre told Francis later, after the president had seen all he wanted to see of the rebels' violent handiwork and had taken his sister and his guards and his commander of the special task force back to the capitol.

She had just taken a shower and removed the grime of the river valley but not the worry. Francis had changed his clothes and raised Joaquim on the radio back at the ranch. He had come to her room, the best the hotel in Sao Costa had to offer, and now he stood before the second-floor window that was open wide so that darkness and rain misted into the room.

From time to time the black sky was rent with a jagged streak of lightning, and the dim lamps flickered. "He scares me, Francis," she said.

"I told you, he's a barracuda."

"But how could he have known that Sean was at the ranch?" Deidre continued to puzzle. "Sean came in the middle of the night. He went nowhere and was seen by no one except your family and staff, Francis. How could Candido have known that?"

"The jungle has ears," he said tonelessly.

"Maybe someone in your house has ears."

He shook his head. "If I started thinking like that, Deidre, I'd have to give up."

"Well, you'd better start thinking like that, Francis. Something is terribly wrong."

A tap sounded at the flimsy door, and Francis moved to open it. "Just bring it in here, please." He motioned the waiter inside with the huge covered tray. "Set it on the table."

After the waiter laid out the napkins and the silver, the covered platters and two plates that had once been lovely but were now faded and chipped, he uncorked the wine and filled two stemmed glasses. That done, he accepted his tip and left with a deep bow and profuse thanks.

"I think I just found out what was wrong," Francis said as he lifted a cover from one of the platters and smiled unhappily.

Laughing, Deidre moved to his back and tiptoed to look over his shoulder. "It's not that bad."

"You wanna bet?"

Francis made a slow, suspicious inspection of the table, peering at the cold sliced beef and pickled beets, the chunks of boiled potato and the great slices of bread made from cracked grains. He made a face.

Following him, she bravely lifted a piece of potato to her nose, sniffed, popped it into her mouth and lifted her glass. "To...everything," she said and washed down the potato with a gulp.

Smiling, he transferred his slow inspection to her as she stood barefooted on the smooth varnished floor. After her bath, she had slipped on the skirt and blouse again, and, seeing the spark of his interest, she twirled slowly around so that the gathers drifted out in a sensual furling tent.

"What kind of toast is that?" he asked as he felt the familiar pull of desire. "To everything?"

Bending over the table again, she speared a beet with a fork and slipped it whole into her mouth. She chewed it quickly and lifted the glass and threw down another swallow of wine. "What do you want to drink to, then?"

Francis picked up a sliver of meat with his fingers and rolled it in a piece of bread. He took a great bite and began chewing it. The meat was tough. It took him so long that Deidre placed a fist on her hip and teasingly counted off the seconds.

After he got it swallowed, he made a face and drained the glass of wine. Deidre laughed as he sank to one of the chairs as if the ordeal had exhausted him. Then she smilingly took one of the napkins and, fluffing it out, tied up her hair in a turban. He didn't smile as he watched her reach between her legs to catch the tail of the skirt. Drawing it through, she fastened it at her waist in the manner of an earthy peasant serving girl.

Watching him watch her, she refilled his glass with wine. A smile toyed with the edges of her mouth.

"You didn't toast anything," she said, and slid sensually into the chair opposite him.

Over the rim of his glass, Francis grew more and more solemn. He studied her for so long that Deidre forgot about food. She was aware of the wine's warmth, the soft, slow turning of the ceiling fan, the rumble of thunder in the distance.

"Lean over here," he said, and propped an elbow on the table.

Blinking, she focused on him. "Why?"

"Did you know you've got a scar in your eyebrow?"

She fell willingly into the game. "I've also got one—" she craned to peer at the back of her left elbow "—here."

Tossing back the wine, Francis slapped his glass to the table. He bent and kissed the scar, and Deidre guessed, as she lowered her head so that she felt his curls brushing her chin, that at least one of them was getting a little drunk. When he looked up, she quickly took another sip of wine and pushed up his head with a fingertip. She placed a swift kiss on his neck.

"What was that for?"

"The scar on your neck. I just kissed it."

He refused to let her eyes escape. "Is that what we're doing now? Scar-kissing?"

"Is there such a thing?"

"Maybe we're inventing it."

She giggled and shyly tipped her head to her shoulder. "To tell you the truth, Francis, I'm not sure what we're doing."

"Scar-kissing is an old and respected Irish tradition."

"Really?" The game was more involved now. She cut him a sidelong look. "Then how about this one?"

Rising, she attempted to lift her foot and turn up her heel, but she found that her equilibrium was very badly damaged. Laughing at herself, she hopped on one foot to the edge of the bed and tumbled onto it. Then she dragged herself around and took her foot into her lap with an earnestness that Francis found irresistible.

"Here," she said. "I disobeyed my...father." She sighed. "The folly of childhood."

Francis pushed back from the table and walked across the room with a sure-footed precision she had lacked. Dropping down beside her on the bed, he bent over her foot and found the crescent-shaped line on her heel.

"You disobeyed your father and got this?" he asked as if it were a matter of grave import.

Her reply was appropriately solemn. "A tomato juice can."

He released her foot without remembering to kiss it and said, "I can beat that. I've got a pineapple one."

To his dismay, Francis found himself unable to pull off his boot. Deidre happily straddled his leg and turned backward to grip the riding boot while he planted his other foot firmly on her backside. Both of them groaned with the strain until the boots were off.

After peeling off one sock, he danced around on one foot and turned up the sole of the other. "Pineapple."

Laughing, they tumbled onto the bed, but when Deidre bobbed up onto her knees and stooped to kiss his heel, he, too, rose to his knees and caught her with two handfuls of hair.

"Hey, don't kiss my heel," he softly protested.

Her cheeks were flushed adorably, and her lips were soft and sweetly parted. Her turban had slipped free, and her hair was sliding gently down to her shoulders and across one cheek.

She pushed back her hair with a movement so slow and sensual that Francis thought he would break in half. "Why not?" she huskily challenged. "I like your heels. You have very sexy heels, Francis."

The momentum hurtling them forward had little to do with the wine or the dim lights or the rain hissing outside. Francis guessed that this would have happened if they'd been at the Antarctic or on the moon.

"And everything about you, Deidre Miles, is sexy. You have sexy heels and sexy thoughts whirling around in that sexy little head of yours. I like the sexy way the sides of your mouth tremble when you're preparing to make one of your sexy speeches. And the back of your neck . . . God, the back of your neck is so sexy it breaks my heart."

Deidre was stone-cold sober now. His words didn't surprise her. They were much the same as the ones she felt. But things couldn't get out of hand tonight; she'd been irresponsible enough with this man, and heaven would have to work a miracle to keep her from getting pregnant as it was. If that happened, it was over between them; there was no way she would use the corners of life to trap him.

She turned away, but he moved too quickly and snagged her with an arm around her waist.

"Uh-uh." Like a winsome boy, he drew her back into his lap and placed his chin in the hollow of her neck. "Don't leave me."

When he arched into her, Deidre felt the heat of his desire and didn't know if she could resist him or not. She dipped her head. "Francis, you know what will happen."

"You once told me that you'd make the hurt go away."

She smiled at him, then shook her head. "I wasn't talking about that kind of hurt, Francis."

They were like two frightened children, she thought, clinging together in the woods. When he nuzzled her cheek, asking, searching, she could no more have denied him than she could have stopped the rain. She lifted trembling lips to his and brushed them once, twice. A groan came from deep in his chest. He reached for the kiss, claiming it, and a sudden crack of lightning shot across the sky, and the lamp flickered and went out.

Deidre flinched, but not from fear of the storm outside.

"Sweetheart?" He stopped kissing her, and she bent her head until her chin touched her collarbone.

"Do you want me to leave here, Deidre? Would it make things better if I lived in the States?"

She shook her head and remembered all the things the servants had told her. "These people would die without you, Francis."

He laughed mirthlessly. "No one human being is necessary for life."

"What?" She pretended horror, but he didn't smile. "Oh, I could go on living without you, Deidre. It would hardly be worth the effort, but I could."

Dragging her skirt from between them, Deidre twisted in his lap. She locked her legs around his waist frantically, knowing that she was a fool and would always be a fool where he was concerned.

"Hold me," she pleaded. "Don't stop holding me."

He rocked her back and forth in his arms. "Everybody hurts," he mourned, his words grating against her mouth and her cheek, her ear. "Everyone hurts so much, and I can't do anything to stop it. But maybe together...you make me want to keep on fighting. You put life back into me. Just the sight of your smile is worth more to me than all the love in Paradise."

Weeping, Deidre tried once to find his lips, but he was kissing her face all over and wanting to take everything from her. Finally he leaned back to wipe the tears from her face. She kissed his work-worn hands.

"Are you really here in my life, Deidre?" he asked, gruffly near tears himself. "Or am I dreaming?"

Smiling, smoothing back his curls—*You're a fool, Deidre Miles, a fool, fool, fool*—she slid off his lap and pulled him down so that he stretched out beside her. She drew his head to her breast and held him as one would hold a child. She smoothed her hand over the curve of his side, across the planes of his chest and the column of his throat, his face.

"You're not dreaming," she whispered as his hand closed upon her breast.

He took her own hand and placed it upon the aching throb between his legs. "Sweet Deidre, sweet, sweet Deidre. After all these years..."

Knowing what he needed, what he wanted, and knowing that she couldn't stop herself from giving that much, Deidre worked the button of his pants. She couldn't think past this moment. She couldn't think past the need to be held and touched and filled and loved.

She found his lips in the darkness and kissed them. "Maybe you are dreaming," she whispered to herself as the rasp of his zipper was harsh, then silent. "Maybe we both are."

Chapter Eleven

By the time Joaquim reached the airstrip and waited for the Cessna to land, dusk had fallen. The evening was drowsy. The rain had rinsed everything clean, and now the wind was gently drying everything out. All around him, the peasant huts were softly lighted. Cows lowed contentedly from the pastures. Voices echoed across the valley. Far in the distance he heard the faint whine of the Cessna coming home to roost.

Beyond the fence, the sentries posted by Candido Malta stopped their chattering and drew themselves into formation and watched. Joaquim could feel their gloating through the panels of the Land Rover where he sat smoking. They knew, yet he had known for only an hour, himself.

He forced himself to wait a few minutes more as Deidre dropped down to the runway. She taxied neatly into the hangar, then he got out and walked inside. The sounds of the propeller deafened them for a moment, then the interior sounded like a tomb.

"I was about to set out some flares," he said as he reached up for Deidre's hand and helped her out of the cockpit.

Glad to be back, wanting only the comfort of a scalding shower, Deidre scrubbed at her cheeks and laughed. "Francis insisted on seeing all the fields. The president and his sister came."

"Yes, it was on the news." Joaquim smiled.

But his hesitation was a fraction too long, Deidre thought as her feet got a firmer grip on the floor. Something was wrong.

"Is he all right?" Joaquim murmured from between smiling lips, meaning Francis.

Dipping her head, Deidre watched Francis climbing out on the other side. He stretched, then reached wearily for his hat and settled it low on his brow. She was more attuned to his moods than any other human alive.

"Yes, he's fine," she told Joaquim. "Very tired. Worried. What is it? What's wrong?"

"Not here. Stay close to him."

Joaquim's words hit Deidre like a hammer blow. Only hours before she had thought the worst thing that could happen was not to spend the rest of her life with Francis. Now she had a premonition that there might be no life to spend.

The Hispanic took Francis's case and filled his arms with maps. He placed himself between Francis and the surly sentries as they walked outside to the waiting Rover.

On the floorboard behind the front seats were three rifles. "Don't mind me," she said wryly. "I'll sit back here with the arsenal."

Joaquim didn't get into the driver's seat until they were settled, and he didn't speak until pennons of dust streamed out behind them.

"How did you find it up there?" he questioned as he drove.

In order to be heard, Francis nearly had to shout. "The damage was pretty bad. Men are working round the clock, but I expect it's going to take a while. What are the papers saying about it?"

"Mostly that the president should negotiate with the rebels."

"I don't know. I got the idea that Francisco has just about had it."

The look Joaquim exchanged with Francis was too complex for Deidre to understand. Fear? Excitement? Eagerness?

Francis shook his head. When Joaquim whipped to the side of the road and braked until the engine dropped to an idle, he sat examining his hands on the wheel.

"I have to tell you this here," he said, "because I'm afraid that we shouldn't do much talking at the ranch just now."

The dust that drifted around them and sifted into the Rover had the smell of danger. Francis was suddenly as tight as a wire.

"What?" His reply cracked like a whip.

"Don't ask me, Mac." Joaquim shook his handsome head and dropped it to his hands. "I've done nothing but dissect every word, every single thing we did since it happened. I don't have the slightest idea."

"Since *what* happened?" Francis hissed.

Leaning forward, Deidre placed her hand on Francis's shoulder. He reached back to accept her caution, but he kept his eyes riveted to Joaquim. "What happened?"

"Sometime after you left Sean up near the dam, he was captured. We don't know by whom. He's being held in Panama City."

It was, Deidre supposed, the thing that every man of wealth and importance dreads in the "age of assassins," as Francis had so eloquently put it. The hostage, the symptom of human struggle.

Before she or Francis could speak, Joaquim added, "It seemed to me, Mac, that it was rather a second-rate affair, something more petty than political. I don't really think this is directly connected to the rebels. Maybe that means it's not so dangerous. I don't know."

In horror, Deidre watched Francis's callused hands removing his hat and slowly crushing the felt into a ruinous mass. Then, as if possessed by a demon, he asked coldly, "Has a ransom been demanded?"

"No."

"Is he in a jail?"

"I don't think so, though it was inferred that he would be turned over to the authorities safely if you complied with the demands when they came. They said they would give you forty-eight hours. Should I go to Panama, Mac?"

Francis shook his head. "I don't know. Let's see what we have on this end. I want no one told of this. Not even my parents nor Chris nor any of the family. No one is to know anything."

"Francis, you can't keep this from Mavis and Cleary," Deidre told him over the rumble of the engine.

The angles of his face were hard and merciless when he turned his head. She knew that he could be ruthless when something he loved was threatened.

"If there is a leak," he said without a show of emotion, "perhaps we can learn more from the leak than from the source. We carry on."

Remembering, Deidre shook her head. "I can't, Francis. Tomorrow...I told you about that stupid shopping thing with Isabella. I can't do that now, pretending—"

"Do you think Isabella could be telling tales?" Joaquim interrupted with sharp alarm.

Francis pinched the bridge of his nose. "No one knew where we were going to drop Sean except those of us who were at breakfast that morning."

"I can't believe it's Isabella."

Deidre shrugged helplessly. "Maybe it's one of the gardeners. Or one of the maids. Luiz."

It could be anyone. For the first time since she'd come, Deidre slept in Francis's bed that night. She held him when he clung to her and was grateful that he opened his poor, hurt heart enough to let her in. But very early she rose and tiptoed quietly to her room and dressed in the darkness. She didn't know how she would be able to do this thing Francis wanted. She could bluff for herself, but for another human life?

She didn't know how long she sat in the chair, dozing. When she heard Isabella's soft rap on the door she snapped up her head. The sun was up and thrusting itself grandly into the room. It promised to be a beautiful day.

From the outset, it was obvious that Isabella had never shopped for Lee jeans in her life.

After a half hour in Katz's Department Store in downtown Las Tablas, one of the most cosmopolitan cities west of Rio de Janeiro, offering items for the most discriminating tastes, Deidre knew that what she'd always suspected was true: she had never watched enough old movies on television. She should have paid more attention to Deborah Kerr and Grace Kelly and less to Bell Helicopter and Aero Classics.

She worked hard at being calm and casual as Isabella took her to blouses and pants. But when she turned up the price tag on a T-shirt and saw three digits, she dropped it and coughed discreetly.

"Isabella," she said with her best there's-nothing-wrong-with-me smile, "can you really see me lying on my back beneath the *Albatross* working in this?"

The cool secretarial brows lifted. "Francis said the best. I naturally assumed—"

"To me, casual means cotton. Let's look at something really casual."

"I know just the thing."

Isabella headed straight for the racks of Guess? Deidre had no choice but to try on a pair of prewashed jeans and a blouse. From there, she was spirited away to Ralph Lauren and Liz Claiborne. At the register, after dumping an armful of garments, Isabella fished one of Francis's credit cards from her wallet.

Deidre had to bite her tongue to keep from blurting, *Did you tell anyone where Sean MacIntire was going?* She watched the clerk ring up six hundred dollars on the cash register, while Isabella lit a cigarette and blandly blew smoke at the ceiling.

She mumbled instead about how grim it was to live on lower Greenville Avenue, and when the salesclerk held out two bulging shopping bags, she grabbed them both and trudged after Isabella.

The next stop was lingerie, then shoes and cosmetics. Formal wear was last.

Isabella announced as she scooped up a Dior and measured it against herself in the mirror, "How about this for the state dinner?"

"What state dinner?" Deidre asked through lips that were now the color of Pink Delight.

"The one where Mac makes his big presentation to Francisco Araujo and soothes the presidential feathers."

You mean the one where someone betrays Francis? Deidre wanted to shriek. "I'm sure I'll be home long before then," she said.

With a shrug, Isabella replaced the gown on the rack. "I promised myself when I got divorced and out on my own, the one thing I'd indulge was my love for pretty clothes. Have you always been single?"

Deidre was absorbed with the loungewear in the next section. She answered without looking up from the folds of a flowered djellaba. "I was married for a year."

"Divorce is worse than death, isn't it? At least death is final. With divorce the pain goes on and on. How long has it been?"

Walking over, Isabella fingered the Oscar de la Renta creation. Her nails were the kind one hated a woman for, Deidre thought as she watched them, long and indestructible and as red as her own cheeks.

"I never was divorced." She tucked her own abused hands deeply into the crumples of the shopping bag.

The djellaba lay for a moment in Isabella's loose grip. "I'm sorry. I misunderstood. Here I've been rattling on with my foot ankle-deep in my mouth. Please forgive me."

When the woman closed her fingers about her wrist, Deidre didn't know who felt more awkward. She shook her head. "It's not like that at all. I really wasn't ever married."

"But—"

"He was irresistible," Deidre explained with a shrug and a laughing, self-deprecating grimace. "And I was eighteen. He wanted to be married in a church. You tell me, what starving eighteen-year-old girl could resist a man who wanted to be married in a church?"

Laughing, Isabella crossed herself. "I understand completely."

"One year later I discovered he already had a wife." Before Isabella could gasp, Deidre lowered her head. She couldn't believe she was revealing this. Only one person in the world besides the detectives knew about John Desmond's bigamy.

She charged frantically on. "In Springfield, Tennessee, would you believe it? They had two children. Girls. They looked just like him. I saw pictures. One day he'd walked off and left them."

As incredible as it was, right in the middle of ladies' ready-to-wear, Isabella placed the de la Renta upon the shopping bags and folded Deidre in her arms.

Maybe she'd needed the cleansing of confession. She was suddenly ashamed that she'd suspected Isabella. After teary sentences that didn't go anywhere, they both leaned back and laughed through their tears.

"Men are such sons of bitches," Isabella said enthusiastically and released Deidre to grope about in her bag for a tissue.

Deidre nodded. "I hate them all. No, I don't really. I guess I honestly like men. Or I would if I found one who had his head on straight."

"I knew one once."

"Really? What happened to him?"

"I don't know. He just kind of . . . faded away."

"Ah, an old soldier," Deidre observed in sepulchral tones.

Whether it was the shopping or the weeping, they both laughed again. When they could speak, Isabella said through her clogged sinuses on the way to the cash register, "I know just what we should do, Deidre."

"As long as it isn't fattening." Deidre sniffed, dumbfounded that the clerk was actually ringing up the djellaba.

"Drat," Isabella said and replaced the credit card. "I was going to suggest fondue."

"Is that a fact?"

Isabella rolled her eyes. "We could put it on Francis's credit card."

Deidre shrugged. "Now, why didn't I think of that?"

Sweeping up her bag, the secretary moved elegantly through the revolving glass doors that opened onto the boulevard. Deidre, keeping a close second, sidestepped shoppers and businessmen on their way to lunch and suffered the horrors of Francis finding out about John Desmond via the grapevine.

Dodging a pack of street punks with long hair and skin-tight jeans, she moved closer to Isabella. "Uh, Isabella, what I said before about my marriage..."

Over the top of the bag from Katz's, the dark eyes smiled. She turned an imaginary key upon her lips. "Don't worry," she told Deidre. "Your secret is safe with me."

Not until much later did Deidre wonder if Isabella could possibly have planned everything—from the shopping trip to the miserable little side trip on the way to the restaurant. It wasn't possible for a human being to predict events so perfectly that they meshed like precision gears, was it?

Like the wrong turn she'd made after they drove away from Katz's; it was an accident, pure and simple. As Isabella hesitated at one intersection, then another, debating the quickest way of getting to the restaurant, Deidre peered out the window at ghetto streets where neon signs advertised the human flesh of the night.

No, there was no way the tableau could have been arranged with the sparkling, pristine tower of the capitol just happening to preside high above the filthy squalor, right above the street where soldiers patrolled and prostitutes tried to keep a few blocks ahead and out of sight, making a mockery of the prosperity Araujo claimed for his government.

Mockery? Uniformed men with automatic rifles paraded up and down the broken sidewalks. They jostled through the crowds and passed garish graffito on the sides of the buildings that expressed hatred for *el Presidente*. Jeeps were parked at intersections with machine guns mounted on the back.

"Your papers, please," one soldier gruffly demanded in Spanish as Isabella stopped the car so he could peer inside as if looking for a smuggled body.

Deidre, too, dragged out her passport and handed it over. The poverty here was unbelievable. She'd heard reports—and who in the United States had not if they watched the evening news at all?—that the Araujo government was famous all over the world for the royal treatment bestowed upon visiting dignitaries.

But now, watching dirty children linger around stoops with starving cats while gaunt-faced mothers screamed at them from windows, Deidre shivered with repulsion.

The soldier pointed with the barrel of his gun toward the street Isabella wanted, and as she jammed her little car into gear, she didn't say a word. When they stopped at a light, a pretty girl with wasted cheeks and bleached punk hair leaned inside and made her proposition.

Isabella muttered a remark that Deidre didn't need Spanish to interpret. The prostitute muttered something unintelligible. Straightening, she moved on to another car.

The man, an American tourist probably, reached across and opened the door for her to crawl inside.

Casual massacre on a grand scale, Deidre thought and looked at Isabella. Now she caught the secretary in the unguarded moment she'd wanted. The beautiful hands were shaking now, and the long, glamorous nails were practically digging into the steering wheel.

When she saw Deidre staring, she smiled. "This is what it's like in this country if you're not Francis MacIntire or Francisco Araujo."

Shocked, Deidre shrugged. No more mention was made of it, and later she wondered if she had imagined it all—not that Isabella once might have been a girl who'd leaned into cars and bargained, but that now, having risen above that, she could have planned for Francis to walk into the restaurant with the small, pretty woman on his arm.

Isabella couldn't have known that Deidre and Cidinha had become friends. If she had, she would never have directed her attention to Cidinha's chignon topped with a black hat from Paris and her midcalf black suit.

"Isn't she pretty?" Isabella said. "Francis will probably marry her. If his mother has anything to do with it, I know he will."

The trip home was interminable. Once back at the ranch, vowing to herself that there was no truth whatsoever to such a statement, Deidre hurried into her room and threw all the expensive clothes into a drawer of the bureau. After pulling on her old work clothes, she climbed into the Land Rover and sent gravel spewing clear back to the veranda as she raced down the drive and out onto the highway to the landing strip, passing every other vehicle on the road.

There, she stormed out onto the field and dared Candido Malta's sentries to say so much as one word. By the time dusk was nearing, she had finished going over the *Alba-*

tross with a fine-toothed comb. The oil had been changed, the instruments all checked and double-checked. Except for the scars on her belly, the *Albatross* was as good as ever.

"Why didn't you let me know you were coming out here?" Joaquim said, startling Deidre so badly that she yelped.

He laughed. "Sorry, didn't mean to frighten you."

Deidre drooped until she could brace her elbows on her knees. "That's all right. I'm finished anyway. This has been one bad day."

"How did it go with Isabella?"

Straightening, weaving a bit on her feet, Deidre wiped her hands and began picking up her tools. "She put me through a wringer. If you're asking me if I learned anything specific about Sean, the answer is no, I didn't."

The tall man collected a handful of wrenches and placed them in a toolbox. He started to speak, then hesitated. "Are you all right, Miss Miles?"

Cocking her head, Deidre swallowed. "Yes. Well, not really. Isabella took me to a lovely restaurant. Francis was there with the secretary of interior."

Joaquim laughed. "Cidinha Araujo? Do I see your eyes getting green?"

Color flooded Deidre's cheeks. "More like my gills. No, I think I ate something that didn't agree with me."

No sooner had the words slipped past her lips than the bitter taste of gall rushed into Deidre's mouth. Embarrassed, she waved Joaquim away and rushed as discreetly as possible to the door of the hangar. There, she slipped out into the darkness and threw up her expensive lunch.

"Are you sure I can't do something?" he said when she stepped back inside.

She queasily shook her head. "It's nothing."

"South American bacteria, perhaps."

"Please don't say that."

That evening, before the hands of the clock had reached eight, Deidre dragged herself to the pretty white bedroom and dropped the mosquito netting into place. Without even taking a bath, she crawled between the sheets. She tried to ignore her body aches. She told herself that she would stay awake until she heard Francis's return, but hardly had her head touched the pillow than she breathed one long sigh and slept.

Chapter Twelve

Clinically speaking, it was impossible to be ecstatically happy and suicidally miserable at the same time. Two days later, when Deidre realized her unfortunate condition at two o'clock in the morning, it only proved her theory: at two o'clock, anything was possible.

At least she was woman enough to admit that she had no one but herself to blame. No, she hadn't made a mistake in calculation, and no, it wouldn't go away. She wasn't going to miraculously start her period, which was a week late, and she wouldn't die from morning sickness. She was pregnant.

She had often wondered if she would ever be so blessed. Hadn't she? Yes, a thousand times yes. She wanted a baby. Sometimes she needed a baby. But, dear God, what was she going to do?

She lay beside Francis. The bedroom was very dark. Beyond the netting were the distant sounds of the jungle. She relished the nearness to Francis as only a woman can for the father of her unborn child, but over and over she heard his words: "The investments you make in children, the heavy dividends you pay—no, never again, Deidre. No more for me."

Of course, if he'd known she was carrying his baby he never would have said such a thing; she had to be sensible. Francis MacIntire had more compassion for human beings than anyone she'd ever known, and he would be, despite his history with Sean, a wonderful father.

But he *had* said the words, and she couldn't go to him now, not when his heart was being ruthlessly crushed because of his son.

Keeping the secret of Sean's abduction from the family was like balancing on the end of a spear. For the past several days, every minute had been an eternity. Joaquim had gone to Panama City, after all, and she could still see the two tall men with their hands clasped and their heads bent as they tried to bolster each other's courage. Then Joaquim had embraced him.

Afterward, she and Francis had attended mass with his family. Faith? Oh yes, she wasn't a complete skeptic. And what about love? Love was so strange—it could be noble or perverse—but it was the only thing between human beings and chaos. Kneeling within the cool walls of the church, she had buried her face in her hands and locked her secret more deeply within her breast.

"Why couldn't Sean have had a nice little clinic like everyone else?" Francis had asked tonight as he sat heavily upon the edge of his bed.

"Because his father isn't like anyone else," she told him flatly as she undressed. "What do you expect?"

He watched her in silence. She felt no embarrassment in removing her clothes and dropping the gown over her head.

The fact that his parents were asleep in another part of the house no longer concerned her. Francis concerned her.

When she stepped between his legs and drew his head to her waist, the tension left him by degrees. She stood stroking the back of his neck.

"That thing for Araujo is in two days," he said with bitter weariness. "I wish to heaven I'd never started it."

"We'll get through it."

"Smiling?"

"I didn't say that."

"Deidre, I don't want you so close to me right now."

Deidre felt the blood withdrawing from her arms and legs. "It's a little late for that, Francis."

"I may have to do..."

"What?"

"Things."

"What things?"

"Hard things."

Not for a moment did Deidre believe that he was incapable of it. From the first moment when he'd slapped Juan Geisel's face, she had known he was capable of doing whatever was necessary.

Bending, she placed a kiss on his temple. "I love you. I can't stop that, even if you do hard things."

His only reply was to tighten his arms fiercely about her waist. She wondered if part of him didn't guess that his blood was part of her now.

"I pray God he's safe tonight," he said quietly, like a boy lost. "If there's any dying to be done, I hope it's me, Deidre, not him."

Deidre knew that if she shed one tear it would be the end of their fragile hold upon sanity. "Francis, I'm going to tell you something I've never told anyone before. When my mother lay in the hospital, dying, at the end I stood by her bed almost constantly, and there were times when her eyes followed me around the room. She couldn't speak, but I knew that if she could she would have asked me to pull out all the tubes and lines that were keeping her alive. I was eighteen years old, and I knew what she wanted, and I couldn't do it because all my life I'd been trained to obey the rules. I've always regretted that, Francis. You told me that first day, life is a bitch, and we fight for the wrong things. We try to keep terror away and hold on to the scraps of sanity we have. You start fighting, and someone dies. One death leads to another. But somewhere there has to be a balance. The tyrants and the assassins can't take the world, Francis. Somewhere there has to be someone to stop them. I can't stop them. I couldn't even spare my own mother a few moments of suffering. Whatever happens, darling man, I won't stop loving you. You can do hard things, and you can push me away, but I will still love you. I'm sorry, but that's all I can do."

A long moment passed, and presently he released her and brushed his face with the back of her hand. "Come to bed," he said.

When she lay beside him, he slipped a leg heavily across her thighs and laid his head upon her breast, pulling her closer and shaping his hand about the curve without any overtures of lovemaking, simply because to do so comforted him.

"Go to sleep, my love," she whispered and combed through his curls with her fingers until she grew too drowsy to talk. "Go to sleep."

Now, slipping from the bed, she shivered and wrapped her arms about herself. "I have never loved anyone so much," she whispered to the shadows that enfolded his length. "And never has anyone made me so unhappy."

Silently she returned to her own room. She would find a way somehow to do the right thing, but first she had to learn what that thing was.

For three weeks Rio Tepuí had known that President Araujo and his enormous retinue would descend upon their town in a swarm. Politics aside, it would be a financial boon. An influx of money would pour into the modest shops and meat markets and wine shops and hotels.

While Francis lived through the eternity of each hour, the hotels were going through a frenzy of cleanings and polishings and orderings. The houses and shops that lined the small, quiet streets were like women preparing their faces for a grand event. Holes were patched, and new shrubbery was planted. Painters worked through the rain from daylight until dusk. Bakers and grocers and photographers made lavish plans.

For his family, Francis took a suite at the same hotel Araujo and his retinue would occupy. It would be their home base for the day. Along with the wives, Deidre took her dress and a small case of feminine articles.

Soon the suite was buried beneath an avalanche of boxes that spilled clothes and garment bags and shoes and hair dryers and electric rollers. All this, Deidre thought, for a few hours at dinner with a man whose tiny crown was teetering upon his head.

She stood at the window and shut out the chatter of Pat and Amanda and Mavis as she watched a parade winding through the streets. Francis was attending a press conference with the president. Cleary was in one of the bedrooms resting. Sean? Only God knew where Sean was.

Below her as she watched, women wearing black dresses trimmed with borders and sashes of bright red and green danced upon floats. At each step their headdresses bobbed, and their necklaces of silver swung. The men were trimmed out with feathers and bells. They held instruments that made a dry brittle sound. On foot, they whirled and weaved and made music that carried for blocks.

"Deidre?"

Mavis's soft query snatched Deidre from her sad musing. She turned. "Yes, what is it?"

"This package came for you, dear."

As Mavis extended a large, gift-wrapped box, Chris and Travis made an explosive entrance into the suite. For a moment sheer bedlam reigned.

"Who is it from?" Deidre quietly asked the older woman.

Mavis was watching her with a gentle, knowledgeable smile, and for an instant Deidre wondered if the woman had guessed about her grandson, Sean. Or maybe she was guessing about the grandchild not yet born.

She said, "You'll have to read the card. I don't know."

Beneath the large satin bow, Deidre fished out a crisp envelope. On the outside was an embossed label that read Edward's: Rio de Janeiro, Rio Tepuí.

"Edward's," she softly repeated.

Mavis laughed softly. "The best shop in town. We all buy our clothes there."

"Why, it's from Francis." Deidre slipped the card from the envelope. *My darling, after all these years... I never knew what love was.*

Before she could stop the tears, they splashed upon the smooth white card and blurred the bold scrawl. Mavis gently took the paper and gestured at the box. With trembling hands, Deidre fished through the rustling tissue, glancing up momentarily to see if anyone was watching.

Inside, a gown of rich emerald-green was layered with tissue. She drew a surprised breath. Never in her life had she seen such a gown.

"Oh," Mavis sighed. "Hold it up, dear."

Deidre obediently lifted it from its nest, and a graceful skirt of thousands of tiny pleats unfolded to the floor. The scoop neck and shoulders were trimmed in golden braid, and around the bottom of the long, slender sleeves the braid was repeated.

Not moving, Deidre closed her eyes. She simply could not betray herself with tears before Francis's mother, and when the older woman's thin hand closed over her own, she blinked the moistness back.

"I have known my son for so many years," Mavis said quietly beneath the commotion on the other side of the room, "and he still surprises me."

Deidre's jaw slackened.

"Francis is so generous. He's always given everyone all they could possibly want. But someone—myself or Isabella, sometimes Amanda—always took care of the details like gifts for birthdays and anniversaries. Even those for his wife. I think this is a first, Deidre. You'll be beautiful."

As Deidre changed later that evening, after having labored for over an hour with her hands and her nails and her hair that was caught up on her head in a large, loose doughnut, she slipped into the privacy of one of the bathrooms and slithered into the luscious coolness of the dress.

Mavis was right. She did look very pretty. She lowered herself to the tiny boudoir stool and stared at her reflection in the mirror, and she placed her hands across her belly.

"Oh, Francis," she whispered. "Your son is in terrible trouble somewhere, and I carry within me a child. How do I smile for you tonight? How do I tell you what's in my heart?"

A soft tap at the door made her hurry to blot her eyes without ruining her mascara. "Yes," she called quickly. "Yes, what is it?"

The door opened, and in the mirror Deidre met his tired blue eyes.

He was wearing a tuxedo, and instead of it complementing his rugged, untamed frame, he complemented the clothes. He was every bit the august, distinguished gentleman, but she knew him far too well by now to miss the tension of his muscles beneath his clothes. He was like an overwound spring.

Without a word, he stepped inside, and she, turning, went into his arms. Deidre clung to him all along his sinewy length and sighed as his hollowed face touched hers. He offered her no caresses, but his hands cradled the back of her head and neck. From between parted lips she whimpered as he kissed her deeply and long.

Finally he pressed his head against hers and took her scent into his lungs. "Stay close to me tonight," he whispered hoarsely into her hair. "I take back what I said. Stay close to me tonight. I just need to know you're there."

Her reply was to wrap her arms tightly about him. Life was suddenly better. He was here, holding her.

Captain Candido Malta always tended to business first. Not until he had made sure that the hotel's security was tight and foolproof did he allow himself to relax and take one small drink.

It wouldn't be an easy night. Restaurants were overbooked all over town. Every hotel was filled, and stores and shops were doing a booming business. A long line of cabs was outside, dropping fares. Crowds were strolling in, weaving here and there in an attempt to see the president when he arrived. The lobby was packed, and there were lines waiting to get into the two restaurants.

Around the elevator, people kept collecting. At the registration desk, bells rang and the service staff was going crazy. Yes, tonight his men would earn their money.

"I'll be back in fifteen minutes," he told Juan Geisel, who stood near one of the military cars parked beside the southern entrance.

The corporal gave him a sharp salute, and Candido reached into his pocket for a key that he had picked up at the desk early in the afternoon. Before he walked inside, he gave a final glance at the streets in all directions. He had men posted everywhere.

After satisfying himself, he shouldered his way through the crowd and took the elevator to the third floor. The carpet, he detected when the door swept open, had been freshly shampooed. He smiled. He appreciated orderliness in all things.

No one in the hall seemed to notice him as he walked the full length of it and made a turn. When he came to room 320, he stopped and threw a look over both shoulders. The key fit easily into the lock, and as he walked through the door he smelled the familiar perfume.

She was coming out of the bedroom as he shut the door, having heard him enter. The only thing she was wearing was a pair of four-inch black heels. She had left her hair down, and it spilled to her waist, as glossily black as the hair above her legs. Her breasts were large and full, proudly nippled.

"I don't have much time," he said and handed her his quirt while he began undressing.

"You never do," Isabella complained mildly.

Deidre hated sitting at the president's table. As she looked out over the room and its two hundred guests sitting at beautifully tended tables, she had no idea how many shared Francis's concerns about the country's leadership. Araujo had not done very well tonight. Though he had spoken gracefully enough, chairs began scraping noisily on the floor, and people exchanged furtive glances and spoke behind their hands.

Now, thankful that the man was taking his bows, Deidre obligingly clapped along with the rest. Beside her, Francis looked tight-lipped and angry. She turned to see Cidinha a dozen seats away. She was lovely in her pale yellow gown, but her eyes kept darting toward Francis and the members of her brother's cabinet, who were sprinkled everywhere.

Finally, the applause stopped. Deidre looked at Francisco Araujo and thought he looked pale and relieved it was over.

"What do you think?" she asked Francis on a sigh as she turned.

Francis looked like a man standing on the very brink of hell. "The man's mad," he said between his frozen smile.

"What!"

"Didn't you just hear that he'd accepted the resignation of Alvar Galvez? These people will kill him for that."

Deidre could have told him that she didn't have the foggiest notion who Alvar Galvez even was, so she could hardly find it in her heart to worry about him. Most of the president's political remarks had passed over her head. But she did comprehend Francis's alarm, and now she understood Cidinha's shuttered worry as she sought Francis's eyes from across the room.

Deidre laid her hand upon the ruffled cuff peeping beneath Francis's sleeve. She asked briskly, "What do you want me to do?"

Cidinha was making her way toward them as people clustered around the president, voicing questions. Soon they would be shouting.

"I've got to get to a telephone," Francis said quickly. "Will you be all right if I leave you?"

Amid the talk of guests and the flurry of the waiters, Francis rose to meet Cidinha, and Deidre, too, came to her feet, but she tactfully turned away. This is what it would be like, wouldn't it? If she were Francis's wife, she would always be seeing his back.

After the two of them exchanged some words, Cidinha extended her hand, and Deidre politely took it. "You're positively radiant tonight, Señorita Miles," she said.

Deidre mumbled something she hoped was passable and continued to watch the guests, as did Francis and Cidinha. Araujo had surrounded himself with nonthreatening people tonight. The journalists who had been invited were half a dozen friendly ones who always gave the president good press. The hostile press had had to wait in the parking lot.

But even the friends were beginning to slip daggers into their questions. Cidinha could hardly disguise her alarm. "We're in trouble," she said under her breath to Francis. "I don't dare speak to any of the others. Once word leaks out about this, I don't know what we'll do. We've got to get him out of here."

"I need to know what's going on at the capitol," Francis said. "Give me ten minutes."

Nausea rose unexpectedly in Deidre's throat as she watched him go. He had meant this affair as a way for Araujo to reconcile some of his differences with his people. He now blamed himself for its failure.

The room was too hot. She had to get outside for a moment. When Cidinha touched her hand and sought her eyes, she hesitated.

"Señorita," she said so softly that Deidre had to bend her head, "do you remember what we spoke of the last time we met?"

Throwing a glance for Francis but finding him gone, Deidre smiled uncertainly. "Yes, Ms. Secretary, I do."

"Is everything . . ." Cidinha nervously moistened her lips and touched the rim of her glasses. "Is everything the same? In good condition?"

She was talking about the *Albatross*. Deidre didn't want to be a part of that, but Francis was part of it, and therefore, she had to be.

"Yes," she said. "Everything is in good condition."

"If I needed you—" Cidinha chose her words carefully beneath the noise of the room "—if our country needed to place someone in a position of safety, to prevent a tragedy, do you think you could be of service?"

Incredibly, the woman was asking if she could fly Francisco Araujo out of the country! Deidre drew in a quick breath. "Does Francis know about this?"

"He knows that it might be the only way."

"Then yes, if I can help, I will."

"I must warn you that there may be repercussions later. I don't think so, but one never knows about people. But I promise you that the U.S. ambassador will know about this beforehand. He will inform your country. At all costs, we must maintain our relationship there."

How strange it was, Deidre thought. A person could sit by the television in the United States and see news clips and make judgments, but people were still people. She extended her hand.

Accepting it, Cidinha said softly, "He isn't a bad man, *señorita*, just a tired, sick one."

As Cidinha moved back to her brother's side, Deidre understood where Francisco Araujo had gotten his strength through the years. From across the room, Mavis and Cleary were watching her with confusion. She worked her way toward them to say hello. But when they questioned her about Cidinha Araujo, she smiled and moved toward the door.

As soon as she stepped outside, cool air lifted her spirits and cleared her head.

"May I help you, *señorita*?" a security guard asked from behind her.

Spinning around, she gasped. "I'm fine. I just needed some fresh air."

"Please remain in the lobby." He continued his patrol.

Hardly thirty seconds had passed before she realized that the wretch had reported her. Walking toward her, resplendent in his uniform, was Captain Candido Malta. A cold smile was on his mouth, and with an insulting flick of his quirt, he stepped before her and inclined his head.

"Good evening, Señorita Miles," he said. "May I say that you are the most beautiful woman here this evening."

Angry, she refused to let him intimidate her. "I hardly believe you've seen every woman here this evening, Captain. Perhaps there is one more beautiful than I."

"Ah, but you are wrong. I told you before that I know everything and everyone."

"Really?"

"I absolutely guarantee it."

She jutted her chin and tried to settle her stomach with a deep breath. "Well then, I'll be sure to extend my congratulations to your dogs of war at the hangar, Captain. And when you learn to read minds, let me know. I'll extend my congratulations to you, too."

He laughed at her attempts to irritate him. Shrugging, he fondled the length of his quirt. She turned to leave him.

"While we're on the subject of sentries, *señorita* . . ."

"Yes?" Deidre looked over her shoulder.

"I might mention in passing that you could exert a bit more discretion out at the hangar. I pride myself on keeping high standards among my men."

Blistering heat swept over the top of her scooped neckline and into Deidre's throat. *Francis will kill you for that!* she wanted to shriek at him, but she lifted her head instead and said icily, "It's too bad you don't include decency in those standards, Captain."

His smile slapped her across the face. "You speak to me about decency, *señorita*? You, who married a man with one wife already and who are now dangling yourself beneath the nose of another? Tsk, tsk. I think you should tend to the mote in your own eye before you try to remove the one in mine."

"Isabella," Francis said icily from the doorway of her hotel room, "you have ten seconds to tell me where Sean is."

Isabella did not look surprised to see him. He stepped into the room and shut the door. He did not touch her, and he was silent for a moment.

She didn't move. "I didn't intend to do it, Mac. Not in the beginning."

"What did Candido do with Sean?"

"I don't know."

"I don't believe you."

Her lips trembled. "Before I tell you, I want you to know that I have always loved you."

Stepping toward her, he took her jaw in his hand. "Don't make me hurt you."

"I have no doubt that if you were forced into a choice between killing me and saving Sean, you would not hesitate. But I don't know where Sean is being held. Only Candido knows that. And if he thinks I betrayed him, I am ruined," she said quietly. "You'll protect me against him, won't you?" she asked Francis.

Releasing her, he walked to the door. Once there, he turned. "I'll give you the same protection you gave me, Isabella."

Francis shut the door in her face. Now he must find Deidre and ask her if she would fly Araujo out of the country. The man had been foolish and stupid, but he didn't deserve to die.

"I've never flown the *Albatross* at night," Deidre told Francis when he asked her. The A-26 had no proper instruments, no radar. "Can't we wait until dawn?"

"We could," he said unhappily. "But I don't think we can."

After Francis made arrangements with his parents—she knew he told them some gentle lie—he drove her home and they changed clothes. Full circle, she thought as she climbed into her flight suit and zipped up.

Not until she was in the security of the pilot's seat and Francis was waiting in the copilot's seat did she ask him. Outside, his men were setting up flares to mark the length of the airstrip. It was now three o'clock in the morning. She was very tired.

"I don't want you to violate your honor, Francis," she said as she watched the twinkling line of flares grow longer, "but I have to know something."

He sighed. "Cidinha and I made a bargain tonight," he told her, seeming to dredge the words out of his throat. "There are people who would assassinate Francisco for what he said. There are those who want to fight, and this is the excuse they need. To prevent that, and to save his life, we're going to fly him to Panama, where he'll be reported hospitalized for a few weeks. In the meantime, I expect that

Cidinha may assume some kind of power. Frankly, I expect Araujo to resign. At any rate, the rebels will pull back a little, and maybe the conservatives will call off their military. I'm hoping. She's hoping.''

"Not the Phillipines all over again?"

"Maybe. I don't know, sweetheart. Right now I can only think like a father. I want my family safe. I want Sean safe and alive."

"But you don't know where he is."

"Cidinha will know when she gets here."

"How?"

"Believe me, Deidre, she has ways. Candido will be lucky to get out of the country alive when she gets through with him. Francisco was the one who kept Candido on, not Cidinha. She's always despised him."

Francis leaned forward and took her face in his hands. He kissed her tenderly. "We walk awfully close to the fire here, my darling. I have no blood on my hands, I assure you."

"I know that," she whispered, "but I think some of the people you associate with do."

"You think they don't get blood on their hands in the good old U.S. of A.?"

"I know, I know, but...so much is happening here. I still don't like your green hell, Mr. MacIntire."

"Yes," he said and kissed her eyes and her trembling mouth, tracing the frame of her bones in the darkness, "but it likes you."

Cidinha Araujo brought her brother to the airstrip in a convoy of jeeps. Just before dawn, the *Albatross* was loaded with its burden of men and materials. All Francisco's personal effects were on board, and two dozen men. Deidre knew in her heart that the man would not be coming back.

He was going into exile. But at least he would not be a name on a headstone.

With Francis by her side, she flew them out. The dawn rose up out of the clouds with a vengeance, and when, hours later, she brought them down at the Panama International Airport, she felt as if she had been through the Spanish Inquisition. Every muscle in her body screamed for attention. She hadn't dared eat for fear of losing it, and bitter black coffee sloshed drearily around in her stomach.

All in all, things went remarkably well. People were there to meet the president, and he conducted himself with remarkable dignity, all things considered.

But now Francis had only one thing on his mind: Sean. The moment they walked across the sunny expanse of tarmac and reached the door that opened onto the concourse, a voice shouted, "MacIntire!"

The pressure of Francis's hand on hers tightened as they watched Joaquim making his way toward them.

Francis smiled. He was pale but composed, a bit too tough-looking behind dark sunglasses, Deidre thought. He shook hands with his friend and filled him in on what had happened at Rio Tepuí.

Joaquim told him, "I know that, Mac. Shortly after the president's debacle, I was contacted and told to meet a man. Hello, Miss Miles. It's good to see you."

"Who?"

"It doesn't matter at this point. What does matter is that I met him. He told me that he had received orders to turn Sean over to us."

"Where is Sean?"

"He's here at the airport, Mac."

"Here? Thank God. How is he? I want to see him."

"He's fine, Mac. Shaken, but okay. The trouble is, as a safeguard his captors reported him to the Panamanian authorities as a smuggler. Everyone and his dog is looking for the boy. They've been one inch behind him all the way. We've got to get Sean out of this airport with no trace. I've been working on it all morning, and for twenty thousand dollars I can buy us some people who—"

Ten wonderful bells went off in Deidre's head at once. As tired as she was, she twirled around in a happy pirouette and laughed out loud. Both men turned to look at her, probably concluding that she had finally lost her mind.

She turned up her palms at them. "Let me get this straight. You want to smuggle Sean out of this airport, and you're willing to pay twenty thousand dollars to do it?"

Their wide eyes were laser beams burning into her.

She smiled sweetly. "Where do you want to take him?"

"Baja," Joaquim said, frowning.

"Mexico City," Francis said.

Deidre let her shoulders drop with a sigh and resettled the strap of her flight bag on one shoulder. Nicolas Noreiga had to be around the airport somewhere. "Can you give me a few minutes?"

"What're you going to do?" Francis growled, more himself than he'd been in days.

Rising up on her toes, she kissed his jaw, then rubbed the rough stubble of beard. "Trust me."

Nicolas Noreiga hadn't changed. When Deidre found him at Gate Seven and walked up and tapped him on the shoulder, she thought she must have been the one who'd changed.

He pulled off his cap and squinted at her with bloodshot eyes. "Don't you remember me, Señor Noreiga?" she asked.

Several seconds ticked past as he scratched the end of his nose. Then a slow smile drew one side of his mouth up.

"The lady from Hollywood, California. Of course I re-member you, *señorita*. Welcome to Panama."

Deidre grimaced. "I'm not from Hollywood, *señor*. And I'm pressed for time today. I wanted to ask you a question."

Like a cloak-and-dagger man, he ducked his head. "A question?"

"Do you still know this friend of yours at the top, *señor*? The one who can be bribed from time to time?"

Nicolas strolled out into the sunshine and squinted up at a jet thundering through the sky. He pursed his mouth, and Deidre considered the twenty thousand dollars at her disposal.

"What would you like to buy, *señorita*?"

"We are ready to depart in the A-26. Our crew will be four. Perhaps you might see that the records say three."

He pretended to consider the matter seriously. "Ah, you say you would be willing to pay for this favor?"

"How much would it cost, if such a thing could be done?"

"Well, what you ask is very serious. Perhaps I might get into real trouble. *Aflicción*."

"I give you my word, there is absolutely nothing that has been done wrong here. Nothing. I would swear on my mother's grave, on a Bible. We just need to save a man's life, that's all. He is a good man. He's a doctor."

"Oh, I see. Well, in that case . . ."

"How much?"

"Hmm . . . I am slow to answer. Let us say, four, five thousand to do this. *Sí*, five thousand would do it."

Deidre's frugal nature battled to assert itself. "Three."

"Four. What a hard one you are. I will lose much money because of this."

"I know, I know. Stay right here. Don't move. I'll be back."

"Oh, that is what the Terminator said."

Deidre screwed up her face. "What?"

"The Terminator. Arnold Schwarzenegger? The big guy? Forget it, *señorita*."

She laughed as she went to find Francis.

Chapter Thirteen

No, Francis," Deidre told him when Sean was safely in the *Albatross*, and Joaquim had climbed into the bomber along with him. "I don't want you to come to Dallas with me. This is something I need to do by myself."

They stood outside the cockpit, and Francis felt as if life had turned on him and bared fangs. Just when everything was put to rights and God was in his heaven and he was at peace with the world—almost—she was telling him that she had to return to Dallas alone.

"I won't let you."

"I have to."

"This is the wrong time for this, damn it," he said. He pushed her back so that she was standing beneath the red letters that had once been painted so neatly. "We need to get out of here before something happens."

"Francis, listen to me."

"We'll be married tomorrow. Hell, if that's what's bothering you, I'll hire a pilot to fly this thing and we'll be married here, today. I love you, Deidre. I'm not letting you go back to settle some business that can just as easily be settled from Santiago."

What she could *not* do, Deidre wanted miserably to say as she memorized everything about him—the sweet, familiar way he had rolled his sleeves back to his elbows above the strong, sculptural forearms that were braced beside her face, the curls fluttering in the wind, the blunted brows, the rumpled bush pants, the scuffed boots—was tell him about the baby. Not until she was sure she could bear trapping him with it.

Swearing she would not cry or let her desperation show, she rose up on her toes and kissed him. His arms were instantly around her, nearly crushing her.

"I couldn't have done all this without you," he groaned against her ear.

"Yes you could."

"Wrecking people's lives, maybe. I love Sean. I love them all, but you're what I dream about. You can't take my dream away."

He was tearing the heart out of her! Deidre clung fiercely to his neck. "It'll only be for a few days, Francis. Please, don't make this harder. I need just a little time...just a little time to go inside myself. Please understand."

"Mac," Joaquim called out.

Francis made a desperate motion with one hand. "I've got to go. Come on, now."

Francis jerked his head toward the plane, then back to her, and Deidre drew her mouth into the facsimile of a smile. She couldn't let him see. She couldn't let him guess.

She tipped her head in a sassy way. "Are you sure you can fly this thing, jungle man?"

He didn't find her comment the least bit funny. His voice drilled into her with accusation. "Are you sure you can turn around and walk into that airport? You love me too much. You can't do it."

With her pulse slamming through her body, Deidre started inching backward. She wouldn't cry. On her shoulder was her flight bag. She wouldn't cry. In it was all the money she needed or wanted. She wouldn't cry. Inside her was something she would die to hold on to. Tears sprang into her eyes. She would work it out. Maybe she could talk to Phillip. Phillip had four kids.

"I'll call you tomorrow." She strangled on the words and blinked furiously. "I promise."

Francis thought he would never forgive her as he placed his boot upon the ladder. And he couldn't bear to watch her walk into the terminal. Where had he gone wrong? What had he done? Why was she exacting this terrible price when he was torn between two people he loved?

Feeling very old, he climbed up into the cockpit and took his seat. "Are you okay?" he yelled back to Sean, the words coming out more sharply than he intended.

"Yeah, Dad. I'm okay."

Francis exchanged a dour look with Joaquim. His friend shook his head.

Grimacing, Francis reached for the headphones and dragged them on. "Hell," he muttered.

Joaquim's fingers clasped Francis's wrist. He gave the wrist an encouraging shake. "Give her a few days, Mac. It'll be all right."

"Yeah, yeah."

"She's got a lot on her mind right now. Everything's happened so quickly, and let's face it, this hasn't been one of your ordinary vacations in the tropics."

Francis stared bitterly at the flight panel. He sighed heavily. "A man comes to believe things, you know?"

"When she's feeling better, Mac."

"Yes, I know." A long pause spun out. Francis threw Joaquim a sidelong glance. "What do you mean, feeling better?"

"She's sick, Mac. Can't you see that? And not just in the morning—it's all day long. Frankly, I think—"

"Morning?"

"Mac—"

In the flash of a drowning man's vision, Francis saw it all. He remembered the words he'd said to her that night in the stable. He remembered every gesture, every hesitation, every misleading sigh. God help him, how had he been so blind? And she'd borne it by herself....

Stumbling to his feet, he threw his son a pleading look. "Sean, I—"

Sean had to smile. Good old Dad? Having the hots for Deidre Miles? "Go after her, Dad."

"But, I don't know how.... I've got to get you out of here." Francis dragged his hand through the tangle of his hair. "I don't want you to think ... Oh, hell."

Joaquim broke in. "I'll get us a pilot, Mac. Hey, that Noreiga guy? I daresay he can get one in half an hour. I'll sweeten the pot. He might get one in fifteen minutes."

Guilt caught Francis by the ankles and hung on. "Sean, I'll make this up to you."

The haggard young man stooped and moved up to the pilot's chair. "I'm not an invalid, you know," he said to Joaquim. "*I'll* fly us out of here." Then he turned to his father.

"Dad," he said as tears rolled down his face, "you don't make anything up to me. I'll spend the rest of my days trying to make it up to you."

"Sean—"

"No. It wasn't your fault. Now, go get her before her plane takes off."

For the first time Francis looked at his son as a man, as a man who had made mistakes but who had tried and would keep on trying. Without a word he closed his arms around Sean and held him with a fierce love.

He guessed they were both crying as he grabbed his jacket, then climbed down the ladder and sprinted across the tarmac until his hip was screaming with pain.

Don't you dare take off, he willed the pilot of the plane she would be boarding. *Don't you dare.*

If Deidre hadn't been sitting in the waiting area with her face buried in her hands, she might have seen Francis racing down the concourse, dodging people and making them bump into one another and then ducking into a tiny cocktail lounge. The middle-aged woman beside her did. She even saw him come out of the lounge with a clumsy bundle tucked under his arm, and she heard a group of boys cup their hands and yell, "Hey, Crocodile Dundee!"

When Deidre heard the flurry of activity, she raised her face and saw heads all around her turning. She heard mutterings from a few seats behind her. "Pardon me...so sorry...oops, excuse me, please."

And then Francis was towering over her, and her mouth was dropping open in astonishment. On his face was a mixture of frustration and amusement, and he looked as much like a mischievous boy as the ivory smuggler she'd once thought him.

She glanced over her shoulder to find people watching her.

"Flight one-eight-four now boarding at gate six," the announcer's sterile voice intoned. "Will all those passengers holding first-class..."

Though her flight was obviously boarding, the woman beside Deidre stared as if riveted to her seat. When Francis lifted her purse from the end table and handed it to her, she gasped and snatched it to her bosom as if he'd been about to steal it.

"Excuse us, madam," he said and smiled.

She threw him a glare.

Deidre finally snapped her mouth shut. "Francis, people are... What're you doing here?"

"What do you think?"

"Everyone is staring."

Looking up, Francis grinned at his audience, then ignored them. "Be still," he said softly to Deidre and dragged a crumpled white cloth from beneath his arm and threw it haphazardly upon the little table where the woman's purse had been.

In amazement, Deidre saw him fumble about in the folds of his jacket and withdraw a bottle of wine and a rose that had fallen out of its little vase. People on their way to board were distracted by the small drama, and they craned over other people's shoulders in an effort to see him replace the rose.

So hot from embarrassment that she could hardly keep still, Deidre tried to smile and muttered under her breath, "Have you lost your mind?"

"Only for a moment, darling. Only for a moment."

"Will you stop this? We'll be arrested or something."

"I'll stop it if you will."

"What?"

The crowd had grown. Francis, unperturbed, arranged the table more neatly, shifted the rose to a more strategic position, and set down the two glasses that had cost him in the neighborhood of two hundred dollars. Satisfied with the table, and, as if no one existed but the two of them, he bent at her feet and took her hands tenderly in his rough ones.

"You are the one perfect spot in my life," he said softly. "I want to marry you, Deidre Miles. I want to be the father of your children. I want to be—"

"Flight one-eight-four now boarding at gate six..."

"Your plane's leaving, miss," the woman in the next seat whispered.

Francis turned quelling eyes upon the woman, and she drew fearfully back. He said to Deidre, "You can't live without me, lassie. You know it, and I know it. Say yes."

If she could have spoken a word, Deidre would have told him yes before now. With tears streaming down her face, she nodded and wiped her eyes on the sleeve of her jumpsuit. She didn't care how he'd found out, only that he knew and wanted their baby.

Swallowing, she laughed through the tears. "I really do have to go to Dallas, Francis, but yes, I will marry you. I will give you the prettiest black-haired Irish child you ever saw."

"Oh, brother," some unseen woman murmured.

"Shut up," another said and sniffed.

When Francis finally came to his feet, Deidre thought at least fifty people must have sighed with relief as they tore themselves away and trudged toward the door where the flight attendants were waiting.

"Well, come on, then," Francis said and grabbed her flight bag. "We'll miss our plane."

He tunneled them a path to the ticket booth and lifted Deidre's ticket from her trembling hands. "Two seats together, please," he told the ticket agent, and smiled down at Deidre.

"But this is for one, sir," the man protested.

Without turning around, Francis told him, "There's been a mistake. We had reservations for two."

"But, sir—"

Turning, Francis leaned upon the booth and looked at him as if he were Juan Geisel. "Two, please. Together."

The man smiled nervously. "Just a moment." He returned almost immediately. "Yes. Take this, and this. But you'll have to hurry, sir. Your plane is about to take off."

"Wonderful," Francis said and left the tickets on the counter as he took Deidre into his arms and kissed her.

Deidre hugged him with all her might and opened her eyes to see the ticket agent disapproving mightily. "I think we're holding up traffic, Francis," she whispered.

"Wonderful," he said again, and chuckled as he grabbed the tickets and steered her toward the waiting flight attendant.

"Oh, mister!" The woman behind them was clutching her purse and waving the bottle of wine. "You forgot this."

"Keep it," Francis called over his shoulder as he thrust the tickets into the hands of the smiling attendant.

"Watch your step, sir," the attendant urged.

Francis peered down the end of his nose and lifted his brows. "Of course I will. I'm going to be a father."

Smiling, Deidre nudged him forward.

The woman who brought up the rear rolled her eyes at the laughing flight attendant and muttered, "At his age, I should think he would know better."

*   *   *   *   *

Take 4 Silhouette Intimate Moments novels
and a surprise gift
FREE

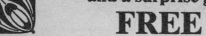

Then preview 4 brand-new Silhouette Intimate Moments novels—delivered to your door as soon as they come off the presses! If you decide to keep them, you pay just $2.49 each*—a 9% saving off the retail price, *with no additional charges for postage and handling!*

Silhouette Intimate Moments novels are not for everyone. They were created to give you a more detailed, more exciting reading experience, filled with romantic fantasy, intense sensuality and stirring passion.

Start with 4 Silhouette Intimate Moments novels and a surprise gift absolutely FREE. They're yours to keep without obligation. You can always return a shipment and cancel at any time.

Simply fill out and return the coupon today!

*$2.50 each plus 49¢ postage and handling per shipment in Canada.

ATTRACTIVE, SPACE SAVING BOOK RACK

Display your most prized novels on this handsome and sturdy book rack. The hand-rubbed walnut finish will blend into your library decor with quiet elegance, providing a practical organizer for your favorite hard-or soft-covered books.

Only $9.95

Approximately 16" x 8" when assembled

Assembles in seconds!

To order, rush your name, address and zip code, along with a check or money order for $10.70* ($9.95 plus 75¢ postage and handling) payable to *Silhouette Books.*

Silhouette Books
Book Rack Offer
901 Fuhrmann Blvd.
P.O. Box 1396
Buffalo, NY 14269-1396

Offer not available in Canada.

BKR-2A

*New York and Iowa residents add appropriate sales tax.

COMING NEXT MONTH

#409 A CERTAIN SMILE—Lynda Trent
Impulsive widow Megan Wayne and divorced father Reid Spencer didn't have
marriage in mind, but what harm could come if their friendship turned into
something stronger? Reid's two teenage daughters didn't intend to let them
find out....

#410 FINAL VERDICT—Pat Warren
Prosecutor Tony Adams's upbringing had built him a strong case against lasting
love. Could attorney Sheila North's evidence to the contrary weaken his
defenses and free his emotions from solitary confinement?

#411 THUNDERSTRUCK—Pamela Toth
Crew member Honey Collingsworth accepted the risks of hydroplane racing.
Still, when her brother and dashing defector Alex Checkhov competed,
churning up old hatred, she feared for their lives...and her heart.

#412 RUN AWAY HOME—Marianne Shock
Proud landowner Burke Julienne knew that to restless vagabond
Savannah Jones, the lush Julienne estate was just another truck stop. Yet
he found her mesmerizing, and he prayed that one day Savannah would trade
freedom for love.

#413 A NATURAL WOMAN—Caitlin Cross
When farmer's daughter Vana Linnier abruptly became a sophisticated
celebrity, she desperately needed some plain old-fashioned horse sense to cope
with her jealous sister and her disapproving but desirable boss, Sky Van Dusen.

#414 BELONGING—Dixie Browning
Saxon Evanshaw returned home to a host of family fiascos and the lovely but
stealthy estate manager, Gale Chandler. Who was she really? Where were the
missing family treasures? And would Gale's beauty rob him of his senses?

AVAILABLE THIS MONTH:

Starting in October...

SHADOWS ON THE NILE

by

Heather Graham Pozzessere

A romantic short story in six installments from best-selling author Heather Graham Pozzessere.

The first chapter of this intriguing romance will appear in all Silhouette titles published in October. The remaining five chapters will appear, one per month, in Silhouette Intimate Moments' titles for November through March '88.

Don't miss "*Shadows on the Nile*"—a special treat, coming to you in October. Only from Silhouette Books.

Be There!

IMSS-1